"WHAT DO YOU THINK HAPPENED HERE, CAPTAIN?"

"That's what I mean to find out," Kirk said. "Spock?"

The Vulcan was riveted by a bizarre structure in the center of the square. An elaborate apparatus, which appeared to have been cobbled together from various cannibalized bits of technology, framed a shimmering triangular void filled with coruscating lights and colors that hurt Kirk's eyes to look upon. A touch of vertigo made him feel slightly dizzy.

"Fascinating," Spock observed.

If the strobing colors caused Spock any discomfort, his lean, ascetic features betrayed no sign of it. Simple Vulcan stoicism, Kirk wondered, or were Spock's inner eyelids providing him with an extra degree of protection from the disturbing spectacle?

Probably a bit of both, Kirk guessed.

"What is it, Spock?"

Spock scanned the void with his tricorder. "If my readings are correct, this appears to be a dimensional rift of some sort. It is also the source of the exotic gravimetric distortions we detected from orbit." He perused the readouts on the tricorder. "Further study is required, but preliminary data suggests that some variety of artificial gravity is being employed to tear open a gap in the space-time continuum, possibly opening a passage to another reality."

STAR TREK®

THE ORIGINAL SERIES

THE WEIGHT OF WORLDS

Greg Cox

Based upon *Star Trek*
created by Gene Roddenberry

POCKET BOOKS

New York   London   Toronto   Sydney   New Delhi

Pocket Books
A Division of Simon & Schuster, Inc.
1230 Avenue of the Americas
New York, NY 10020

This book is a work of fiction. Names, characters, places, and incidents either are products of the author's imagination or are used fictitiously. Any resemblance to actual events or locales or persons, living or dead, is entirely coincidental.

This book is published by Pocket Books, a division of Simon & Schuster, Inc., under exclusive license from CBS Studios Inc.

First Pocket Books paperback edition April 2013

POCKET and colophon are registered trademarks of Simon & Schuster, Inc.

For information about special discounts for bulk purchases, please contact Simon & Schuster Special Sales at 1-866-506-1949 or business@simonandschuster.com.

The Simon & Schuster Speakers Bureau can bring authors to your live event. For more information or to book an event, contact the Simon & Schuster Speakers Bureau at 1-866-248-3049 or visit our website at www.simonspeakers.com.

Manufactured in the United States of America

10 9 8 7 6 5 4 3 2 1

ISBN 978-1-5011-4631-2

To Shore Leave, Norwescon,
VikingCon, Lunacon, Philcon,
and all the other fannish gatherings
that have been my comfort zone
for over thirty years now.

PROLOGUE

"Madam President! I need to talk to you about the latest allocations budget. The stellar evolution project cannot monopolize the subspace telescope like this. I need time on the apparatus for my own research!"

Doctor Elena Collins held up her hand to fend off the Tellarite's blustering indignation. "Please, Mav. Not so early. At least let me enjoy my morning tea."

A handsome woman in her early sixties, with long, snowy white hair, she was taking her usual post-breakfast constitutional around the campus. It was a cool, clear morning, approaching the planet's vernal equinox, and the faintly violet sunlight showed off the Institute's grounds and architecture to pleasing effect. Research centers, laboratories, libraries, galleries, an observatory, auditorium, and fully equipped gymnasium rose gracefully from the campus's spacious lawns and courtyards, which were graced with outdoor art installations representing numerous cultures and traditions, both classical and cutting-edge. Even as she strolled down one of the tree-lined pathways winding through the campus, dogged by her irascible colleague, an amateur band was rehearsing on the east lawn. The group boasted a notably eclectic range of instruments, including everything from a Vulcan lyre to a bagpipe and bone flute, while their music sounded like a daring fusion of Klingon opera, Argellian belly-dancing rhythms, Denobulan show tunes, and old-fashioned Kentucky bluegrass. A holographic sculpture of Tarbolde's *Nightingale Woman* danced atop a pedestal behind the musicians, moving in time to the melody. Sipping her tea, a citrusy blend she had discovered during her sabbatical on Tiburon a few years back, she paused to take in the familiar sights and sounds.

She felt very much at home.

The Ephrata Institute was an advanced academic think tank on the outer fringes of the Federation, attracting scholars from all over the quadrant who wished to pursue the life of the mind far from the distractions of civilization. After a somewhat peripatetic career, bouncing from one planet to another, Elena had finally put down roots when she agreed to take over as the Institute's administrator. She had yet to regret that decision, despite the best efforts of prickly geniuses like Mav.

"But, Doctor Collins," he persisted, "you must realize this is intolerable." His porcine face was flushed with anger. Stubby claws waved a flashing data slate in her face. "Professor Kabrol has booked the subspace telescope for most of the next semester, leaving little time for the rest of us." Steam jetted from his snout.

"Typical Orion piracy, if you ask me. Pure, unadulterated brigandage."

"Professor Mav!" Elena said sternly. She put on her most disapproving face, the one that had kept a couple of generations of unruly undergraduates in line. She had found it worked on misbehaving academics as well. "You know we do not tolerate such bigoted sentiments around here. That was unworthy of you . . . and the hallowed traditions of this institution."

For over forty Standard years, the Institute had prided itself on its notably diverse population, which welcomed humanoid—and occasionally nonhumanoid—species from every sector of the quadrant. Just looking around her this morning, she could see humans, Andorians, Tellarites, Deltans, and other sentient life-forms going about their business in more or less perfect harmony. Indeed, Mav had clearly forgotten that Elena's own partner, a distinguished poet, was one-quarter Orion, as evidenced by the subtle jade undertones of her complexion.

Thank providence that Yvete did not overhear Mav's intemperate remark, Elena thought, *or there would be hell to pay.*

To his credit, Mav seemed suitably abashed by her reprimand.

"My sincere apologies," he said gruffly. "I forgot myself. No slur was intended. I am simply passionate about my work, as you know, and can get incensed when I encounter obstacles to completing my research."

"I quite understand," she said, adopting a more conciliatory tone now that she had made her point. "Let us consider the matter forgotten." She reached out and graciously accepted the data slate. "In the meantime, I promise to review the allocation requests and see what I can do to accommodate both you and Professor Kabrol. The universe is not going anywhere, as far as I know, so there should be time enough for both of you to study it—in your own fashions."

Her assurances seemed to mollify the Tellarite cosmologist, at least for now.

"Thank you, Madam President. That's all I was asking."

Until next time, she thought, repressing a weary sigh. Riding herd on a whole passel of temperamental academics, artists, and scientists, all of whom believed that their latest project was the most important thing since Zefram Cochrane broke the warp barrier, could be a challenge, but she wouldn't have it any other way. If nothing else, it made for a highly stimulating environment, albeit a sometimes exhausting one.

"Walk with me," she suggested. "I'm curious to hear more about your recent investigations into cosmological anomalies."

His face lit up, his previous bad humor swept away by her interest. He really was passionate about his work, as was everyone else at Ephrata. It was one of the things that made the Institute such a rewarding place to live and work.

"I would be honored, Madam President. You'll be pleased to know that I am currently developing a revolutionary new theory about the possibility of fluidic space. Imagine that, if you will: an entire subdimensional continuum in which space consists of a liquid rather than a vacuum!"

"How fascinating. Tell me more."

Collins sipped her tea and nodded as he lectured enthusiastically. They continued across the campus toward the observatory. Purple ivy and creepers adorned the steel, glass, and marble walls of the buildings around them. The Institute was nestled in a cozy valley between two gently rising hills. The bulk of the academic facilities were located in the valley, while faculty and visitor housing occupied the wooded slopes. Elena's own home, which she shared with Yvete, was a cozy bungalow nestled between leafy trees that were already changing color with the season. Fallen leaves, blowing across the campus, crackled beneath her tread.

A bell chimed, tolling the hour. Elena recalled that she had a meeting with the head of the geology department after lunch. Something about launching another expedition to explore the planet's inner core. There was even talk of a foreign exchange program with the Hortas on Janus IV. . . .

"Mind you, fluidic space is only a theory now, but it's possible that we might be able to find evidence to support our conceptual models by taking readings from a very specific variety of quantum singularity, which is why is I urgently require more time on the subspace telescope—"

A sudden clap of thunder, coming out of nowhere, startled them both. The wind whipped up without warning, blowing Collins's hair across her face. Tree branches rustled loudly. Fallen leaves skated through the air. The sky, which had been clear and lavender only moments before, was invaded by roiling burgundy clouds that billowed into being directly above the campus. Energy discharges flashed ominously within the rapidly burgeoning clouds. It was both spectacular and frightening.

"What the devil?" Collins whispered.

Gasps and exclamations, erupting all around her, indicated that she and Mav weren't the only ones caught off guard by the unexpected turbulence. All eyes, antennae, and psychic receptors turned toward the seething atmospheric disturbances above. The pulsating clouds blotted out the sun, turning the day dim. The band put down their instruments, unable to compete with the brewing tempest. Mav sniffed the air. His nostrils flared.

"The wind," he announced. "It smells . . . wrong."

The president could smell it too. There was a distinct whiff of ozone in the air, indicative of some sort of ionization effect. Goosebumps broke out over her skin. Tiny hairs stood up along the back of her neck.

"What is this?" Mav asked. He nervously pawed at

THE WEIGHT OF WORLDS

the ground with his heel, digging a short trench in the lawn. "Where did this come from?"

"I don't know," Collins said, equally baffled and concerned. This region of Ephrata IV was known for its mild and temperate climate. Elena had never witnessed weather like this in all the years she had resided on the planet. Certainly, Meteorology had not predicted any major storms in the offing. Unlike the more developed population centers at the heart of the Federation, Ephrata was not equipped with full climate-control stations. They had never seemed necessary before. . . .

Was this an emergency situation? She plucked a communicator from her belt. "Collins here," she said crisply, raising her voice to be heard over the wind and shouting. "Get me Environmental Sciences!"

A burst of static greeted her hail.

"Hello?" she attempted. "Anybody?"

Angry pops and crackles assailed her ears. Scowling, she put down the communicator. Whatever this disturbance was, it was apparently interfering with their communications as well.

Terrific, she thought.

Plasma bolts, crackling with crimson energy, blasted down from the sky, striking the campus. A decorative fountain, of third-dynasty Elasian design, was blown apart by a blast, the sparkling liquid metal in its basin boiling over. Another bolt took out the corner of the Phlox Library. Flying rubble rained down on the campus. Smoke and flames added to the turbulent atmosphere. Startled gasps gave way to screams as men, women, neuters, and androgynes ran for cover. Pandemonium consumed the Institute.

"No," Collins whispered, aghast. "This can't be happening."

A jagged energy bolt shattered the walkway in front of her, only a few meters away. Bits of powdered masonry pelted her face; the brightness of the discharge left spots before her eyes. The teacup slipped from her fingers, crashing unnoticed onto the paving stones. Her ears rang.

"My work!" Mav exclaimed. His piggish eyes bulged from their sockets as yet another bolt hit the main cosmology complex. A wall of ivy burst into flames. "I must save my work!"

Abandoning the president, he raced frantically toward the burning building. She reeled about, trying to figure out where she was needed most. Her eyes still watered from the plasma flash. The wind whipped her long hair about, further obscuring her vision. She angrily brushed it aside. The spreading smoke irritated her nose and throat. She coughed hoarsely.

I have to do something, she thought, *but what?*

As nearly as she could tell, the disturbances were zeroing in on the main square at the center of the Institute, which was attracting the bulk of the plasma strikes. The churning mass of clouds overhead also appeared to be converging on the center square. She heard screams and shouts from that direction. A chill ran down her spine as she remembered that Yvete typically conducted an outdoor poetry jam in the square every morning.

Yvete!

She raced across the campus, passing heartbreaking scenes of chaos and destruction along the way. Overwhelmed medics and security staff, who had never before coped with an emergency on this scale, hurried to the aid of the injured. Automated fire-suppression systems struggled to control the blazes. Directed force fields were employed to cut off the flames' oxygen, but the fires were outracing the fields. Elena wished that she had scheduled more emergency drills.

But would that truly have made any difference? How on Earth—or Ephrata—could you prepare for something like this?

It was a nightmare.

By the time she arrived at Pearl Square, so called for the nacreous white tiles paving the large courtyard, all hell had broken loose. Scientists and scholars were pouring out of the endangered buildings, clutching data slates, microtapes, jars of biological specimens, irreplaceable archaeological artifacts, and even old-fashioned books and papers. A plasma bolt decapitated an imposing silicon statue of Richard Daystrom, as though outraged by that tormented genius's tragic fall. Emergency sirens blared, adding to the cacophony. As if anyone couldn't tell that there was a catastrophe under way!

And then the gravity went mad.

The weight of worlds crashed down on Elena, who suddenly felt as though she had just gained two hundred kilograms. Ephrata's gravity, which was roughly ninety-seven percent Earth-normal, increased to near Jovian proportions, at least where she was standing. Her limbs felt like solid duranium; she could barely lift her feet. It took all her effort not to drop onto the tiles. All her blood seemed to rush to her feet. She felt dizzy and light-headed. Her lungs labored to breathe.

How—? I can't . . .

The weight was unbearable, until, just as quickly as it had fallen upon her, the crushing gravity evaporated and she abruptly felt light as air. The abrupt transition turned her stomach. Her gorge rose, and she clenched her teeth to keep from vomiting.

What is this? Collins thought. The scientist in her desperately tried to make sense of what she was experiencing. Was this a freak natural phenomenon, or some sort of artificial gravity mishap? Had there been an accident at the applied physics lab? She wasn't aware of any experiment that could have triggered a disaster like this, but maybe somebody had carelessly violated the safety protocols?

Heads would roll if that was the case, assuming the entire Institute wasn't about to disappear into a

wormhole or singularity. The natural laws govern-
ing mass and attraction were being rewritten all
around her.

Glancing about in horror, she saw random gravity
fluctuations wreaking havoc on people and property.
The photonic arts gallery collapsed under its weight,
sinking deep into the earth. A fleeing historian lost
touch with the ground and, shrieking in terror, drifted
off into the sky like a lost helium balloon. Elena
watched him disappear into the violent plasma storm
overhead. Blinding flashes threatened to incinerate
him, if he didn't achieve escape velocity first.

Nor was the unfortunate historian alone in his
plight. Afflicted with negative gravity, various friends
and colleagues became unmoored from the planet,
along with random bits of debris and rubble, only
to abruptly regain their weight at terminal heights.
Dagmar Polasky, an award-winning geneticist and
playwright, rose as high as the upper stories of Trang
Hall before suddenly plummeting like a meteor back
down onto the square. A smoking crater mercifully
concealed her remains.

The shocking tragedy drove home the risk to those
she loved.

"Yvete?"

Collins searched for her partner amid the tumult.
At first she couldn't find her, and for a few horrible
moments, she feared that Yvete had been lost to the
sky like those others. Panicked colleagues, fleeing

the devastation, bumped and jostled Elena, blocking her view of the square. She forced her way through the mob toward the formerly peaceful corner where Yvete typically held her poetry jams, in the shade of a levitating abstract sculpture. She shouted hoarsely, choking on the smoke and soot.

"Yvete! *Yvete!*"

Just when she had about given up hope, she spotted the precious poet lying prone on the tiles, seemingly pinned to the ground by an overdose of gravity. The mangled remains of the kinetic sculpture, which had once consisted of floating geometric shapes constantly reorganizing themselves into different configurations, lay in a heap nearby. It looked as though Yvete had gotten out from underneath it just in time. A lifeless tentacle, jutting out from beneath the wreckage, revealed that someone else had not been so lucky.

"Elena?"

Yvete struggled to lift her head from the tiles. Her speech was garbled, as though her tongue was weighed down as well. One arm appeared to be broken. But at least she was alive!

If only for the moment.

Letting out a sigh of relief, Elena started toward her, only to be stopped short by an urgent cry.

"Doctor Collins! Over here!"

She turned to see Officer Hevlas, the head of campus security, limping toward her. Soot covered the Andorian's face, darkening his ordinarily pale blue features. His antennae were in a tizzy, unable to cope with the sensory overload. Turquoise blood leaked from a cut in his forehead. His usually immaculate tan uniform was torn and rumpled.

He looked just as shell-shocked as she felt. Hevlas had been in charge of security for at least a decade, she knew, and in that time he'd seldom had to deal with anything more serious than a few overenthusiastic celebrations or, at worse, a brawl between feuding academics or rival departments. He had once lost a tooth during a dust-up between the Preserver theory advocates and some hard-line Hodgkin's Law devotees, but that was nothing compared to the carnage facing them now. His entire staff numbered fewer than a dozen.

We're not equipped to deal with this, she realized. *None of us are.*

"Madam President!"

Collins hesitated, torn between her need to rush to Yvete's side and her duty to the Institute. Her anguished gaze swung from Hevlas to Yvete and back again. "What is it?" she called out to Hevlas. "What can I do?"

"Look!" he exclaimed. He pointed, with both his fingers and his antennae, at the center of the square. "Something's happening!"

A large oval reflecting pool served as the nucleus of Pearl Square. Rippling aquamarine waters provided an oasis of tranquility at the very heart of the Institute.

On sunny days, Elena often took her lunch by the pool. When the wind blew just right, the Brownian motion of the waters, lapping against osmotic crystals embedded in the basin, caused the pool to literally *sing*.

Now it was screaming.

The plasma bolts converged on the pool, as though drawn to it by some electromagnetic, or perhaps gravitational, force. Concentrated blasts fused the wailing water into a silent sheet of black glass, surrounded by a ring of molten slag. Steam rose from the murdered pool.

But that was just the beginning.

"Do you feel that?" Hevlas asked her. His voice quavered in a way she had never heard before. "In the air?"

"Yes," she whispered.

It was impossible to miss. Weird, indefinable sensations set her nerve endings tingling. A peculiar vibration in the air set her teeth and bones humming. The goosebumps returned in force. She felt nauseous again.

Now what? she wondered.

Reality rippled above the steaming black mirror. At first, Collins thought that maybe her eyes were deceiving her, that it was just a trick of the light, but, no, there was definitely *something* flickering about a meter above the fused remains of the reflecting pool. It started small, no larger than a pinprick, but rapidly expanded, tearing open a hole in the fabric of the universe. Eldritch colors strobed inside the rift, hurting her eyes. Diamond-shaped, the rift expanded and contracted like a pulsating heart, growing measurably larger with each expansion. The harsh yellow light of another dimension spilled through the rift.

"What is it?" Hevlas asked. His hand went to the type-1 phaser holstered at his hip. "Where did it come from?"

"I wish I knew," she said. A theoretical physicist by education, before she found her true calling as an administrator, Collins struggled to interpret what she was seeing. A micro-wormhole? A quantum filament distortion? A Lazarus corridor? Despite the danger and tragic loss of life, she couldn't help but be intrigued by the phenomenon, even as she dreaded what it might portend. She had joked earlier that the universe wasn't going anywhere, but now, staring into this unnatural gap in the space-time continuum, she wasn't quite so sure about that.

Remind me to knock on wood next time, she thought.

One small consolation: the gravitational fluxes and plasma discharges seemed to taper off as the rift manifested. The sky above remained cloudy and turbulent, and the air still smelled of smoke and ozone, but at least the destructive tempest had died down. A hush fell over the square, broken only by the crackling of the flames and the whimpers and moans of the wounded. Collins prayed that the worst was over, but knew better than to count on that.

If only they knew what was coming next.

"Elena?"

No longer pinned by gravity, Yvete staggered over to join them, cradling her injured arm against her chest. Her lovely face was scuffed and scratched, but Elena was grateful for her survival. She placed an arm around Yvete's slender waist as they leaned against each other for support. Yvette was pale and trembling. Her face was more ashen than green.

"Sri Winchdu," she murmured. "He pushed me out of the way just in time. . . . He . . . he didn't make it himself. . . ."

Elena remembered the motionless tentacle protruding from beneath the fallen sculpture. She shuddered to think how many others might have perished as well.

"I know."

But now was not the time to mourn or tally the dead, not while the unnatural rift continued to pulse at the heart of the Institute. No longer growing in size, the diamond-shaped gap sank halfway into the glazed black mirror below, so that it formed a large triangular portal about the size of a large pair of double doors. The same painfully psychedelic colors continued to swirl violently within the rift; it was like looking into the face of a Medusan.

"Careful!" Hevlas said sharply. "Something's coming through!"

He was right. Blurry figures could be glimpsed through the shimmering colors. They seemed small and distant at first, as though many kilometers away, but time and space and perspective appeared to be distorted by passage through the rift. In a matter of moments, a cadre of darkly clad humanoids emerged from the portal, setting foot on the glassy remains of the reflecting pool, which cracked loudly beneath their weight.

The aliens were at least two meters in height, wearing belted black tunics and boots. Layers of overlapping silver scales armored their skin. Segmented limbs had a vaguely crustacean look. Glossy black eyes, lacking any visible irises, were more striking than the small, beak-like protuberances that barely registered as noses. A mane of translucent golden spines, like the tentacles of a sea anemone, framed their masculine-looking faces in the place of hair or fur. Hinged jaws hung open as the aliens chanted and marched in unison. An errant breeze carried a smoky aroma, like burnt paper, from the aliens. Green sashes, ranging in hue from chartreuse to jade, stretched diagonally across their chests. Collins wondered if the various shades of green denoted rank.

This was more than just an academic concern; she needed to figure out who was in charge.

An advance guard arrived first, fanning out to secure the area immediately around the rift. Polished obsidian batons, roughly thirty centimeters long, were clipped to their belts, but no other weapons were in evidence. Elena prayed that was a good sign.

"Who?" Yvete whispered.

Elena had no idea. She had traveled widely in her time, and had studied even more, but this was no species known to her. She suspected they were not known to this *universe.*

"Get back!" Hevlas advised. Drawing his phaser, he took up a defensive posture between the intruders and the faculty. A handful of his junior officers, looking distinctly the worse for wear, fanned out behind him. Elena guessed that the rest of the security staff was dead, injured, or dealing with fires, casualties, and other emergencies all across the campus. "Better let us handle this, Madam President."

Collins had her own thoughts about that, but before she could respond, one last alien emerged from the rift. His measured pace and commanding bearing instantly pegged him as the expedition's leader. He also appeared somewhat taller and older. His "beard" of wriggling tentacles was fuller and more imposing, while his higher status was denoted by a striped sash that incorporated every shade of green, as well as by a waist-length black cape with dark green lining. A four-fingered hand clutched a meter-long black lance that appeared to be a larger and more ornate version of the batons worn by his men. Jade and turquoise rings marked off sections of the shaft, while the sharpened head of the lance resembled a large obsidian teardrop. His silver face bore a severe expression. Lustrous black eyes looked about with what appeared to be disapproval. He cut off his men's chanting with a wave of his hand, then stamped the foot of his lance against the cracked black mirror beneath him.

"Rejoice!" he declared, speaking standard English with an odd accent. His voice was deep and reverberating. "I am Sokis, warrior-priest of the Crusade. We bring you Truth and Harmony—before it is too late!"

"Truth?" Hevlas snarled, enraged by the death and havoc unleashed by the strangers' arrival. He raised his phaser. "I'll show you enlightenment!"

"Stand down, Officer!" Elena placed a restraining hand on his arm. His phaser, per Institute regulations, was set permanently on stun, but just the same, she had no intention of allowing him to shoot first and ask questions later. "Hold your fire . . . for now."

The Andorian's arm trembled beneath her grip. He kept his finger on the trigger of his weapon. "But . . ."

She understood his fear and anger. Her own heart grieved for the dead and the wounded, as well as for the devastation unleashed on the Institute, but if this was a first-contact situation, it needed to be handled accordingly. As horrific as the day's event had been, it would be even more tragic if their first encounter with visitors from another dimension ended in violence.

"We don't know for certain that this was an attack," she reminded him. "For all we know, the . . . disturbances . . . might have just been an unexpected side effect of their passage here. A tragic byproduct of opening that rift."

"Or maybe they just didn't care," Hevlas said.

"Possibly," she conceded. "But we won't know that unless we ask." She increased her pressure on his arm. "Stand down, Officer."

He reluctantly lowered his weapon, and signaled his people to do the same. "I don't like this," he muttered.

"Duly noted." She reluctantly let go of Yvete and started forward. "Let's try talking to them first."

Yvete reached out with her good arm and laid her hand on Elena's shoulder. "Are you sure about this?"

"Not in the least," Elena confessed, but what choice did she have? Hadn't she just been lecturing Mav on the importance of working peacefully with beings from other worlds and cultures? She had a chance here to make contact, and maybe even initiate a fruitful exchange of knowledge and beliefs, with a previously unknown alien race, possibly from an entirely different plane of reality. How could she possibly turn away from that opportunity out of fear and suspicion? "But this is what Ephrata is all about."

Yvette nodded and withdrew her hand. "Be careful, my love."

"Just write a nice poem about me if this doesn't work out."

Her mouth dry, Collins approached the strangers. She held out open palms in what she hoped was a universal gesture of peace. She swallowed hard, wishing she'd fortified herself with something a little stronger than tea.

"Greetings. Welcome to Ephrata. On behalf of my people, I—"

"Silence!" Sokis barked. "We have no interest in your false knowledge and lies. We come to save you, not sully our ears with your heresies."

"I don't understand," Elena said, still hoping to establish a dialogue. She wiped her sweaty palms on her slacks. "Save us from what?"

"The End of all things. But fear not, for we bring the weight of the Truth to this fractured realm."

He raised his lance. The opaque black shaft lit up from within with a flickering jade-green radiance. The head of the lance spun along its vertical axis. A low whine, not unlike the chant the aliens had keened earlier, emanated from the weapon. The glowing lance cast dark-green shadows on the square.

"*Tezha,*" Hevlas swore. "I've had enough of this."

He fired his phaser at Sokis. A sapphire beam shot across the courtyard, only to fall short of its target. An invisible force tugged on the beam, dragging it down to the ground, where it discharged harmlessly against the pearly tiles, leaving not even a scorch mark behind.

The Andorian's jaw dropped. He gaped in shock.

"Son of an Aenar!"

Artificial gravity, Collins realized, *employed as a*

shield. Her mind boggled at the concept. *Theoretically possible, I suppose, but . . .*

"Let there be no more defiance," Sokis declared. "Bow down before the weight of Truth."

He waved his lance at Collins and the others. Weaponized gravity swept across the campus, driving the survivors to the ground. What felt like hundreds of kilograms yanked Elena down onto the floor of the square, holding her fast. Her face was pressed against the tiles as she lay prostrate before the invaders, unable to lift a finger.

The Crusade had come to Ephrata.

ONE

Captain's Log. Stardate 6012.9.

The Enterprise *has concluded a successful week charting the Wyvern system, a region devoid of intelligent life but full of fascinating planets, moons, asteroid belts, and radiation fields, or so my first officer informs me. In the meantime, with no immediate crisis on the horizon, the crew is looking forward to some much-needed recreation . . .*

"Mister Spock," Lieutenant Uhura said. "Do you have a minute?"

The Vulcan science officer looked up from his scanner. "At our present cruising speed, we are not expected to arrive at Starbase 13 for another 72.03 hours. You have my attention for as many minutes as you require. How can I assist you?"

It was a relatively quiet moment on the bridge. The *U.S.S. Enterprise* was cruising at warp 2 through the interstellar void, with the Wyvern system receding in the ship's aft sensors. Captain James T. Kirk listened casually to the conversation behind him as he reviewed the latest maintenance reports from engineering. A yeoman offered him a fresh cup of coffee, which he gratefully accepted.

"Oh, I doubt this will take 72.03 hours," Uhura quipped. She wandered away from the communications station to confer with Spock at his post. "I'm just organizing this year's holiday party, and I wanted your input."

Spock arched an eyebrow. "I am not certain that I am the appropriate officer to consult on such a matter. Levity is hardly the Vulcan way."

That's putting it lightly, Kirk thought. He wondered what Uhura was about.

"Well, that's what I wanted to ask you about," she said. "As usual, the holiday party embraces the varied cultures and traditions of the ship's entire crew, celebrating Christmas, Hanukkah, Kwanza, Diwali, Ramadan, *mololo zam,* and the Saturnian Blessing of the Rings, but I admit that I'm not terribly familiar with the customs of your people, Mister Spock. Are there any Vulcan holidays or rituals you would like us to include in the festivities?"

Kirk rotated the captain's chair around to observe Spock's science station. The general chatter on the bridge died down, the better to eavesdrop on this increasingly intriguing conversation. Kirk suspected that Chekov and Sulu and the rest of the bridge crew were listening in as well. Even though they had all been serving beside Spock for at least four years now, there was still much they didn't know about Vulcan life and customs. Spock, like the rest of his people, tended to be rather close-lipped on the subject.

"You need not trouble yourself on my behalf, Lieutenant," he said, "although you are to be applauded for your efforts at inclusiveness, which are very much in keeping with the Vulcan philosophy of IDIC."

Infinite diversity in infinite combinations, Kirk translated mentally. He was quite familiar with the motto, which was one of the fundamental touchstones of Vulcan civilization. It had also been one of the guiding principles behind the formation of the Federation itself. No small surprise, considering that Vulcan, along with Earth, was a founding member of the UFP.

"So you *never* celebrated any holidays at home?" Uhura pressed. "Not even when you were growing up?"

"That is not entirely the case," Spock admitted. "My father occasionally indulged my mother's fondness for certain Terran holidays, most notably the human custom of St. Valentine's Day."

Uhura reacted with delight to this unexpected revelation. "Why, Mister Spock, that's positively romantic!"

"On the contrary," he stated, "it is simply logical. In a universe populated by myriad species and cultures, respecting and accommodating each other's disparate traditions is the only rational response."

"Well said, Mister Spock," Kirk said, joining the discussion. "I believe it was George Bernard Shaw who famously stated that a barbarian was someone who confused the customs of his own tribe with the laws of the universe. Or words to that effect."

Kirk half expected Spock to make some gibe about humans being well equipped to comment on the topic of barbarism, but the Vulcan refrained, possibly because Doctor McCoy was not in earshot. Bones was presently holding down the fort in sickbay, dealing with an outbreak of Therbian fever among the crew, which meant there was nobody on the bridge to provoke.

"A most civilized sentiment," Spock said instead, "particularly for an Earthman of his generation."

"What about you, Captain?" Uhura asked. "Can we expect you at the party?"

"Er, we'll see," he hedged. After the Helen Noel incident a few years back, he was still a bit leery of holiday parties. Such celebrations were good for morale, but too much fraternization could lead to some awkward moments afterward. *Thank goodness Helen eventually transferred over to the* Reliant, he thought. "It depends on what my schedule is looking like."

Uhura wasn't going to let him off that easy.

"I'm sure the whole crew is hoping you'll attend, sir. It wouldn't be the same without you."

She had a point, he admitted. Maybe if he just made an appearance?

"Well, I certainly wouldn't want to disappoint the crew—"

An urgent chime from the communications station interrupted him. Uhura hurried back to her post and adjusted her earpiece. All talk of parties and holidays was instantly put aside as she resumed her duties with her usual brisk professionalism.

"Captain," she reported urgently, "we're receiving an emergency distress signal from Ephrata IV."

"Ephrata?" he echoed. "The Institute?"

It had to be. As far as he knew, there were no other colonies or settlements in the Ephrata system. Indeed, the Institute had chosen Ephrata IV because of its remote and isolated location, far from the hustle and bustle of more populated systems. Seclusion was considered more conducive to serious study and contemplation.

"Put it on the screen," he ordered.

Uhura consulted her control panel and displays. "I'm trying, sir, but there's interference with the visual component of the signal. I'm mostly getting audio only." She turned toward the main viewer at the front of the bridge. "Coming through now."

On the screen, a burst of visual snow replaced a view of the starry vista they had been traversing. The head and shoulders of a humanoid figure could be only dimly glimpsed through the chaff. A feminine voice, punctuated by static, cried out in obvious distress:

"Help us! This is the Ephrata Institute, requesting immediate assistance. . . ." Crackles and pops obscured the audio, so that only snippets could be heard. " . . . disaster . . . casualties . . . gravity of the situation . . ."

Kirk thought he recognized the voice. He leaned

forward in his seat, trying in vain to make out the figure's features.

"Elena?"

Doctor Collins was an old family friend from Iowa who had often played bridge with his parents when Kirk was growing up. Last he heard, she had accepted a position as president of the Ephrata Institute. He couldn't remember the last time he'd seen her in person. Probably at Sam's and Aurelan's funeral. As he recalled, she'd come all the way from Alpha Centauri to attend his brother's and sister-in-law's memorial services on Deneva. Kirk had been touched by her thoughtfulness.

"Elena!" he said. "What's happening? What's the nature of your emergency?"

"It's no use, Captain," Uhura said. "This signal was sent days ago. We're only just now receiving the signal." She fiddled with her controls. "Unable to establish direct communication with Ephrata at this time."

"Keep trying."

Frustration gnawed at Kirk. Out here on the final frontier, remote settlements like the one on Ephrata were often cut off from relief or communication for days, weeks, or even months at a time. For all he knew, the disaster at the Institute had come and gone—and Elena and the other scholars were already dead or dying.

"*Emergency!*" she repeated. "*Gravity . . . the weight of worlds . . . help us. . . .*"

The transmission ended abruptly. Nothing but snow and static filled the screen.

"Uhura?"

"That's all, Captain." She hit a switch, and an endless sea of open space returned to the viewer. "The signal appears to have been cut off at the source."

"Understood." Kirk would have liked more information, but his course was clear. Their routine call on Starbase 13 would have to wait. "Mister Sulu, set a course for Ephrata IV. Warp factor 6."

"Aye, aye, sir." The helmsman consulted the astrogator located at the helm and navigation stations. "Estimated time to Ephrata system thirty-nine hours, seventeen minutes."

Damn it, Kirk thought. He found himself wishing that the Institute had chosen a location somewhat less off the beaten track. "Any chance that another vessel might have already responded to that distress signal?"

"Unlikely, Captain," Spock reported. "As you know, Ephrata IV is isolated by design. The *Enterprise* is the only Federation starship in this sector, and the odds that a private or commercial vessel would be in their vicinity are roughly seven hundred sixty to one."

"I was afraid of that," Kirk said. Aside from the typically precise probability, Spock hadn't told him anything he didn't already suspect. The *Enterprise* was probably the only chance those people had, if they were still alive to be rescued. He turned to his first officer for guidance. "Your thoughts?"

"There is insufficient data to reach any definite conclusions," Spock said. He called up the latest reports and information on Ephrata from the ship's memory banks and swiftly reviewed the relevant material. "The Ephrata Institute appears to have been thriving. There is no indication that the settlement was encountering any significant difficulties. A supply ship, the *Yakima*, visited the planet six months ago and reported nothing untoward. The Institute's primary output was academic papers and research studies."

"And then what happened?" Kirk wondered aloud. "An epidemic? A natural disaster? An alien attack?"

"The last is improbable," Spock said. "The Ephrata system is safely distant from the Klingon, Romulan, and Tholian borders. And the surrounding systems contain no potentially hostile species with warp capacity."

Kirk wanted to believe him. "What about some enemy unknown to us?"

"Always possible, Captain, but it is uncertain where precisely such a threat would originate." Spock eyed Kirk with concern, and a hint of compassion. "I take it you know Doctor Collins?"

"Very well," Kirk admitted, but did not elaborate. There would be time enough to fill in Spock and McCoy on his personal connection to this crisis; the rest of the crew didn't need to worry about their captain being emotionally compromised. Kirk stared at the distant stars ahead, mentally willing them nearer. Thirty-nine long hours stretched out before him. He briefly considered upping their speed to warp 7, even over Scotty's inevitable protests, but thought better of it. Warp 7 would place too great a strain on the ship and its resources, and they had no idea what they were in for once they reached Ephrata. He didn't want to face the crisis ahead, whatever it was, with a ship and crew at anything less than peak efficiency, ready for anything.

"Total population on Ephrata?" he asked.

Spock had the data at his fingertips. "Seven hundred and eighty-six, plus or minus various guest lecturers and teaching assistants."

"Nearly eight hundred souls," Kirk repeated. *Including Elena Collins.*

He wondered how many, if any, of the scholars were still alive. And what exactly he would find on Ephrata IV.

TWO

"Still no luck, Captain," Uhura reported. *"The Institute is not responding to any of our hails."*

"Understood," Kirk said into the intercom in the ship's main transporter room. His finger pressed down on the speaker button. "Looks like we're going to have to get our answers on the ground."

The *Enterprise* had entered orbit around Ephrata IV less than half an hour ago. Although the ship's sensors had detected over a thousand humanoid life-forms on the planet, all efforts to make contact with Elena Collins or anyone else at the Institute had met with failure. Peculiar gravimetric distortions, emanating from the center of the campus, had interfered with the ship's long-range scanners, making a closer look at the site problematic. All they could tell for sure was that the Institute was still there—and still inhabited.

That's something, Kirk thought, but he still didn't like the idea of beaming in blind. *Why aren't they responding?*

Nearly forty hours had passed since they had first received the distress signal. He was anxious to find out what state the Institute was in.

"*Good luck, Captain,*" Uhura said.

"Thank you, Lieutenant. Kirk out."

He stepped away from the intercom to join the rest of the landing party, who were ready to beam down to the planet. Spock and Sulu waited on the transporter platform, accompanied by Ensign Fawzia Yaseen, an experienced security officer who had recently transferred over from the *U.S.S. Sally Ride.* She was an attractive woman of Middle Eastern descent. Her regulation red uniform flattered her trim, athletic figure.

Also on hand was a notably cantankerous party crasher.

"Damn it, Jim," Doctor Leonard McCoy protested. "Why won't you let me beam down with you? There could be injured in need of treatment!"

"We don't know that, Bones," Kirk replied. "In the meantime, I need you to take care of those sick crew members . . . and yourself."

Although treatable, Therbian fever was a nasty bug that had not spared McCoy himself. His weathered face was more haggard than usual. Puffy bags hung beneath his eyes, and he braced himself against the transporter controls as though slightly unsteady on his feet. His voice was hoarse, his nose stuffy, and his chest sounded congested. Wheezes and coughs punctuated his arguments. He had been working himself ragged, over Nurse Chapel's protests, to take care of his patients, even while getting over his own bout with the disease.

"I have things under control," McCoy insisted. "My patients are all responding to treatment and should be back on their feet in a day or so. Sickbay can spare me long enough to find out what's going on down there."

Kirk believed him, but also knew that McCoy already had a lot on his plate—and could use some rest.

"Just let us get the lay of the land first," Kirk said. "If your services are required, you're only a transporter beam away."

"I've heard that before," McCoy grumbled, "usually right before some hostile aliens trap you in a force field."

"In which case, you are safer aboard the ship, Doctor," Spock pointed out. "Particularly in your present condition."

"Who says I want to be safe, you cold-blooded, pointy-eared computer? And if I wanted your medical opinion . . . well, trust me, that's never going to happen."

"My decision stands, Bones." Kirk tried to lighten the moment with a quip. "Besides, I thought you didn't like house calls . . . or transporters."

"That's beside the point and you know it," McCoy said, but knew when to back down. Not even the ship's doctor could change Kirk's mind when it was made up. "At least take Chapel with you, just in case."

Kirk respected the nurse's abilities, but felt she could better serve the ship in sickbay at the moment, if only to look after McCoy and make sure the doctor didn't end up in worse shape than his patients. It would be just like McCoy to neglect his health in favor of others.

"Not necessary," he said. "Yaseen here is a trained combat medic. Isn't that so, Ensign?"

"Yes, sir," she said, standing stiffly at attention. A fully equipped medkit, slung over her shoulder, accompanied the type-2 phaser pistol at her hip. "If you say so, sir."

"At ease, Ensign," Kirk said. "Your record speaks for itself."

He had reviewed her file when her name had turned up on the duty roster. Yaseen had performed admirably during a siege on Brubaker Prime, keeping several injured crew members alive until reinforcements could arrive. She had been rewarded with a commendation—and a transfer to the *Enterprise*.

"Well, I still don't like it," Bones said. "No offense, Ensign."

"None taken, sir," Yaseen said.

"Your preferences are not material, Doctor," Spock added, taking advantage of the opportunity to tweak McCoy. "The captain has made his decision."

"Easy for you to say," McCoy groused. "You're not being left behind like a broken hypospray."

Kirk decided to cut the banter short. "We need a doctor, you'll be the first to know." He hopped onto the platform beside the others. "Mister Kyle, you have the coordinates for the Institute?"

"Yes, Captain." Kyle manned the transporter controls in place of Scotty, who was currently in command of the bridge. "I should be able to place you right in the middle of the campus."

"Good," Kirk said. "Beam us down."

"Aye, aye, sir."

The familiar whine of the transporter effect arose as the landing party dissolved into energy. The sound lingered in Kirk's ears as he rematerialized on the planet below.

It was dark.

Although it had been midafternoon by shipboard reckoning, it was the wee hours of the morning in this time zone on the planet. Ordinarily, Kirk would beam down to a hemisphere facing the sun, or else delay his arrival until it was a decent hour at a planet's main population center, colony, or capital, but that had not been an option this time. He'd needed to go where the Institute was, and he wasn't about to wait for dawn to rise in this part of the world. If that meant disturbing the Institute in the middle of the night, so be it.

They were greeted by a cool autumn breeze upon materializing. As predicted, they had touched down in a large courtyard in the center of the campus. Although it was quiet now, it was obvious that some manner of catastrophe had struck the Institute in the recent past. The square's outdoor lamps were dark and/or toppled, so that only a crescent moon provided any light to see by. Peering about, Kirk saw that several of the surrounding buildings had undergone significant damage, with evidence of both fires and explosions. Rubble was strewn across the square. A heap of mangled metal and crystal looked as though it had once been some sort of sculpture. An empty pedestal had been stripped of whatever statute had once posed upon it. Scorch marks, resembling those left behind by disruptor blasts, blackened cracked walls, overturned trees, and even portions of the pearly tiles beneath their feet. The floor of the square was pitted with craters and shattered masonry. Kirk was reminded of Cestus III . . . after the Gorn attack.

No bodies, he noted with relief. Although, judging from the scenery, it was hard to imagine that there hadn't been some fatalities.

"My God," Sulu said, gazing about at the wreckage. His hand went instinctively to the type-1 phaser on his belt. "What do you think happened here, Captain?"

"That's what I mean to find out," Kirk said. "Spock?"

The Vulcan was riveted by a bizarre structure in the center of the square. An elaborate apparatus, which appeared to have been cobbled together from various cannibalized bits of technology, framed a shimmering triangular void filled with coruscating lights and colors that hurt Kirk's eyes to look upon. A touch of vertigo made him feel slightly dizzy.

"Fascinating," Spock observed.

If the strobing colors caused Spock any discomfort, his lean, ascetic features betrayed no sign of it. Simple Vulcan stoicism, Kirk wondered, or were Spock's inner eyelids providing him with an extra degree of protection from the disturbing spectacle?

Probably a bit of both, Kirk guessed.

"What is it, Spock?"

Spock scanned the void with his tricorder. "If my readings are correct, this appears to be a dimensional rift of some sort. It is also the source of the exotic gravimetric distortions we detected from orbit." He perused the readouts on the tricorder. "Further study is required, but preliminary data suggests that some variety of artificial gravity is being employed to tear open a gap in the space-time continuum, possibly opening a passage to another reality."

Kirk tensed. On rare occasions, the *Enterprise* had encountered such phenomena before. Danger had usually resulted.

"Is that possible?" the captain asked.

"Theoretically," Spock said. "Gravity itself, from a certain perspective, is simply a curvature in space-time. That being the case, it is more than possible that applied gravity could distort or even rupture the fabric of reality. However, the amount of energy, and control, required to create and maintain such a rift is staggering to consider—and currently far beyond the abilities of the Federation or any of its rivals."

Kirk cautiously circled the rift. Oddly, it appeared

as a triangular portal from every angle, rising up from a cracked black mirror that darkly reflected the iridescent colors within the rift. Sulu and Yaseen watched his back as he inspected the portal, even as their curious eyes were drawn to the puzzling phenomenon as well. None of them knew quite what to make of it.

"What about this apparatus?" Kirk asked. "Can you tell who built it?"

"Negative, Captain." Spock inspected the mechanism from a safe distance, taking care not to touch it. "The technology is unfamiliar to me."

That's saying a lot, Kirk thought. There wasn't much that his science officer didn't know when it came to high-tech hardware, both conventional and exotic. Spock had often been known to figure out the operation of alien computers and control panels on a crash basis, which had saved the *Enterprise*'s bacon on more than one occasion. *Like that time on Miramanee's world.*

"This *is* a research facility," Sulu observed. He glanced at the darkened buildings surrounding the square. "Maybe some sort of experiment that went awry?"

"Doubtful," Spock stated. "During our voyage here, I reviewed the most recent scientific papers and reports generated by the Institute. There was nothing of this nature under way."

"Perhaps an unpublished discovery or breakthrough?" Kirk suggested. "That hadn't been made public yet?"

"Possible," Spock said, "but unlikely. As I said, the technology does not conform to any known scientific disciplines or engineering principles. It is as though it sprang out of nowhere." He eyed the rift speculatively. "Or perhaps from somewhere unknown to us."

"Another dimension?" Kirk said.

Spock nodded. "With its own technology and sciences."

"I see."

Kirk was both intrigued and alarmed by the prospect. He recalled Spock's observation days ago that there were no hostile alien races in the vicinity of Ephrata. But what if an attack had come not from across space, but from an adjacent reality? Stranger things had happened. Kirk himself had once exchanged places with his counterpart from a brutal mirror universe. And then there was that business with Lazarus . . .

Yaseen glanced around the deserted square. "But where is everybody?"

"That's what I want to know," Kirk said grimly. Even considering the hour, it was worrisome that there appeared to be no activity going on in any of the surrounding buildings. You would expect at least a few dedicated researchers or academics to be burning the midnight oil . . . unless something had shut down the Institute entirely. Back at the Academy, there was always somebody working or studying, no matter the hour. Ditto for the *Enterprise*.

Where is Elena? Did something happen to her?

Turning his attention away from the triangular rift, he contemplated the faculty housing on the hills. Cozy bungalows, pagodas, and geodesic domes reflected a range of architectural styles and cultural influences. He gestured toward the western slope.

"According to the ship's computer, Doctor Collins's residence is that way. Let's start there."

"That may not be necessary, Captain." Spock lowered his tricorder and squinted into the shadows surrounding them. "We appear to have company."

Dozens of figures entered the square from all directions, emerging from the damaged buildings and unlighted pathways. In the faint moonlight, it was difficult to make out their faces, but they appeared humanoid enough, and were dressed in worn civilian attire. Kirk estimated at least seven hundred survivors.

Looks like those life-forms readings were accurate, he concluded, relieved by the sight of the survivors. Perhaps the disaster had not been as devastating as he had feared, and there had been fewer fatalities. *I could live with that.*

"Hello," he called out to reassure the Ephratans. "We're from the *Enterprise*. . . ."

His voice trailed off as the approaching figures stepped into the light. To his surprise, every member of the crowd wore the same burnished silver mask. Only their eyes were visible through the masks, which were affixed to their faces somehow. Protruding beaks made room for noses and snouts of various sizes. Hinged jaws allowed for speech and respiration. A metallic gold fringe framed the faces of the men. Eerily homogeneous in nature, the masks seemed to erase the survivors' individualities even as they concealed their identities. There was something distinctly unsettling about them.

"Captain?" Sulu asked. His hand remained glued to his phaser.

"Stand fast, Lieutenant." Kirk wished he had more in the way of an explanation to offer the helmsman. "Remember, this is a relief mission."

"Yes, sir."

The crowd closed in on the landing party, surrounding them. It was clear that, beneath their masks, any number of alien races were represented in the assemblage. Their hands and paws and tails gripped a variety of improvised weapons: twisted metal rods, rocks and chunks of rubble, heavy tree branches, hammers, a steak knife, a laser scalpel . . .

Simply for self-defense?

"Phasers on stun," Kirk instructed. "But hold your fire."

He scanned the crowd, searching for a familiar . . . face? The masks frustrated his efforts, but his eyes zeroed in on one particular figure in the forefront of the crowd. A mane of lustrous white hair distinguished a masked woman whose gait and build stirred Kirk's memory.

"Doctor Collins? Elena?"

"Accept the Truth!" she said fervently, her voice slightly muffled by the mask. Crazed blue eyes gleamed behind the disguise. She clutched what looked like an antique Troyian dagger, possibly salvaged from the Institute's xenoarchaeology department. "Surrender to the Truth . . . or face obliteration!"

"What?" Kirk recognized the voice, but not the zealous tone. Elena Collins had always been a very sensible, level-headed individual, as she would have to be to run an institution like Ephrata. He had seldom known her to raise her voice. "We received a distress signal. What is the nature of your emergency?"

"The end of all things is nigh. Only the Truth can save you!"

"Captain?" Sulu repeated. "I'm not liking the sound of this."

You and me both, Kirk thought. Memories of Beta III surfaced from the past. He was getting an uncomfortably Landru-like vibe from the masked survivors, who began chanting an atonal hymn or dirge in a language Kirk didn't recognize. Even the universal translator seemed stymied by the unearthly refrain. "Spock?"

"The music is not to my taste," he replied, "but beyond that I have little to offer." He put away his tricorder, slinging the strap over his shoulder, and drew his phaser. "I suspect, however, that Doctor Collins and the other Ephratans are not themselves."

"I would hope not," Yaseen said. "'Cause I'm picking up a real whiff of crazy here."

Kirk had the same feeling.

"We have cast aside the deceits of this universe!" Elena insisted. "Surrender to the Truth and you will survive the coming cataclysm!"

"Not until someone tells me what is going on!" Kirk said, losing his patience. It was as though the entire population had become possessed by some kind of religious mania. "I want some solid, concrete answers."

"We have seen the Truth," she repeated, unhelpfully. The chanting grew louder and more militant. She brandished the ancient dagger. "As will you!"

The masked zealots, including Elena, charged at the landing party from all sides. They waved their makeshift weapons in the air. Unnervingly, they kept on chanting.

"Fire!" Kirk ordered. "Stun only!"

Phaser beams swept in arcs over the attacking crowd, dropping the first wave of assailants to the ground, where they were immediately trampled on by the zealots behind them, who displayed no fear of the landing party's superior firepower. Kirk and the others formed a tight circle, their backs to each other, as they defended themselves against the crazed mob. Kirk winced as a beam from his own type-1 phaser stunned Elena Collins, causing her to crumple to the ground. His jaw clenched.

This is all wrong, he thought. *We came to rescue these people, not battle them!*

"Captain." Spock calmly fended off attacks from the east. "Might I suggest a strategic retreat?"

"Logical as ever, Mister Spock." Kirk used his free hand to unhook his communicator from his belt. He flipped it open with a practiced motion and held it to his lips. "Scotty. Beam us up!"

Static crackled from the device.

"Scotty? Kyle? Uhura?"

There was no response.

"I can't make contact with the ship!" Kirk shouted. "We're cut off!"

Sulu held his own against the mob. "This just keeps getting better and bet—"

A phaser beam, flashing out of the crowd, hit Sulu, knocking him out in mid-sentence. The helmsman collapsed onto the scorched pearly tiles.

"Hikaru!"

Yaseen swept her phaser in a wider arc, trying to compensate for Sulu's absence, while simultaneously crouching to check on their downed comrade. She placed her fingers against his neck.

"He's alive," she reported. "Just stunned."

Kirk was glad to hear it. *They want to convert us,* he guessed, *not kill us.*

He was none too keen on either prospect.

Another beam shot from the same direction, barely missing Kirk. He could feel the phased energy sizzle past his ear. The beam continued past its target to strike a zealot charging from the opposite direction. The stunned attacker—a Tellarite from the looks of him—was dropped in his tracks.

Kirk was grateful for the assist, but wasn't about to give the enemy sniper another shot. Clubs and knives were bad enough; they didn't need a phaser blasting at them as well. Tracking the origin of the beam, Kirk spotted the shooter: a masked security officer whose twitching blue antennae betrayed his Andorian roots. The uniformed sniper elbowed his way through the crowd, trying to get a clear shot at the Starfleet officers. His fellow zealots jostled and obstructed him, interfering with his aim. These were academics, not soldiers, Kirk remembered; their tactics left something to be desired.

A gap opened in the crowd. The Andorian aimed at Kirk.

Kirk was faster.

A sapphire beam struck at literally the speed of light. The Andorian toppled backward, his type-1 phaser flying from his fingers. The weapon, as well as the Andorian's unconscious form, was swallowed up by the rioting mob. Kirk hoped that the other zealots were too crazed to retrieve it.

We should be so lucky, he thought.

Despite their advantage in training and arms, the situation was becoming increasingly untenable. Sulu was already down and the chanting zealots kept on coming. Kirk was already sick of that damn anthem.

"Captain!" Yaseen shouted. "To your right!"

A masked Orion woman, scrambling up the side of a large pile of rubble, threw herself at Kirk from above. She sailed above the sweeping phaser beams keeping the other zealots at bay. A green fist was wrapped around a polished metal chisel. Kirk dodged the attack just in time, twisting out of the way of the chisel as the woman crashed to the ground within the landing party's defensive circle. Fueled by fanaticism, the Orion sprang nimbly to her feet, slashing wildly with her weapon. Intent on Kirk, she overlooked Spock, who pinched her neck with one hand while continuously firing his phaser with the other. The masked woman slid to the ground, landing only a few centimeters away from Sulu. Kirk wondered what her name was, and who she had been . . . before.

"A more defensible location may be order," Spock observed.

Kirk was inclined to agree. His eyes searched the ruined campus as he repelled the never-ending zealots with his phaser. His gaze went at first to the shimmering rift at the center of the square. Its iridescent depths offered a possible route to . . . where?

No, Kirk thought. *I don't think we're quite that desperate yet.*

A darkened library to their left struck him as a more promising option. The two-story building appeared structurally sound, and its open doorway was less than fifty meters away. A colonnaded portico also offered potential cover from any future phaser blasts.

Kirk couldn't rule out the possibility that there were
more sidearms in the mob.

"Over there!" he ordered. "That library!"

A few dozen zealots teemed between them and
their destination; they would have to clear a path
through the massed hostiles, without actually hurting
anyone, Kirk reminded himself. As Spock had put it,
the survivors were not themselves. *Elena* had not been
herself. They couldn't risk using their phasers at any
higher settings.

Something's been done to these people, Kirk thought.
*I don't know how or by whom, but it's not their fault. We
don't even know who the real enemy is yet.*

Sulu was still out cold, making their retreat more
complicated. Yaseen bent to lift him, but Spock had
another idea.

"Allow me, Ensign."

"I can manage, sir," Yaseen insisted.

"No doubt," Spock said. "But you are not a Vulcan.
Under the circumstances, it is only logical that we take
advantage of my natural strength."

Yaseen shrugged. "Can't argue with that, sir." She
stepped back, providing cover with her phaser, while
Spock easily hefted Sulu onto his shoulders in a fire-
man's carry. "Thank you, sir."

"Watch our backs, Ensign," Kirk instructed, taking
point. With Spock and Sulu between them, he set his
sights on the library. He kept his phaser set on stun.
Here's hoping that's enough.

He didn't get a chance to find out.

"Infidels! Halt your defiance!"

The crowd parted to reveal a tall, caped alien standing on the empty pedestal. He was an imposing humanoid, over two meters tall, whose scaly skin had a metallic silver sheen. A pair of lustrous ebony eyes peered out of a smooth, inhuman countenance with only a slight beak of a nose. A hinged jaw reminded Kirk of a Moray eel. Clear golden spines "bearded" his face.

Kirk didn't recognize the species.

A belted black tunic, made of a satiny black material, clothed the alien's broad torso, exposing silvery, segmented limbs and joints. A striped green sash stretched across his chest, matching the green-lined cloak hanging from his shoulders. One hand grasped a gleaming black lance. Metallic rings girded the weapon's shaft. A polished black teardrop was mounted at its business end.

A squadron of similar aliens, numbering at least fifty soldiers, flanked their commander, whose status was evident by his more ornate attire, weaponry, and fringe. The other intruders had smaller beards, no cloaks, and were armed merely with short obsidian batons. They appeared to be male, although sex could be tricky to determine when dealing with an unknown alien species. Kirk had been fooled before.

Not that it mattered right now.

He noted the obvious resemblance between the

aliens' silver faces and the masks worn by the brainwashed survivors. It was as though the varied members of the Institute had surrendered their individual identities to emulate the strangers—or had been forced to.

Here at last was the true face of the enemy.

"You have done well, my adopted kin," the alien commander addressed the masked devotees. His deep, resounding voice made a Klingon sound like a soprano by comparison. "Your newfound devotion to the Truth does you credit. But it appears stronger measures are required to liberate these visitors from the lies of this false universe."

Kirk wondered why the invaders had not shown themselves earlier. He suspected that the aliens had used the converted academics as cannon fodder, possibly to gauge the landing party's defenses. It was possible the entire battle had been nothing but a test. His blood simmered at the thought of Elena and the others being exploited so callously, not to mention the attack on Sulu.

"Who are you?" he demanded. "What have you done to these people?"

"I am Sokis of Ialat, warrior-priest of the Crusade," the alien stated. "And I have come to save you all from the destruction to come."

"Seems to me you're the ones who brought destruction here," Kirk said. "And you're going to have to answer for that."

"I answer only to the Truth!" Sokis thundered. "As passed down to us since the beginning of time!"

"We'll see about that."

Kirk saw no point in trying to reason with a fanatic, at least not while the landing party was in jeopardy. He had already seen enough of the Crusade's handiwork to know that he couldn't allow Sokis to get the upper hand. He could attempt to make peace with the Crusaders later, after he had freed the Institute from their control—and guaranteed the safety of his people.

He aimed his phaser at Sokis. It was still set on stun, but the alien didn't need to know that. Yaseen watched his back, as instructed.

"On behalf of Starfleet and the United Federation of Planets," Kirk said firmly, "I am ordering you to lay down your weapons and tell me how to release your hold on these people. You have no right to impose your 'Truth' upon them!"

Sokis shook his head sadly.

"You are blinded by falsity. The lies must be crushed from you!"

He raised his lance, which took on an ominous green glow. The weapon keened shrilly. Kirk knew a threat when he saw one.

"Fire!" Kirk unleashed a phaser beam at Sokis, hoping to take out the leader of the invaders before matters could escalate further. But his beam fell short of its target, bending downward to strike the pavement at the foot of the pedestal. Discharged energy flashed harmlessly against the pearly tiles. Kirk gaped in surprise. He had never seen a phaser beam diverted like that. It was as though it had been pulled down to the earth by some irresistible force.

What had Spock said earlier about applied artificial gravity?

Yaseen swore under her breath.

"Fascinating," Spock observed. "Captain, I believe . . ."

A moment later, Kirk experienced the same irresistible force. A massive weight descended upon him. His phaser became too heavy to hold; it was like trying to lift a shuttlecraft with one hand. His arm dropped to his side. The phaser tore itself from his grip, crashing onto the pavement hard to enough the crack the pearl tiles. His knees buckled, unable to support his own weight, and he dropped to the ground beside his weapon. He felt as though he had just beamed from a zero-g environment to a Class-J gravity well. His own weight pinned him to the earth, and the same thing was happening to Spock and Yaseen and Sulu.

"Feel the weight of the Truth!" Sokis preached. "You cannot escape it!"

For the time being, that seemed to be the case.

THREE

"No word from the landing party," Uhura reported, after scanning every frequency. She looked up from her console. "I'm worried, Mister Scott."

"Aye." Lieutenant Commander Montgomery Scott occupied the captain's chair on the bridge of the *Enterprise.* His rugged face bore a grave expression. "I cannae blame you there, Lieutenant. I'm worried, too."

Ephrata IV rotated on the main viewer, its assorted seas and continents offering no clue as to what was transpiring on the planet's surface. Over forty-five minutes had passed since Captain Kirk and the rest of the landing party had beamed down from the *Enterprise,* but there had been no updates from them since. Nor had Uhura been able to make contact with anyone at the Institute.

She didn't like it. As the ship's senior communications officer, Uhura took it personally when her hails went unanswered. Silence meant that she couldn't keep the captain and crew informed and in touch, which was what her job was all about.

Is this Institute unable to respond, she wondered, *or unwilling?*

"Do you think we should send down a search party, Mister Scott?" Chekov asked from his post at navigation. A thick Russian accent proudly proclaimed his heritage. "I volunteer to beam down."

"You can count me in, too, sir," added Lieutenant Fisher, who had taken Sulu's place at the helm. He was a sturdy redhead from New Sonoma. "If you think the captain might need reinforcements."

Scotty weighed his options before replying.

"I appreciate your spirit, laddies," he said finally. "But let's give the captain a little more time before we send another landing party into heaven knows what with nary a clue as to the situation down there." He consulted the chronometer on the right armrest of the chair. "The landing party's next scheduled check-in is approximately fifteen minutes from now." He settled back into his chair. "We'll hold fast until then."

"But what if the captain is in trouble?" Chekov asked with the impatience of youth. "And can't call for help?"

In truth, that possibility had occurred to Uhura as well. She wasn't going to breathe easy until she heard from the landing party. They all knew how dangerous beaming down to a planet could be, especially in response to a distress signal.

"Have a wee bit of faith in our comrades," Scotty gently admonished the young ensign. "Captain Kirk and Mister Spock have been in tight spots before, and they've already got Sulu and that Yaseen lassie to lend them a hand if needs be. Don't forget that, Ensign."

"Yes, sir," Chekov said.

"In the meantime," Scotty said, "keep our shields raised until we find out just what kind of emergency we're dealing with." He eyed the planet on the viewer with a healthy degree of caution. "We don't want to get caught with our pants down."

"I thought you preferred kilts, Mister Scott," Uhura said, hoping to lighten the mood.

"Only on special occasions, lass."

Despite his reassuring tone, Uhura could tell he was as worried as the rest of them. Reading body language was another form of communication that she excelled at, and right now the burden of command weighed visibly on Scotty as he grimly contemplated the spinning purple-green world below. She knew he had to be balancing his duty to protect the ship against his concern for their too-silent crewmates down on the planet.

She didn't envy him.

Kirk blacked out for a time. By the time he gradually regained consciousness, the sky above the Institute was lightening and dawn could be glimpsed rising in the west. Turquoise and lavender fingers streaked the horizon, as seen through the gaps in the Institute's various buildings. Kirk was briefly disoriented, until he remembered that Ephrata IV rotated clockwise, not unlike Venus back in the Sol System.

He found himself lying prone on the pearl square.

He felt bruised and sore from his collision with the pavement, but the awful, crushing weight seemed to have evaporated. He tentatively lifted his head from the tiles; it didn't feel like it weighed a ton anymore. He could breathe more easily.

"Rise!" a loud, basso-profundo voice commanded. "But know that the Truth can strike you down at the first sign of defiance."

Sokis stood before the triangular rift, holding his lance. His fellow Crusaders stood at attention, but struck Kirk as superfluous. Their commander had already demonstrated that he had enough power to subdue a small landing party at least. Masked converts watched from the sidelines. Kirk recalled how eagerly they had attacked before.

"Yes," he said. "I think we got the message."

He staggered to his feet, assessing the situation. Despite some aches and pains, he appeared to be in one piece, with no bones broken. A quick inventory, however, revealed that both his phaser and his communicator were gone. He assumed that the Crusaders had confiscated them while he out cold.

Figures, he thought. That was to be expected.

"Are you well, Captain?" a familiar voice asked.

Glancing to the right, he saw that Spock had also recovered from their literally massive defeat. Greenish scrapes and bruises blemished his face, but the Vulcan displayed no obvious signs of discomfort. He stood calmly only a few meters away from Kirk, guarded by two looming Crusaders. Kirk noted that Spock's tricorder had been confiscated as well—and that two of their comrades were missing.

"Where are Sulu and Yaseen?" he demanded.

"They are no longer your concern," Sokis said.

"The hell they aren't!" Kirk glared angrily at Sokis. It took a fair amount of self-control not to lunge at the self-described "warrior-priest," even though Kirk knew he had to be smarter than that. "I'm Captain James T. Kirk of the *U.S.S. Enterprise,* and those people are my responsibility."

"Not any longer," Sokis said. "But you need not fear for your kin. They will be safe once they accept the Truth."

Kirk's temper was fraying by the minute. Diplomacy came second to the safety of his crew.

"That's not good enough," he said. "What do you mean by that? And don't give me any more cryptic mumbo-jumbo about the 'Truth' or the end of everything."

Sokis's expression darkened.

"'Mumbo-jumbo'?" His argent features registered offense. His segmented knuckles tightened around his lance. "You dare mock the Truth?"

Spock spoke up.

"Perhaps if you care to enlighten us, we can better appreciate your truth, as well as your purpose on this planet."

His diplomatic tone appeared to appease Sokis.

"So be it," he said. "I sometimes forget that this benighted universe of yours has been cut off from the Truth, and lost in lies and illusions, until our coming. You cannot be blamed for your ignorance."

"That's very big of you," Kirk said, while resisting the temptation to demand answers from Sokis again. Following Spock's lead, he decided it might be more effective to encourage the prickly warrior-priest to proselytize instead. One way or another, they needed to find out more about the Crusade and its agenda. "Please, tell us more."

Sokis nodded.

"Know that the Truth was passed down to us by our heavenly ancestors, the first of the Ialatl, who built creation for us, their descendants. We serve our mighty God-King, whose sacred bloodline stretches back to the dawn of the universe. For countless generations, the Ialatl have known nothing but the Truth. It weighs us down, holds our feet to the path of harmony."

Kirk had seen where that path led—to the invasion of Ephrata and the attack on his people—but he refrained from comment . . . for now.

"I see," he said. "But what brings you here? What does your truth have to do with us?"

Sokis eyed Kirk suspiciously, as though wary of some veiled challenge in the captain's queries.

Kirk wondered if he'd pushed too hard.

"Indeed," Spock added. "Your purpose here is of great interest to us."

Kirk cracked a smile. Spock had a talent for diplomacy, perhaps inherited from his distinguished father. *Probably wouldn't make a bad ambassador,* Kirk thought, *if and when he ever opts out of Starfleet.*

Sokis accepted the implied apology.

"The prophecies of our ancestors have long warned of a day, at the close of this present cycle of being, when all of creation will be destroyed and re-created. It is also said that only those who surrender to the Truth will be reborn in the new universe to come."

The Crusaders' beliefs had a vaguely familiar ring. Kirk was aware that various cultures, throughout history and across the galaxy, had anticipated similar apocalypses. Personally, he tended to be leery of doomsday prophecies. He didn't believe in no-win scenarios.

"For most of our history," Sokis continued, "we believed that the end was long distant. There were even some foolish skeptics who believed that the prophecies were mere myth and poetry. But then the ancestors granted our scientists the knowledge to rend the fabric of creation, and we discovered your false universe hiding behind a veil. Clearly, this was a sign that the prophecies were coming true at last."

"Clearly," Kirk said. "But, again, what has that to do with us?"

Sokis regarded Kirk as though he were a child—or an idiot.

"Do you not understand? Time is running out,

and your people must embrace the Truth or they will be lost." He swept out his arm at the occupied campus around them. "We brave this false universe not for our sake, but for yours. We come not to conquer you, but to deliver you all!"

"The way you 'delivered' these people here?" Kirk spotted Elena Collins among the faceless zealots. Her silver mask denied her humanity. He was relieved to see that she had not been trampled in last night's crush, but he was appalled at the way she—and the other brilliant residents of the Institute—had apparently been brainwashed by the Crusaders. He couldn't believe that they had all surrendered to this alien creed without question. There had to be something more to it.

"They are but the beginning," Sokis declared. "Our mission is to bring the Truth to as many of your worlds as we can before the end arrives . . . . and a new creation is born."

"And if those worlds do not welcome your teachings?" Spock asked. "What then?"

Sokis did not seem to regard that as a possibility. "The Truth cannot be denied."

"And what about doubt, dissent, diversity?" Kirk challenged him. "Don't these things exist in your universe?"

He raised his voice in hopes that his words would touch the masked spectators, despite whatever the Crusaders had done to them. It was a long shot, perhaps, but who knew? Maybe there was still a chance to reach the Elena he knew. . . .

"Not any longer," Sokis said. "We have eliminated such evils. Ours is a society of perfect harmony, in accordance with the timeless wisdom of the ancestors. As ordained, the weight of the Truth holds us fast and keeps us from straying into error."

"Then I am surprised that you have achieved such breakthroughs in gravity control," Spock said. "Without doubt, or the willingness to question established dogma, revolutionary scientific discoveries are unlikely, if not impossible."

Spoken like a Vulcan, Kirk thought. *And a scientist.*

"Doubt is not required," Sokis countered, "only divine inspiration. When the time was right, the ancestors saw to it that we discovered a way to reach your fragmented realm, so that we could bring you the Truth."

Kirk decided Sokis needed a reality check—about this reality.

"If you think the Federation, with all its myriad worlds, is just going to roll over for your 'Crusade,' then maybe you don't understand our universe as well as you think you do," he scoffed. "And somehow I don't think the Klingons or the Romulans or the Tholians are going to be in hurry to accept your truth either, although you're welcome to try, if you're feeling suicidal."

Sokis's mane of spines flared outward, stiffening

in anger. They turned a darker shade of gold. He stomped his lance on the tiles. Retractable claws extended from his fingertips.

"Ungrateful creatures!" he roared. "Unless you submit to the Truth, you are doomed to oblivion. Can you not grasp that we are your only hope for rebirth?"

Kirk gestured at the damaged buildings and rubble surrounding them. The Ephrata Institute had once been a temple of learning and culture, but apparently the Crusade had no respect for any knowledge beyond their own. The wanton vandalism offended Kirk deeply.

"You'll forgive me if I fail to appreciate your altruistic motives, especially when two of my people are missing!"

I probably shouldn't provoke him, Kirk thought, but he had seldom been one to curb his tongue when faced with petty tyrants, bullies, and injustice. He was a soldier, not a diplomat, at least where the safety of his crew was concerned. *I think I've heard quite enough from this fanatic.*

Sokis's temper flared as well.

"Blind fools!" He gripped his lance with both hands and swung the business end toward Kirk and Spock. The point began to spin fiercely. A greenish glow radiated from the lance. A rising whine sounded like a phaser on overload. "Feel the full weight of the Truth!"

Kirk braced himself for another gravity attack.

Without his phaser, there was little he could do to defend himself. He just hoped that Sokis wasn't planning to flatten them to pancakes this time around.

"High Brother!" one of the other Crusaders cried out. "Curb your wrath!"

Sokis halted, puzzled by the interruption. His head swiveled toward the other alien even as his weapon remained energized and pointed at Kirk and Spock.

"Brother Maxah?"

The other Ialatl appeared younger than the caped warrior-priest. His fringe-like "beard" was shorter and less dramatic. The scales covering his skin were smaller and less rigid. His face was a duller shade of silver. His voice was deep, but not as stentorian as his leader's.

"Forgive me, High Brother," he said. "I well understand your impatience with these infidels. But I believe Ialat is waiting. . . ."

A look of frustration came over Sokis's saturnine features. His baleful gaze shifted back toward Kirk, and he let out an indignant huff before turning his lance back toward the sky. Kirk repressed a sigh of relief as the keening weapon powered down.

"Alas, you are correct," Sokis said. He struggled visibly to compose himself as he glared at the prisoners. "Were it up to me, I would make examples of you both by punishing you for your sacrilege here before your fellow creatures." He looked as though he was still sorely tempted to do so. "But your judgment lies elsewhere."

Spock arched an eyebrow. "And where might that be?"

Sokis swung his lance toward the rift.

"Those above me have decreed that you be sent on to the true realm, Ialat, where the God-King himself desires your presence."

He sounded jealous. Kirk guessed that a summons from the "God-King" was not to be taken lightly.

"And why is that?" Kirk asked. "What does he want with us?"

Various troubling possibilities came to mind. Did Sokis's superiors hope to extract strategic information on the Federation's defenses from him and Spock, or were they simply intended to be trophies, paraded through the streets in celebration of the Crusade's first victory? Or were they to be specimens in some alien menagerie like poor Chris Pike?

"That is not for me to know or question," Sokis replied. "I but submit to the will of the God-King . . . as shall you."

"We'll see about that," Kirk said.

Sokis scowled, still irked by the captain's attitude.

"You should consider yourselves blessed," he scolded. "You are being granted a great privilege, never before bestowed upon any denizens of your realm: to pass from this false universe to the true realm beyond the portal."

"I confess that I am intrigued by the prospect," Spock said. He examined the shimmering rift. "Am I correct in assuming that you employed artificial gravity to create a passage from one space-time continuum to another? And that the apparatus surrounding the rift, which appears to have been constructed after the fact, serves to help maintain the rift and prevent it from closing?"

That's Spock for you, Kirk thought, admiring his friend's indefatigable scientific curiosity, even in the face of unknown perils. *Always figuring things out.*

Sokis was less impressed by Spock's quizzical nature.

"The workings of the portal need not concern you," he said impatiently. "And I grow weary of your incessant questions." He called out to his minions. "Send them through!"

Crusaders came up behind Kirk and Spock, prodding them with their batons. Kirk's skin crawled as they were marched toward the portal. Peculiar sensations washed over him as they approached the rift, raising the hairs at the back of his neck. Unnatural colors, some of which he couldn't even name, made his eyes water and throb. Bile rose at the back of his throat. This rift was a distortion of time and space that wasn't meant to exist; his whole body was telling him to stay away from it.

Not that they had much choice.

"It seems, Mister Spock, we are going from the frying pan into the proverbial fire."

"A less than comforting idiom," Spock replied. "I

prefer to think that we are making significant progress toward locating the root source of our present
dilemma."

Kirk couldn't help smiling, despite the unsettling
presence of the rift. He took considerable comfort
in knowing that, whatever lay ahead, his first officer
would be at his side as usual.

"A commendably positive attitude, Mister Spock."

"And, I would hope, a logical one."

Their banter did not go over well with their armed
escorts.

"Still your heathen tongues!" the guard behind
Kirk ordered, jabbing Kirk in the back with his baton.
It took Kirk a moment to realize that it was the same
young Crusader who had interrupted Sokis a few
minutes ago. He leaned forward and whispered in
Kirk's ear. "Be not afraid. Allies await you on the other
side."

A deft hand furtively slipped a small metallic
object beneath the waistband of Kirk's trousers. Kirk
recognized the weight and feel of it immediately.

My phaser.

Kirk carefully concealed his surprise at this unexpected development, even as his mind raced to figure
out its implications. Maybe Sokis's Crusade did not
have as many adherents as the unquestioning warrior-
priest believed?

Interesting, Kirk thought.

But first the portal waited. Kirk gritted his teeth

against the nauseating sensations emanating from the rift. He averted his eyes from the strobing colors. All in all, he preferred the *Enterprise*'s transporter.

"Prepare yourselves, deluded creatures," Sokis boomed, throwing out his arms dramatically, "for the only true realm!"

Kirk glanced over at Spock, who displayed not a trace of discomfort or trepidation. Kirk envied his Vulcan calm—and inner eyelids.

He forced himself to keep his own eyes open as they were thrust roughly through the rift.

Here goes nothing, Kirk thought.

He just wished he knew what had become of Sulu and Yaseen.

FOUR

The museum had seen better days. Shelves had been stripped clean of microtapes. Computer terminals had been trashed. Display cases, which might once have held priceless artifacts or documents, had been emptied—and apparently with extreme prejudice. Shards of broken pottery and shattered idols littered the floor, along with shredded and trampled parchments. Chairs and tables were overturned. Phaser burns blackened the walls. Frames held torn and mutilated canvases. The remains of what looked like an authentic pre-warp Arcturian tapestry were strewn about the room.

Sulu was sickened by the wanton vandalism.

"How's your head?" Yaseen asked.

They were pinned to the floor by their own weight, barely able to move a muscle. Flat on their backs, staring up at a high domed ceiling and the upper galleries of the museum, they lay side-by-side but in opposite directions, so that Sulu's head was even with Yaseen's boots. A skylight let in the violet sunlight. He was hungry and thirsty and would have killed for a refreshing cup of tea. A misty green nimbus enveloped them like a low-hanging fog.

"Better." He still had a bit of a headache from being phasered, but the effect was fading. "Thanks for asking."

He was grateful for her company. To be honest, he had noticed her as soon as she'd transferred aboard and had been looking forward to the opportunity to get to know her better. Granted, this wasn't exactly what he'd had in mind. . . .

"So how are you liking your first landing party with the *Enterprise*?"

"Somewhat heavy going," she quipped. "Your rescue missions always this . . . complicated?"

She had filled him in on everything that had transpired after he was stunned by that phaser blast, including the appearance of the alien Crusaders. The only thing she didn't know was what had become of Captain Kirk and Mister Spock.

"Remind me to tell you about the time an alien virus made me think I was d'Artagnan."

A fuzzy memory, of prancing shirtless through the corridors of the *Enterprise* with sword in hand, challenging bewildered crewmates to duels, surfaced from the past. He had been a long time living that down.

"Like the musketeer?" She sounded intrigued, despite their present circumstances. "I'm going to hold you to that." She grunted as she strained unsuccessfully to break the hold of the gravity trap. Her back arched but failed to lift her from the floor. "Especially since it doesn't look like we're going anywhere soon."

Sulu tested their unusual restraints as well. He

wasn't literally paralyzed, but he might as well have been. Human muscles simply weren't built to function in this kind of gravity. With effort, he managed to slightly tilt his head to one side so he could glimpse Yaseen out of the corner of his eye.

"I know what you mean," he said. "You might as well save your energy. We're pretty much anchored here."

She gave up her fight against gravity. She sagged against the floor, gasping with exertion.

"What do you think happened here?" Her chipper tone faltered for a moment. "To those people?"

Sulu remembered the masked zealots, chanting in unison.

"I'm guessing they were brainwashed somehow," he said. "Via telepathic mind control, hypnosis, drugs, alien spores. . . . I don't know."

"It has to be something like that," she agreed. "No matter how persuasive these aliens are, I can't believe that *all* of those people could turn into fanatics so readily." She managed to shudder at the memory. "I mean, don't get me wrong. I grew up in a Za'Huli colony on Hayak V. I still believe in the teachings of the twelve celestial messengers, and have been known to offer up a prayer or two in a tricky situation, but even back home we never thought that we had *all* the answers, or that there weren't new revelations to be found out there in the great, big universe. We weren't like . . . those people in the square."

"I know," he said. "That was pretty disturbing."

"You ever seen anything like this before?"

"Unfortunately, yes."

A troubling sense of déjà vu preyed on his nerves. He couldn't help remembering Beta III, where a godlike computer program had captured the minds and souls of the lobotomized populace. Sulu himself had fallen under the sway of "Landru," an experience he was in no hurry to repeat.

I'll be damned if I let myself get turned into a brainwashed puppet again!

"But things got better, right?" Yaseen asked.

"Usually," he assured her. "Thanks to the captain."

"What do you think has happened to him and Mister Spock?" She fought again against the artificial gravity. "It kills me to think that they're in trouble . . . and we're stuck here, doing nothing."

"Ditto," he said. "I'd rather hug a Horta than be sidelined like this."

Before he could say more, the museum doors slid open and a solitary Crusader entered. The silver alien matched Yaseen's description of the invaders. Sulu lifted his head and took his first look at the enemy. He saw with alarm that the Crusader was bearing two ominous silver masks, identical to the ones worn by the "converted" residents of Ephrata. The masks' obvious resemblance to the alien's own features did not escape his notice.

Uh-oh, he thought. *This can't be good.*

Yaseen twisted her head toward the intruder. "If

you think we're going to wear those ugly masks, you're sadly mistaken."

"What she said," Sulu agreed.

Despite their bravado, he feared the worst, and not just for himself and Yaseen. How could they help the captain and Spock, and alert the *Enterprise,* if they were converted into masked zealots as well? Memories of Landru sent a chill down his spine.

"Fear not," the Crusader said, gazing down at them. He lowered his voice and glanced around furtively, as though fearful of being observed. He put the masks aside, placing them on an empty shelf. He fingered the baton at his waist. "I've come to release you."

Okay, I didn't see this coming, Sulu thought. Hope surged in his chest, even as he remained wary of the alien's intentions. *This had better not be a trick.*

"Come again?" Yaseen said simply.

"Patience," the Crusader said.

He removed his baton from his belt and waved it at them like a magic wand. It briefly flashed green before turning black and opaque again. All at once, the oppressive weight departed along with the phosphorescent green nimbus. Sulu sprang to his feet like John Carter of Mars, feeling light as a feather. He had once taken part in a low-g fencing tournament on Earth's moon. This felt even better.

Yaseen scrambled to her feet beside him. She smoothed out her cherry-red skirt.

"Things are looking up, d'Artagnan," she said with a wink. "All for one and one for all."

Sulu checked out their third musketeer. The towering Crusader had at least ten centimeters on them. A smoky odor wafted from him. He returned his baton to his belt.

"Who are you?" Sulu asked. "Why are you doing this?"

"Call me Maxah," the alien said. "As to why, look about you." A sweeping gesture encompassed the wreckage and emptied shelves around them. "My people did this, destroying knowledge, eradicating art and culture, burning books and scrolls, rewriting history, simply to expunge any 'dangerous' ideas that might question our ancient truths."

Sulu envisioned the Crusaders—and the masked converts—ransacking the museum. His blood boiled at the thought. What Maxah was describing went against everything Starfleet stood for.

"And you have a problem with this?" Yaseen asked.

"You must understand," Maxah said. "We Ialatl were not always like this. I was a librarian . . . before." Guilt contorted his face. "I cannot stand by while the Crusade spreads this madness to another universe. It is bad enough that my own people have come to fear anything new or different, while eagerly anticipating the end of all things."

Sulu's fears of trickery receded. The anguished Crusader struck him as both sincere and passionate. *I think we can trust him.*

"But what happened to your people?" Yaseen asked. "What changed you?"

"You did," he said ruefully. "Your universe."

Sulu didn't understand. "What do you mean?"

"There is no time to explain." Maxah glanced nervously at the doorway, which had slid shut behind him. "I was sent to convert you. They must believe I succeeded." He hastily retrieved the silver masks from the shelf. "Put these on."

"Not so fast," Sulu said, regarding the masks warily. His earlier suspicions began to resurface. "What if this is a trick?"

"I could have masked you at any time," Maxah pointed out. "Why would I go to such lengths to win your trust if I merely intended to let the masks convert you as they did your kin."

"The masks?" Yaseen said. "They warped those people's minds?"

"Yes," he confessed. "They emit an electromagnetic signal that manipulates brain waves and provokes a powerful religious response in the temporal lobes. But you need not be concerned. I have deactivated these masks so that they will not remove your ability to think for yourselves."

"Good to know," Sulu said. He accepted the mask, but hesitated before donning it. The memory of those brainwashed Ephratans was hard to get past, not to mention his own past experiences with mind control, not just on Beta III but on Pyris VII as well. He could live without becoming a zombie once again.

Heavy footsteps sounded outside the door.

"The others!" Maxah said urgently. "They're coming. You must trust me. Put on the masks!"

Looks like we don't have much choice, Sulu thought. He exchanged a look with Yaseen. "We on the same page here?"

She nodded back at him. "Ready when you are, d'Artagnan."

They put the masks on together. Sulu swallowed hard, half expecting to start chanting a hymn to the Truth at any moment, but nothing happened except that the cold metal felt cool against his face. A weak attractive force held the mask in place.

"Praise the messengers," Yaseen whispered, offering up a heartfelt prayer of thanks. She reached over and squeezed his hand. "Don't worry. I'm still me. You?"

"Do you hear me chanting?"

A moment later, the doors slid open to admit two more Crusaders, both of whom seemed older and more intimidating than Maxah. Sulu let go of Yaseen's hand. He held his breath.

"Is it done?" one of the newcomers asked Maxah. "High Brother Sokis grows impatient."

Maxah indicated the masked captives. He shot the Starfleet officers a warning look.

"They have seen the Truth," he lied, before addressing the supposed converts. "Is that not so?"

Sulu remembered the masked zealots that had confronted them last night. He hoped he got this right.

"The Truth will save us," he parroted. His voice rang with counterfeit fervor. He forced his eyes wider. "All else is lies."

Yaseen played along. "There is no other Truth."

Sulu wished he knew more about the finer points of the aliens' theology, but their vague declarations of faith seemed to convince the other Crusaders.

"Well done," the tallest Crusader said. He had a fuller growth of spines around his face. "Come, adoptees. The High Brother awaits you."

Sulu and Yaseen let themselves be escorted to the exit, but Maxah lingered behind in the pillaged museum.

"Are you not joining us, brother?" the senior Crusader asked.

Maxah shook his head. "My duties call me elsewhere."

Wait a second, Sulu thought. Maxah wasn't sticking with them? Sulu didn't like the sound of that. He was reluctant to lose their only ally so soon.

"Hold fast to the Truth, brothers and sister," Maxah said. He activated his baton, which lifted him off the debris-strewn floor of the museum toward the skylight above. He disappeared into the lavender-tinted heavens, abandoning Sulu and Yaseen to their own devices.

Sulu's mask concealed his dismay.

So much for the Three Musketeers. . . .

FIVE

James Kirk kept his eyes open through the rift. This was easier than he expected, given that the passage took place in what felt like a heartbeat. One moment he was in the occupied square on Ephrata IV, the next he was . . . somewhere else.

The first thing he noticed was the heat. The weather had been cool and fall-like at the Institute, but it was mercilessly hot and humid here. The sweltering heat hit him like a blast from an unshielded plasma conduit. Momentarily blinded by the glare, he lifted his hand to shield his eyes. He felt as though he had beamed directly from a climate-controlled starbase to Atlanta, Georgia, in the middle of July. Or maybe one of the equatorial swamps on Nova Amazonia.

At least Spock won't mind the heat, Kirk thought, *even if it's a bit damper than Vulcan's Forge.*

The next thing he noticed, once his eyes adjusted, was the view. The other side of the portal was located atop what appeared to be a large floating pyramid overlooking a sprawling, modern-looking megalopolis that spread out for kilometers in all directions. Gleaming steel and stone-faced structures, large enough to rival the grandest skyscrapers and spaceports back on Earth, made it clear that this was no minor colony or outpost. Kirk spied courtyards, high-rises, auditoriums, open-air markets, and even what looked to be an immense sports stadium. The cityscape was dominated by another pyramid: a fifty-story ziggurat, crafted of polished black marble or obsidian, which rested atop a steep plateau at the center of the city. It struck Kirk as older than the rest of the city, which had possibly grown up around it. Its elevated position would have made it the most defensible location in days gone by, not unlike a medieval fortress back in Earth's feudal era. He wondered if it was a palace or a temple or both.

They do *have a God-King,* he remembered. *I have a sneaking suspicion I know where he hangs his hat . . . or crown.*

Teeming crowds populated the streets and sidewalks below, or else traversed the sky via gravity-defying trams and floating walkways. If anything, antigrav technology seemed to be applied even more extensively here than anywhere in the Federation, except maybe Stratos. Levitating sculptures, depicting colossal kings and heroes, floated above the parks and plazas, unmoored to any earthly pedestals. Sleek, aerodynamic gliders, of various models and designs, zipped from place to place. Although the people looked like shiny, silver insects from this height, Kirk got the impression that they belonged to the same species as the Crusaders. Were only Ialatl welcome here?

"Impressive," Spock observed.

Kirk had to agree. This was a quite a city, especially compared to the modest campus on Ephrata, or, for that matter, most of the remote colonies and starbases the *Enterprise* usually encountered out on the fringes of known space. The thriving metropolis was clearly a major population center, maybe even the capital of a vast kingdom or empire.

The view is almost worth the trip, Kirk thought.

Almost.

"Welcome to Ialat," a husky voice greeted them. "The one true realm in all of creation."

The voice belonged to what Kirk assumed to be a female Crusader, the first he had seen. Instead of a beard, she had only a short row of spines bisecting her otherwise smooth cranium, while her figure suggested that the Ialatl were at least partially mammalian. Like Sokis, she wore a belted black tunic and cape. An ornate pendant, composed of concentric circles of obsidian, jade, and turquoise, hung from her neck. A mesh glove of lacy black filaments partially veiled her right hand. She was as tall as the male Crusaders, perhaps even more so. Kirk caught a whiff of a pleasantly smoky aroma.

She was flanked by three male Crusaders, who regarded Kirk and Spock with various combinations of suspicion, curiosity, and distaste. Additional

Crusaders, each armed with variants of the lance wielded by Sokis, guarded the portal itself, while also keeping an eye on the proceedings. The Crusade was clearly not taking any chances, particularly where the portal was concerned.

Probably not a good time to reach for my phaser, Kirk decided. He would have to wait for a more opportune moment, and hope that the guards didn't think to search him first. Kirk still had no idea why that young Crusader had furtively returned his phaser to him, but he intended to make the most of it. *Assuming I get the chance.*

"And you are?" he asked.

"I am Vlisora, High Priestess of the royal temple." She gestured toward the shining black ziggurat Kirk had noticed before. "I am here to escort you to the temple, as demanded by the God-King."

"Very well," Kirk said. "I look forward to speaking to whoever is in charge. Perhaps we can still find a way to work out our differences."

"One does not speak to the God-King," she corrected him. "One listens . . . and obeys."

"That hardly seems conducive to a productive dialogue," Spock observed, eliciting a frown from Vlisora. A Crusader stepped forward menacingly. "But, of course, we appreciate your guidance when it comes to matters of court etiquette."

There's that Vulcan diplomacy again, Kirk thought. *Sarek would be proud.*

"As well you should," she said, appeased. She turned toward the portal's guards. "Disengage the barrier so that we may depart."

Barrier?

Kirk didn't see any barrier.

"Yes, High Priestess." The guard activated his lance, and Kirk felt a tremor in the gravity. A bubble of air rippled around them. Crackling energy dissipated. A hot breeze crossed an invisible boundary. "You may pass safely, Priestess."

Kirk and Spock traded looks. Clearly, the portal was guarded by more than just armed sentries. It was apparently shielded as well, and access to it was strictly controlled. No unauthorized trips were allowed.

Talk about strict border control, he thought.

A possibility occurred to the captain. Was this the only portal? Spock had mentioned that tremendous resources would be required to breach the dimensional barrier. Kirk wondered if the entire pyramid was devoted to that purpose. He glanced back at the enigmatic alien technology framing the portal. It appeared much more elaborate and grandiose than the improvised, cobbled-together version back on Ephrata. Burnished steel plates, inscribed with alien symbols, hid whatever circuits, crystals, or conductors were threaded inside the towering apparatus. Reflective black disks, inlaid within angled metal beams, spun continuously to generate a pulsing green aura. Thick cables, thrumming with energy, spread out from the portal like the half-buried roots of a world tree before sinking beneath the surface of the roof. Although the rift itself was the same size as the one on Ephrata, this portal was at least five times bigger than the Guardian of Forever. It was a substantial feat of engineering.

This *portal creates the rift,* Kirk theorized. *The one on Ephrata just anchors the other end of the passage.*

Or so he speculated. No doubt Spock had his own thoughts on the matter. Kirk hoped they would have a chance to compare notes soon. In the meantime, the intense security measures could make returning to their own universe more difficult should the opportunity arise.

I guess we'll have to cross that barrier when we come to it.

"Many thanks, brother," Vlisora said, before leading Kirk and Spock away from the portal to a sunken circular depression a few meters away. The level floor of the ring was only a couple of centimeters below the roof of the pyramid. She stepped inside the circle. Her guards saw to it that their captives followed. The ring, which was the size of a standard transporter platform, accommodated Vlisora, Kirk, Spock, and the guards.

"There is a no-fly zone in force around the portal," she explained, "so we have a short distance to traverse. Our transport waits below."

"How convenient," Kirk said.

She touched the obsidian pendant, and the ring

began to sink below the top of the pyramid, taking its passengers with it. *Some kind of elevator or turbolift,* Kirk realized, as they descended vertically through the heart of the pyramid. Despite her apology for the delay, the ride was both swift and smooth. Illuminated steel walls, punctuated by occasional silver doors, seemed to rush past as the ring carried them downward. Kirk became aware of a persistent steady hum in the background, as well as a buzz of harnessed energy in the air. You could literally feel the surging power contained within the pyramid, in your bones and teeth and skin. More and more, Kirk got the sense that the entire vast pyramid existed to generate the portal above.

"Do you feel that, Spock?" he asked.

"It would be impossible not to," the Vulcan replied. "Whatever we may think of our captors' attitudes, we should not underestimate their technology or ingenuity."

"The Truth has brought us peace and prosperity," Vlisora explained, "and now it has given us the means to rescue your own worlds from oblivion."

"So I keep hearing," Kirk said. "But I'm not convinced."

He waited tensely for the guards to search him and find the concealed phaser, but so far that hadn't happened. It seemed the Crusaders were confident that their "brothers" on the other side of the portal had already seen to disarming their prisoners. Still, that didn't mean that there wouldn't be more stringent precautions once they arrived at the temple of the God-King. Kirk would be surprised if they weren't searched again before being admitted into the presence of a living deity. He needed to take advantage of his phaser before then.

But when?

An electronic chime heralded the end of their descent.

"Ah," Vlisora said. "We are almost there."

Kirk expected the sinking platform to come to a stop in front of a silver door, but, to his surprise, the platform exited the base of the pyramid and descended another ten meters before halting in midair, at least three hundred meters above a large circular reflecting pool below. The immense base of the pyramid hovered above them in a rather unnerving fashion. Kirk was grateful for the shade, but it was hard to ignore the massive edifice hanging over their heads like the sword of Damocles.

The floating ring went from elevator to loading dock. A waiting flyer pulled up to the edge of the platform. About a third of the size of a standard shuttlecraft, its lacquered silver body was sleek and streamlined for atmospheric travel. A tinted canopy offered a glimpse of the cockpit and controls. An embossed design, worked into the side of the ship, captured the profile of a fierce-looking winged serpent. An actual animal, Kirk wondered, or a mythical creature? Scanning the skies, he failed to spot any actually flying snakes.

I can live with that, he thought.

A side door slid open, offering a further glimpse of the vehicle's compact interior, and a ramp extended from the doorway. A moment later, the pilot emerged and stood by the door.

"Greetings, High Priestess," he addressed Vlisora. Like the other aliens, he eyed Kirk and Spock with naked curiosity. "It is my honor to transport you to the royal temple. Please board at will."

"Many thanks," she replied, approaching the ramp. "And my deepest apologies."

Confusion showed on his face. "Priestess?"

Vlisora rotated the rings on her pendant, like the dials on an antique combination lock, and Kirk heard a low whine. The innermost circle flashed green. Moving quickly, and with no warning aside from her cryptic apology, she lunged forward and shoved the pilot off the platform. Gravity seized him and he plummeted from sight. A frantic screech trailed away as he fell, but could still be heard even as Vlisora called out urgently to Kirk and Spock.

"Now! Defend yourselves!"

Caught off guard by her unexpected betrayal, the three remaining guards reached for their batons. Kirk was startled, too, and shocked by the pilot's abrupt disappearance, but he saw the opportunity he had been waiting for. Rescuing his phaser from hiding, he stunned the first guard, who dropped onto the platform. The second guard retaliated by waving his baton at Kirk, who fully expected to be laid low by another gravity beam.

But nothing happened.

"What in the God-King's name?" The puzzled guard stared at his weapon. Kirk realized that Vlisora must have deactivated the batons somehow.

I can work with that, he thought.

Switching gears, the Crusader raised the baton and charged at Kirk, no doubt hoping to use the weapon as a simple truncheon instead, but Kirk didn't give him a chance. A well-aimed phaser beam took out the second guard as well, leaving only one more to go.

Or so Kirk thought.

He swung his phaser in search of the third Crusader, only to find that Spock had already taken matters in hand by pinching the last guard's neck. The Crusader joined his stunned brothers on the floor of the ring.

"I see you didn't need a phaser," Kirk said.

"Not immediately, but I am pleasantly surprised to find that you have one in your possession." Spock observed the weapon quizzically. "May I inquire how you happened to obtain it?"

Kirk was about to explain about Maxah's sleight of hand back on Ephrata, but Vlisora had more urgent concerns.

"Into the flyer . . . quickly!" She scurried up the ramp. "Follow me if you value your ability to think freely!"

She made a convincing case. Kirk had no idea what her own agenda was, but he was not inclined to look a gift horse—and potential ally—in the mouth. If he was going to confront this dimension's God-King, Kirk preferred to do so on his own terms, and after he had a better sense of what dynamics were at play on this planet. Matters were obviously more complicated than they first appeared.

"After you," he said.

Wasting no time, they hurried into the waiting aircraft and Vlisora sat down at the controls. Kirk rode shotgun while Spock seated himself behind Vlisora, within easy reach of her neck. The door whisked shut behind them and the flyer banked away from the floating platform. A low drone emanated from the aircraft's engines.

"Strap yourselves in," she advised.

A burst of acceleration pressed Kirk back into his seat. Locating a seat belt and safety harness, he clicked them into place. The flyer zoomed out of the shadow of the looming pyramid.

"We have only moments before an alarm is sounded," she explained. "We must make our escape, and discard this flyer, before the Crusaders catch up with us."

"But what's this all about?" he asked. "Why are you doing this?"

"Later," she promised. "All your questions will be answered."

A troubling memory, of the screeching pilot plummeting to his doom, would not wait. "Was it necessary to kill the pilot?"

"He did not die," she assured him. "There are safety measures in place to keep him from achieving terminal velocity. I merely needed to remove him from the equation."

"Some manner of zero-gravity safety net?" Spock surmised.

"Precisely," she replied. "In the event of accidental falls or crashes."

Kirk was glad to hear it, assuming she was telling the truth. It dawned on him that he had never heard the pilot hit bottom, and that the Ialatl certainly seemed to possess the technology to create such a safety net. He decided to give Vlisora the benefit of the doubt and assume that she was not quite as ruthless as she had appeared.

Unlike the Crusaders.

Their flight offered a bird's-eye view of the city. Polished stone facings, resembling basalt, jade, slate, and granite, adorned the shining skyscrapers, ziggurats, coliseums, and monuments. Flyers of various sizes and configurations weaved among the towers and elevated causeways, seemingly disdaining the lower levels of the city, which appeared less heavily populated. Vlisora stayed clear of the heavier air traffic, preferring aerial paths less taken. It was a shame, Kirk reflected, that Sulu had missed out on this flight.

The helmsman was an avid pilot as well, with a special interest in historic aircraft. He would have enjoyed checking out Vlisora's flyer.

Kirk couldn't contain his curiosity. "Where are we going?"

"Better I not say just yet," she began, "in case we are—"

An electronic alarm buzzed from the dashboard, followed by a stern Ialatl voice:

"Attention, miscreants! Your unfathomable rebellion has been found out. Direct your flyer immediately to the coordinates decreed." A sequence of numerical symbols flashed across a lighted display panel on the dashboard. *"And surrender to the God-King's justice!"*

Vlisora blurted a string of obscenities that struck Kirk as rather unsuitable for a priestess. He didn't recognize all the anatomical parts involved, but he got the gist of it. Her finger stabbed a control on the dashboard, muting the transmission.

"Brace yourselves," she said. "We have become the hunted."

High-pitched sirens, screeching like the falling guard, penetrated the cockpit from outside. Five intimidating-looking cruisers swooped down from the sky in pursuit of the flyer. Gleaming black fuselages with jade and silver trim allied them with the Crusade. Their sleek contours caused them to resemble passenger-sized photon torpedoes.

Not the most comforting of comparisons . . .

The dashboard squawked as the Crusaders over-rode the speakers' mute function:

"You cannot escape your guilt. Put down or feel the weight of the Truth!"

Vlisora snorted in derision. "Fools."

"I'm hoping you planned for this," Kirk said.

"In truth, I had expected that we would get farther before my transgressions became known, but the Crusade is reacting faster than I anticipated." She shrugged. "How was I to know they would be so wretchedly efficient?"

The cruisers descended on the flyer in a triangular formation. The nose of the lead cruiser began to spin, while emitting an ominously familiar green glow.

"I believe we are about to come under attack," Spock deduced.

"Indeed," she replied. "For all the good it will do them."

An emerald beam sprayed from the nose of the lead cruiser, targeting the fugitive flyer. Kirk expected a sudden increase in gravity to send the flyer crashing to the ground, but, to his surprise and relief, the beam bounced harmlessly off the flyer's reflective silver skin. The deflected beam struck a floating marble fountain instead, which abruptly sank from view.

"That beam didn't affect us," Kirk observed. "Why?"

"Those idiot Crusaders forgot that this is a royal flyer, in service to the God-King. It is shielded against gravity attacks in order to protect the Divinity and his household from rebel attacks . . . in the unlikely event that the dissidents obtained gravity weapons, that is."

"Rebels?" Kirk echoed. "Dissidents?"

Before she could elaborate, explosions went off throughout the city, both above and below them. A floating basalt monument, consisting of a mammoth bust of some regal Ialatl luminary, blew apart in the sky above a spacious courtyard, which was also levitating high above ground level. Pulverized stone and ash swirled weightlessly in the space formerly occupied by the monument. A water tower toppled over, flooding an elevated causeway below it. Kirk even spotted flames and smoke erupting around the perimeter of the majestic ziggurat Vlisora had identified as the royal temple of the God-King.

"Yes," she confirmed. "Dissidents." She banked away from the turbulent remains of the giant stone bust. The shock wave from another explosion, blowing out the windows of what Kirk hoped was an empty tower, rattled the flyer. "Who are even now attempting to give our pursuers something rather more urgent to attend to."

"Diversions," Spock said. "Intended to aid our escape."

She nodded. "That is the plan. Whether it is sufficient remains to be seen."

The strategy appeared to be working, at least partially. Three of the five cruisers broke formation, veering off from the pursuit. Kirk assumed that they had been called away to deal with the havoc being wreaked by . . . rebel forces?

"It would appear, Captain," Spock said, "that we are caught in the middle of an internal conflict among the Ialatl."

Kirk was reaching the same conclusion, which was both encouraging and disturbing. While there were advantages to making common cause with the rebels against the Crusade, he was troubled by the prospect of getting more deeply involved in the civil strife of an alien culture he knew next to nothing about. The Prime Directive argued against him taking sides here.

But that was a dilemma to wrangle with down the road. At the moment, they still had two Crusader aircraft on their tail. A furious voice railed at them over the speakers:

"Apostate! Infidels! The Crusade will not allow these treacherous attacks on the Truth to go unpunished! Surrender now . . . and beg for the forgiveness of the God-King!"

The remaining Cruisers were gaining on them.

"Can you lose them?" Kirk asked.

"I can try," she said.

Up ahead, an artificial waterfall, at least ten stories high, had been engineered between two identical skyscrapers. This architectural feat became even more impressive when Kirk saw that the frothing white water was actually cascading *up* before falling down on the opposite side to create a perpetual liquid loop.

Vlisora powered the flyer straight through the surging water in hopes of shaking their pursuers. Sheets of water washed over the cockpit, making navigation impossible. Inverted currents buffeted the flyer, rocking its passengers, until the flyer burst from the looping falls into the open air—only to find itself zooming toward a towering granite obelisk.

"Watch out!" Kirk shouted.

"I see it!"

Hastily working the controls, she sent the flyer climbing steeply. The obelisk filled the view from the passenger's seat; they were so close to the solid gray edifice that Kirk could make out the arcane alien pictographs inscribed on the polished stone. He hoped they weren't warnings to stay away.

"Higher!" He couldn't resist playing backseat driver. "We're not going to make it!"

"Yes, we are!" she insisted. "Possibly."

Climbing at top speed, the flyer didn't quite clear the tip of the obelisk. Its stony point scraped the underside of the aircraft, sending a bump up Kirk's spine. He flinched at the impact, as well as the horrendous noise coming from below. The scraping died away as the flyer leveled out several meters above the obelisk.

"You see!" their pilot said triumphantly. "Do not lose faith. Our destiny cannot be denied!"

Spoken like a priestess, Kirk thought. *What destiny?*

The trip through the water-rise had carried them up to an even higher altitude. Kirk glanced back

behind them, hoping that the tumultuous ride had
left the enemy cruisers behind. For a second, he en-
tertained the notion that they were free and clear, but
then the Crusader aircraft shot through the decorative
torrent after them, watery spray trailing in their wake.
Their sirens screeched ever louder.

"Bad news," Kirk reported. "We've still got company."

"Obviously," she snapped.

The flyer accelerated, zipping recklessly through
the endless urban canyons faster than local regulations surely advised, but the relentless cruisers
matched their speed and more. They closed in on the
flyer from above and below, squeezing the fugitive
aircraft in an attempt to herd it toward an elevated
landing pad ahead. Glancing up through the tinted
windshield, Kirk could see the underside of a cruiser
less than a meter above them. This struck him as far
too close for comfort. One wrong move, and a midair collision would bring the chase to a disastrous
conclusion.

"*Attention, renegades! This is your final warning.
Land your vehicle or we will force you down!*"

"Not while this *scrilatyl* can still fly!" she said defiantly. "Or halt at my command!"

She slammed on the brakes and the flyer came
to an abrupt stop, throwing Kirk forward in his seat.
Only the safety harness kept him from smashing
headfirst into the windshield.

He would have appreciated a little warning.

And what in the world was a *scrilatyl?*

The flyer's sudden halt surprised the cruisers, who sped ahead, leaving the stationary flyer behind, even as the stalled aircraft suddenly dropped like a stone toward the city below.

Kirk gasped in alarm.

Spock had no audible reaction.

"Do not fear!" Vlisora exclaimed. "Hold on to your faith!"

Less than a minute of freefall felt like forever before she gunned the engines and the flyer shot backward in reverse, halting its uncontrolled plunge. She narrowly missed the top of another building, then switched into forward gear once more. The flyer rocketed away to the west.

Kirk's heart was pounding in his chest. He'd taken slingshot maneuvers around the sun that were more relaxing than Vlisora's barnstorming acrobatics. He needed a moment to catch his breath.

"Pretty fancy flying," he said, impressed.

"I was a pilot before I was a priestess," she volunteered.

Kirk could believe it.

"An intriguing change of career," Spock observed.

"I felt a calling," she explained, "before—"

"Here they come again!" Kirk interrupted.

Twigging to the fact that they had lost their prey, the cruisers looped back to resume the pursuit. Kirk briefly lost them in the blinding glare of the sun, but then they came up behind the flyer again. Even more alarmingly, reinforcements arrived in the form of two more cruisers that swooped in to join the hunt. Apparently, the rebels' diversionary tactics weren't keeping enough of the Crusaders engaged—or maybe somebody had simply decided that capturing the High Priestess and her alien passengers took priority.

Lucky us, Kirk thought. *We're in demand.*

"Any more tricks up your sleeve?" he asked Vlisora.

Her black eyes scanned the city streets below.

"Hang on," she said. "This is going to be close."

The nose of the flyer dipped precipitously as she dived toward the lower levels of the city at an alarming angle and rate of descent. Kirk's stomach lurched, and he grabbed onto the dashboard to brace himself. His knuckles whitened, and he found himself longing for a decent set of inertial dampers. He hoped the word *kamikaze* was not in her vocabulary.

"You sure you know what you're doing here?" he asked.

Spock seemed to have some misgivings as well. "I believe I would like to hear more about that safety net you mentioned."

"We're flying, not crashing," she insisted.

"That seems a fine distinction in this instance."

She shrugged. "Trust me."

We already are, Kirk thought. *More than I like.*

The flyer weaved between gleaming towers and floating sculptures, taking tighter turns than Kirk would have preferred. The floor of the city rushed up to meet them. A bus-size tram appeared in their path, and the flyer banked sharply to avoid it. They darted toward an oncoming stream of traffic, playing chicken with dozens of civilian vehicles, which peeled off in all directions, yielding the right-of-way to the apparently suicidal flyer and its daredevil pilot. The pursuing cruisers had to take evasive action to avoid being hit by the fleeing aircraft. Sirens screeched while emergency signals beeped and blared.

"You do that on purpose?" Kirk asked.

"Perhaps," she said, "but that wasn't the truly risky part. The greater gamble is almost upon us."

Kirk was almost afraid to ask what she meant. "Which is?"

"Wait and see," she said. "But get ready for— What in perdition?"

The steady drone of the flyer's engine went silent. The control panel flashed briefly, then went black. Vlisora swore again and fiddled with her pendant to no avail. She smacked the dashboard with her fist, but the display panels stayed black. Clearly, this was not part of her plan.

"Misbegotten, ancestor-less scum!"

"What is it?" Kirk asked, although he feared he already knew the answer.

"They've killed the grav lifter remotely!" She glared angrily at the dashboard as though trying to will it back to life. "We're going to have to engage the glider wings manually!"

Beats falling like a rock again, Kirk thought. "How?"

"There's a lever to your right! Find it—but don't pull it yet!"

Kirk didn't need to be told twice. He located the lever, which had a lacquered turquoise sheen. "Got it!"

"We need to deploy them in unison or we'll go into a spin," she explained hastily. "On my count. Three, two, one . . . pull!"

Kirk yanked hard on the lever. It was sticky and required a bit of exertion, but functioned as intended. A scalloped wing, boasting embossed silver scales, swung out to starboard, but not on Vlisora's side. The flyer rolled over and starting spinning along its axis. Kirk's safety restraints stopped him from hitting the ceiling.

"Your wing!" he shouted at Vlisora. "What's wrong with your wing?"

"It's jammed! It won't budge!"

She tugged on the lever as the flyer went into a death spiral. Kirk wondered just what the limits of the city's zero-g safety net was—and how exactly this was going to reduce their odds of making a clean escape. Even if they survived the crash, would they be left waiting for the authorities to come scoop them up?

"Allow me," Spock said. Reaching from the back seat, he grabbed the lever and added his Vulcan strength to hers. The stubborn lever yielded to their combined efforts, and the portside wing extended.

"Blessed be your mighty ancestors!" Vlisora exclaimed. Working the manual controls, she halted their barrel roll and brought the flyer back under control, even as it continued to dive toward the floor of the city, which was getting ever closer.

So were the cruisers, which were rapidly eating up the gap between themselves and the flyer. The additional cruisers significantly increased their odds of snaring the flyer, Kirk realized; with four vehicles at their disposal, they could trap the flyer in a fully three-dimensional squeeze play, cutting off every avenue of escape. Vlisora wasn't going to be able to go into reverse or drop away next time.

"These skies are getting pretty unfriendly," he said. "What happens if they catch us?"

"Let us not find out!"

Kirk scoured the streets and alleys below for anything resembling a landing strip. A low steel overpass, connected to two adjacent skyscrapers, loomed directly ahead. Empty tracks disappeared into a lightless black tunnel entrance underneath the bridge. A derelict bullet train, overrun with vines and creepers, rested on an adjacent track. Some sort of underground rail system?

Vlisora aimed the flyer straight at the forbidding black cavity, which looked to be about half the size of the hangar deck's space doors back on the *Enterprise.* Kirk hurriedly tried to estimate the width of the tunnel entrance as compared to the wingspan of the flyer.

Unsurprisingly, Spock got there first.

"With all due respect," he told Vlisora, "I do not

believe we have sufficient clearance for what you appear to be attempting."

"Not in the least." She did not veer from her approach to the tunnel. "If you ever pray to your own deities, ancestors, or ineffable cosmic forces, now would be a good time to do so."

The tunnel entrance, swelling before them like the event horizon of a voracious black star, was only meters away. The flyer's speed and momentum carried them straight toward it. They could not turn away now if they wanted to.

"Ducking is also advisable," she added.

The flyer threaded the tunnel entrance, more or less. The wings were torn off on both sides, the gleaming ceramics screeching in anguish. Sparks flew from beneath the crippled flyer as it touched down roughly on the track and slid down a sharp incline at approximately a forty-five-degree angle. The Stygian depths of the tunnel swallowed them, and Kirk was bounced violently in his seat before the flyer finally skidded to a stop deep beneath the city. The only faint glimmers of daylight came from the tunnel entrance behind and above them.

Talk about a bumpy landing, Kirk thought.

He took a second to catch his breath—and smelled smoke. Glancing around him, he saw that the sides and bottom of the flyer were on fire. Sparks spurted from exposed circuitry. Orange flames licked at the sides of the now-wingless aircraft.

"Everybody out!" he shouted.

He checked on Vlisora, ready to assist her or even carry her if necessary, but she was already moving of her own accord. To his relief, Spock was both conscious and mobile as well.

"We seem to have survived another hostile encounter with gravity," the Vulcan observed wryly, "albeit of a more conventional variety." He sniffed the air. "Combustion, however, remains an issue."

Vlisora popped the canopy, and all three passengers scrambled out of the cockpit. They stumbled away from the smoldering flyer.

"Any chance it could explode?" Kirk asked.

"I don't believe so," Vlisora said, somewhat less than confidently. "But I was a pilot, not a mechanic."

Kirk kept a close eye on the flyer, just in case they needed to dive for cover. Borrowing Vlisora's cloak, he used it beat out the sputtering flames before checking himself for injuries. Aside from a few new bumps and bruises, he was still in working condition. "Everybody in one piece?"

"Yes, Captain," Spock said. "Quite unlike our aircraft."

"I am intact as well," Vlisora said. She did not ask for her scorched cloak back. Her satiny black tunic was rumpled and torn in places. "It seems my divine ancestors were watching out for us all."

Kirk was inclined to give more credit to her own expert, if somewhat reckless, piloting.

"I understand that you're a priestess of some sort, but you may be trusting a little too heavily on your ancestors' good graces, not to mention the power of prayer. On my world, we call that tempting fate."

She shrugged. "And yet we are all still alive, are we not? How miraculous is that?"

Kirk didn't have a ready answer for that, nor did he waste too much time searching for one. They had more immediate concerns.

"Where now?" he asked.

"Follow me," she began, then reeled, clutching her head. She threw out her other hand to brace herself against a sooty tunnel wall. "No," she murmured weakly. "Not so soon. . . ."

Was she suffering from a concussion? Kirk rushed forward and grabbed her shoulders to steady her. "What is it? What's wrong?"

"The God-King," she answered. "He knows of my betrayal . . . and your escape. He is calling for our capture. His command goes forth to all Ialatl. . . ."

Kirk couldn't hear anything and, judging from his curious expression, neither could Spock. Yet Vlisora seemed to be receiving some kind of telepathic alert.

"You can hear him?" Kirk asked. "In your head?"

"We can all hear him. Every Ialatl." She took a deep breath and seemed to regain her balance. "The God-King can speak to us all if he chooses."

"Fascinating," Spock observed.

"Are you all right?" Kirk asked, still holding her

shoulders. She seemed steadier now, but he wanted to be sure. "He can't control you, can he?"

She shook her head. "I cannot avoid hearing him, but I am not compelled to obey his words." She politely disengaged herself from Kirk's grip. "Would that more of my kin exercised that same freedom."

Kirk wanted to know more, but was interrupted by a blaring siren coming from the city above. He heard shouting and pounding footsteps.

"It appears our crash landing did not go unnoticed." Spock looked pointedly at the tunnel entrance. "I believe we can expect company."

"Your weapon!" Vlisora said urgently. The threat of imminent capture seemed to distract her from the demanding voice in her head. "You must use it to seal the tunnel behind us. Can you do that?"

"Yes," Kirk confirmed. He didn't like the idea of burying himself alive—he'd had enough of that on Ardana last year—but they seemed to be running low on options. He had to assume that those cruisers, and the persistent Crusaders inside them, were still hot on their trail.

"Then do so at once!" she said. "There is no time to lose!"

Screeching sirens, and the keening of multiple antigrav engines, could be heard just outside the tunnel. Kirk guessed that the cruisers were touching down up above. Angry shouts and footsteps added to the unmistakable sounds of pursuit.

"Find the infidels!" a furious voice bellowed. "Do not let them elude us!"

Kirk drew his phaser and set it on disrupt. A crimson beam lit up the murky tunnel before striking the roof of the tunnel entrance, which came apart in a rumble of falling steel and masonry. Clouds of dust billowed down the tunnel, adding to the smoky haze left behind by the fire. Kirk backed up instinctively as falling rubble blocked the entrance. Loose scree tumbled down the rails. The sounds of the pursuing Ialatl were drowned out by the cave-in, then lost behind the heaped wall of debris. Echoes resounded through the underground tunnel.

For a second, as the rubble cut them off from the harsh sunlight above, Kirk and the others were cast into utter darkness. Not a sliver of light penetrated the improvised barricade. Kirk completely lost sight of Spock and Vlisora, until the priestess produced a small palm-sized light not unlike the ones Starfleet landing parties used to explore caves, derelict spaceships, night-shrouded planets, and other environments that tested the ocular faculties of most humanoid species. Kirk was grateful for both the light and Vlisora's foresight.

"Will that hold them?" he asked.

"Long enough." She turned her back on the collapsed entrance and began marching farther into the tunnel. "Come with me."

Spock held back for a moment.

"Can we trust her, Captain?"

Kirk understood his first officer's caution. They were getting in deeper and deeper, both literally and figuratively. And they still didn't know who all the players were.

"I'm not sure we have any choice," he said, holstering his phaser. "Unless we want to be left alone in the dark."

Spock sighed. "That would not be an advantageous situation."

"My thoughts exactly," Kirk said.

They took off after her.

SIX

"Mister Scott, I'm receiving an emergency signal from Mister Sulu's communicator!"

Scotty swung around in the captain's chair. "What is it? What does he say?"

"Nothing verbal," she said. "Just an emergency SOS, complete with transporter coordinates."

In an emergency, Starfleet communicators could be used to send a distress signal even when the crew member was too busy or unable to speak. This usually meant that they needed to be beamed out of hot water, pronto.

"He must be in trouble," Chekov exclaimed, stating the obvious.

"Aye," Scotty agreed. "Lower the shields, Mister Chekov." He activated the intercom on the chair's armrest. "Scott to transporter room. Lock onto Mister Sulu's signal and beam him aboard."

"*Aye, sir,*" Kyle replied.

Scotty cut off the transmission. "What about the rest of the landing party?" he asked Uhura. "Captain Kirk and the others?"

Uhura shook her head. "Nothing from them. Only Sulu."

To be honest, she wasn't even sure how the emergency signal had managed to get through the interference down on the planet. Sulu must have figured out a way to boost the signal; it certainly wasn't her doing.

Scotty frowned. Uhura knew he would have preferred to get word of their other missing crewmates as well. "Let's hope Sulu can tell us what the devil is going on," he grumbled.

At least one scheduled check-in had come and gone without word from the planet. Scott had been reluctant to risk another team before they had any sort of clue as to what had happened to the captain and the others, let alone the people at the Institute. Sending more people down blindly could just make the situation worse.

Uhura couldn't blame Scotty for being cautious. *We still don't even know what that original distress signal was about.*

She waited anxiously for an update from the transporter room.

Lieutenant John Kyle locked onto Sulu's signal. He did not hesitate; this was a standard procedure, which he had executed many times before. Standing behind the transporter controls, he watched as a sparkling column of energy materialized above one of the transporter pads, then rapidly coalesced into a humanoid form.

It wasn't Sulu.

A tall silver alien appeared before Kyle's eyes. He hopped quickly off the transporter pad before the startled lieutenant had a chance to beam him back where he came from. The alien glanced around the transporter room, taking in his new surroundings. He clutched a communicator in one hand. Kyle recognized the model. It was Starfleet standard-issue.

Bloody hell, he thought. *We've been tricked.*

Reacting promptly, Kyle hit the intruder alert button. Flashing annunciator lights and blaring klaxons sounded the alarm. He reached beneath his console to retrieve a phaser from the emergency compartment. He had been ambushed in the transporter room before. He wasn't about to let that happen again.

"Stay right where you are!" he ordered the alien. A crisp British accent colored his command. He hit the speaker button on his intercom. "Kyle to Bridge. It's not Sulu! It's someone else."

Glossy black eyes turned toward him.

"Do not obstruct me," the alien warned. "My purpose is urgent beyond your understanding."

"That's not for me to decide," Kyle said. He belatedly noticed the polished black baton in the alien's other hand. "And drop that weapon, mister."

"No," the alien refused. "I cannot allow you to detain me."

The baton glowed green and, all at once, the phaser in Kyle's hand was too heavy to hold. It yanked his arm down, hitting the transporter controls hard enough to dent the sturdy metal casing. He felt the jarring impact all the way up his arm.

"What the—?" He tried to lift the phaser, but it wouldn't budge. "Blast it!"

"Tell your commanding officer to expect me," the alien said. "It is vital that we speak without delay."

He turned toward the door, which whooshed open to admit a pair of racing security officers armed with type-2 phaser pistols. Kyle was impressed by the speed with which they had responded to his alert.

Not that it did any good. With a wave of his glowing baton, which left a dark green blur behind it, the alien somehow caused the two men to collapse onto the floor, where they squirmed helplessly, barely able to move. Like Kyle, they couldn't even lift their weapons.

The alien stepped around them on his way to the door. He exited the transporter room, marching briskly as though he knew exactly where he was going.

"Kyle to the bridge," he notified the others. "We couldn't stop him. He's heading toward you!"

The bridge was on full alert.

"Raise shields!" Scotty ordered, perched tensely at the edge of his seat. "We don't want any more of those rascals beaming aboard!"

"Aye, aye, sir!" Chekov said.

Uhura tuned out the blaring klaxons and flashing red annunciator lights in order to make sense of the multiple reports pouring in from all over the ship.

"Mister Scott," she called out. "The intruder is making his way toward the bridge!"

"Put it on the screen, Lieutenant!"

"Aye, sir."

She directed the feed from the ship's internal monitors to the main viewer. A computer algorithm, of Mister Spock's design, helped filter out any irrelevant images and select the views they needed. She turned her own gaze toward the viewer—and gasped at the sight.

On-screen, an exotic-looking alien of unknown origin was advancing through the *Enterprise*'s busy corridors. Security officers, of varied races and gender, attempted to halt his progress, but met with failure after failure. Phaser beams fell short of their target, striking the floor instead. Burly crew members hit the floor, somehow immobilized by a luminous baton wielded by the intruder. Phosphorescent green auras briefly enveloped their bodies before dissipating into the ether.

"Who the devil?" Scotty exclaimed. He winced every time a deflected phaser beam scorched one of his precious bulkheads.

Uhura had no idea. She had read enough about the Institute and its environs to know that the silver invader was not of any species native to Ephrata IV—or any other planet she was familiar with.

"He seems to know the way," Chekov said, "but how?"

Uhura figured it out.

"He's probably had access to the Institute's libraries, scientists, and engineers. With all that knowledge accumulated in one place, it wouldn't be hard to learn the basic layout of a *Constitution*-class starship."

"Aye," Scotty said grimly. "That's surely the truth of it."

On-screen, the alien forced his way into a turbolift. Nobody seemed to be able to stop him. Bright red doors closed behind him, cutting him off from view. Uhura recalled that there were no monitors in the turbolifts.

"Mister Scott!" Lieutenant Charlene Masters called out from the engineering station. She was an attractive black woman in a blue uniform. Her hair was cut short. "He's taking the turbolift to the bridge."

"Not if I have anything to say about it," Scotty declared. "Seal off the bridge—and shut down that turbolift."

"Aye, sir," Masters said. "Done."

"That's better," Scotty said. "Here's hoping the blackguard has trapped himself."

Uhura received a message from the stalled turbolift. "Mister Scott, the intruder has activated the intercom in the lift. He's demanding to speak to you."

"Is he now?" Scotty's surly expression showed exactly what he thought of intruders who barged aboard the *Enterprise* uninvited. "Pipe him through, Lieutenant."

"Aye, sir."

A deep voice issued from the speakers on the bridge:

"Let me through! I must speak to your command-ing officer. I have urgent news of your captain and your comrades!"

Uhura's interest, which was already acute, ratcheted up another notch. Did this intruder really know what had become of Captain Kirk and the others?

"You're not going anywhere," Scott said firmly, "until you put down your weapon and surrender to our security forces. *Then* maybe we can talk."

"You don't understand! We're running out of time. You must trust me!"

"After you beamed aboard under false pretenses?" Scott replied. "Not bloody likely."

Uhura wondered what had happened to Sulu, and how the alien had obtained his communicator. Did this mean the landing party had been taken captive— or worse?

"You fools!" the voice roared in frustration. *"I'm try-ing to save your entire Federation. Let me through . . . or I'll destroy us all!"*

A sudden shudder shook the ship.

"Sir!" Masters exclaimed. "The turbolift! It's in-creasing in weight. It's tearing loose from its re-straints!"

"What?" Scotty looked at her in shock. "That's nae possible!"

"Maybe not," Lieutenant Philip Ferrari reported from

the science station, which he was manning in Spock's absence. He was a lanky blond with whom Uhura had once shared a shore leave on Shawan V. "I'm picking up some truly bizarre gravitational fluctuations inside the turbolift. They're like nothing I've ever seen before!"

"Kill the gravity in the turbolift!" Scotty ordered. "And seal off that shaft!"

In the unlikely event of an emergency, Uhura knew, force fields and even solid duranium barriers could be used to halt an out-of-control or falling turbolift. She hoped that would be enough.

Another shudder rattled the bridge.

"I don't believe it!," Masters exclaimed. "The lift just tore through the first line of safety barriers. Its weight is increasing by the moment!"

"Please," the intruder begged. *"I don't want to damage your ship . . . but I will if have to!"*

Scott's expression grew darker. He looked around the bridge.

"Anybody got any bright ideas how to stop that turbolift before it tears a hole in the ship?"

A worrisome silence greeted him. Uhura wished she had a solution for him, but what she didn't know about turbolift engineering and gravitational fluxes would fill several databases. Stopping runaway turbolifts was hardly her area of expertise.

"Aye, I was afraid of that." He hit the switch on his intercom. "All right, you made your point. Let's hear what you have to say."

"A wise decision," the voice answered. *"More than you can possibly know."*

"Dramatic much?" Chekov scoffed.

Scotty turned back toward Masters. "All right, Lieutenant. Bring our visitor to us."

"I don't need to, sir." She stared in wonder at her board. "The lift is rising of its own accord."

Security officers, assigned to the bridge, fanned out to cover the entrance. Tension mounted as all eyes turned toward the familiar red doors, which slid open to reveal the alien in the flesh. He strode out onto the bridge, clutching his baton. A mane of golden tentacles fringed his face. His height put even the tallest security officer to shame. He smelled like smoke.

"That's far enough, mister." Scotty rose from his chair to confront the invader. "You want to talk, put down that weapon."

"Not yet," the alien said, unwilling to relinquish his one advantage. "But I mean you no harm. Far to the contrary."

"Tell that to the crew you bushwhacked on the way here," Scotty said. "And who might you be anyway?"

"You can call me Maxah, but that doesn't matter. You must leave this world at once . . . for your galaxy's sake!"

Scotty crossed his arms across his chest. "And why would I want to do that?"

"Please listen to me," Maxah said. "You have to leave orbit before—"

A jolt, far more powerful than before, overpowered the ship's inertial dampers. The prow of the bridge actually dipped forward, almost spilling Uhura from her seat. She grabbed onto her console to keep from falling. Coffee cups, data slates, and other unmoored debris went flying toward the main viewer. Chekov grunted as his gut slammed into the nav controls. Fisher tumbled over the helm. A greenish hue lit up the viewscreen, tinting the image.

What in the world?

"No!" Maxah cried out in despair. He took hold of one of the bright red safety rails surrounding the recessed command area. Despair contorted his argent countenance. "It's too late! They know I'm here!"

They? Uhura wondered. "Who do you mean?"

"What's happening?" Scotty demanded. He lunged across the bridge and threw Maxah up against the rail. "Is this your doing?"

The alien's head drooped forward. His shoulders slumped in defeat.

"No," he whispered, so that Uhura had to strain to hear him. "The gravity cannon. It's locked onto you. We cannot escape."

"Gravity cannon?" Chekov echoed, even as he and Fisher feverishly worked the helm and nav controls to right the ship. The bridge leveled out slowly and jerkily, as though fighting some powerful force. "I've never heard of such a thing."

"It matters not what you've heard," Maxah said

gloomily. "Our moment has passed. The cannon shall not let us go."

"The devil you say." Scotty dropped back into the captain's chair. "Mister Fisher, take us out of orbit."

Uhura caught a tinge of regret beneath his resolve. She knew it had to be killing him to leave Captain Kirk and the others behind, but his first responsibility was the safety of the ship and the crew. Given that they seemed to be under attack from some powerful new weapon, a strategic retreat was clearly in order. Uhura would have made the same call.

Not that it's up to me, she thought. *Thank goodness.*

She waited for the stationary planet to disappear from the viewer, but if anything, Ephrata IV seemed even closer than before. A vibration rattled the ship. A distracting green glow still tinted the viewer.

"Mister Fisher?" Scotty asked. "Why are we still in orbit?"

"I'm trying, sir!" the helmsman said. Perspiration broke out across his forehead as he wrestled with his controls. "But the gravity is too strong. We're locked into a geosynchronous orbit directly above the Institute. We can't break free."

"It's coming from the planet," Ferrari confirmed. "Some kind of targeted gravity beam originating from"—he double-checked his readouts—"the approximate location of the Institute."

The ship's impulse engines whirred loudly as they strained against the pull of the gravity cannon.

Uhura could feel the vibration growing stronger, rising through her seat into her spine. It was like riding one of the old-fashioned roller coasters at New Coney Island.

"More power," Scotty ordered. "Give us all she's got."

Fisher gulped. "Yes, sir."

The roar of the engines increased, but the *Enterprise* remained mired in orbit. The overhead lights flickered. Damage reports—burst plasma conduits, coolant leaks, cracked manifolds, and other mechanical injuries—began flooding Uhura's board, even as she was shaken and tossed about in her seat. She felt as if she were riding a shuttlecraft through heavy turbulence. A jarring bump shook her earpiece loose, and she grabbed it before it hit the floor. She clenched her jaw to keep her teeth from rattling. Bulkheads groaned ominously. The deadly vacuum of space suddenly felt a little bit closer.

"Mister Scott!" Masters said. "The impulse engines are superheating. The containment fields are failing. They can't take it anymore!"

"That's my line, lassie." Scotty jumped to his feet and lurched across the quaking bridge to his usual post at engineering. Masters stepped aside to let him get at the controls. "I've still got a few tricks up my sleeve, the kind they don't teach at the Academy. . . ."

He fiddled with the controls, and an extra surge of power sent the *Enterprise* shooting forward. For a second, it looked as though the ship was actually going to break orbit, but then the ship was yanked backward abruptly, as though it had reached the end of its tether.

"The gravity beam!" Ferrari exclaimed. "It's increasing!"

The abrupt halt was more than the inertial dampers could cope with. People and equipment were thrown across the bridge. Warning lights and displays went into the red zone. Sparks erupted from overloaded consoles. Uhura managed to hang on to her post, but only just barely. A loose data slate landed on the floor near her feet.

"Full reverse!" Scotty shouted, trying to save the ship from being ripped apart. "Reduce pow—"

The engineering console exploded, hurling him across the bridge into the safety rail around the command area. He bounced off the rail onto the floor, where he convulsed in agony. Smoke rose from his scorched red uniform. His face and hands had suffered serious burns as well. His breathing was ragged.

"Bridge to sickbay!" Uhura said, reacting instantly. "Mister Scott has been injured! Report immediately!"

Scotty held himself together long enough to complete his orders. "Reduce power," he said weakly, fighting to stay conscious. "Maintain orbit . . . cannae tear the old girl to pieces. . . ."

He passed out on the floor.

Fisher eased back on the throttle, reducing the strain on the engines. The punishing tremors quieted as the *Enterprise* stopped fighting the "gravity cannon" and eased back into a stable orbit around Ephrata IV. Charlene Masters retrieved an emergency first-aid kit and rushed to Scotty's side. An analgesic hypospray helped ease his pain.

"No!" Maxah wailed from his position by the rail. "This is all your fault!" He shook his fist at the crew. His tentacles writhed in agitation. "Why didn't you listen to me?"

In the tumult, Uhura had almost forgotten about the invader, but he clearly hadn't forgotten about them. She frowned. Things were bad enough without a hysterical alien, armed with a dangerous weapon of unknown potential, losing his marbles all over the bridge.

Something had to be done—and quickly.

The fallen data slate caught her eye. She snatched it up and, without stopping to think about it, whacked Maxah across the back of his head. The slate cracked loudly against his skull, and he staggered forward before falling face-first onto the floor. Limp fingers let go of his baton, which rolled across the floor toward Masters, who turned away from Scotty long enough to grab it.

"Careful with that," Uhura said. "We don't know what that's capable of."

"Yes, Lieutenant." Masters handled the captured weapon gingerly. She looked up at Uhura. "Any other orders?"

"Orders?"

Still coming down from the adrenaline rush of her sneak attack, it took Uhura a moment to notice that all eyes on the bridge had turned toward her. The battered bridge crew gazed at her expectantly. Uhura was momentarily taken aback.

Then it hit her. Now that Lieutenant DeSalle had transferred over to the *Columbia,* she was the senior officer on the bridge.

I'm in command, she realized.

SEVEN

"Why are these tunnels abandoned?" Kirk asked.

He and Spock followed Vlisora through an underground labyrinth of winding tunnels, service corridors, junctions, and loading platforms. Kirk tried to memorize the route, but soon lost track of the confusing twists and turns. Arcane markings, inscribed on the walls in an alien tongue, offered little in the way of direction. He hoped Spock's more analytical mind was faring better, just in case they needed to retrace their steps—without the aid of their current guide.

"Once we conquered gravity," she explained, "my people chose to traverse the sky rather than ride beneath the surface. This vast underground transport system rapidly fell into disuse and was eventually shut down."

Her portable light held back the darkness.

"There was some talk of filling in the tunnels," she recalled with a rueful tone, "or perhaps converting them to another purpose, but then the Crusade arose to devour our society's attention and resources, and less pressing endeavors fell by the wayside." She made her way through the tunnels; she clearly knew exactly where she was going. "Which has proven advantageous for those few of us with other ideas, ones best hidden from the light."

Kirk contemplated the lonely tunnels. They certainly seemed a far cry from the floating pyramid and brilliant daylight he and Spock had first encountered on this world. Their footsteps echoed worryingly in the long cylindrical tubes.

"Will not this Crusade be able to pursue us down here?" Spock glanced back the way they had come. "From what I have seen of your technology, I cannot imagine that a mere cave-in will deter them for long."

Kirk saw his point. If their mastery of artificial gravity could lift an entire pyramid above the city, how hard could it be to clear away some accumulated debris? Even back home, antigrav lifters were often used in excavation efforts.

"True," she said. "Hence the rather circuitous route we have been taking. These tunnels extend beneath the entire surface of Ialat, with multiple overlapping levels and junctions. If the ancestors are with us, we will not be easily found."

Kirk took her word for it. He had little choice but to do so.

"Well, I certainly hope you're not planning to hike all the way around the planet," he said. "I can't speak for my friend here, but I'm only human."

He wasn't joking. Although he was glad to have escaped this world's scorching daylight, the tunnels were still uncomfortably hot and muggy. Sweat glued his shirt to his back. His stomach grumbled. He was tired and sore and his mouth felt as dry as the Mojave; unfortunately, Vlisora did not appear to be carrying a canteen.

He was also worried about his ship and his crew. Hours had passed since he had beamed down to Ephrata IV. Since then he'd lost half his landing party, and the *Enterprise* was now a universe away, possibly unaware of the threat posed by the Crusaders. Kirk would have given anything for a chance to contact his ship.

The Enterprise *is in good hands,* he reminded himself. *Scotty can hold down the fort until I get back.*

"Fear not," Vlisora said. "Our destination draws near."

Kirk was glad to hear it, but he didn't want to wait any longer for answers. "About this Crusade of yours . . ."

"It is not *my* Crusade," she said vehemently. The spines running across the top of her head stiffened, creating a spiky crest. They darkened angrily. "Far from it."

"So you belong to some kind of underground resistance?" he surmised. "No pun intended." He needed to know more about the situation on this world. "Just how many of you are there? And what do you want with us?"

She held up her hand to forestall further questions. "Hold your questions just a while more."

At first, he feared she was stalling, then he saw that they had come to a dead end. One end of what appeared to be a derelict bullet train blocked the track in front of them. Blackened windows concealed the interior of the car. Its tarnished black-and-silver hull was scratched and dented. Alien graffiti revealed that vandalism was not unknown on Ialat, despite the piousness of the Crusade. Filmy orange cobwebs indicated that the train had not carried passengers for some time. Kirk saw no obvious way around it.

"What?" he asked. "Did we take a wrong turn?"

"Wait."

She cautiously approached the train. Raising her hand to her pendant, she spun its concentric circles in a specific sequence. Her deft manipulations produced a series of clicks and chirps. Jade, turquoise, and obsidian rings flashed out a code—but to what purpose?

The train's taillights flared to life, practically blinding Kirk. An amplified voice blared from the car, which was apparently not quite as abandoned as it appeared:

"Your name?"

"It is I, Vlisora." She held up her hand and made a distinctive gesture with her four fingers. "I come bringing guests."

"And your creed?"

"Question everything, even the Truth."

The exchange seemed to satisfy her unseen interrogator. The floodlights dimmed to a less aggressive intensity. A door opened and a ramp extended from the rear of the train. Ialatl, armed with rifles and bayonets of some kind, scurried forth and escorted the new arrivals into the train, where Vlisora was greeted warmly by a male Ialatl who seemed to be in charge. His rumpled, copper-colored attire did not resemble the uniform worn by the Crusaders, nor was there any sash across his chest. Kirk guessed he was a civilian.

"You did it?" He stared at Kirk and Spock in disbelief. "These are the strangers from beyond?"

"See for yourself," she said proudly. "Many thanks for those timely diversions. We would not have eluded the Crusade without them."

"A few valiant compatriots were lost or captured during those efforts," he said gravely. "May the ancestors grant that their sacrifices were not in vain."

"You must have faith that our deliverance is at hand." She introduced her companion to Kirk and Spock. "This is Lasem, the leader of this intrepid band of dissidents and freethinkers."

He saluted the visitors, using the same sign Vlisora had used. His black eyes held an uneasy blend of fear and reverence. The spines around his face tensed warily, but did not flare outward in anger.

"Welcome to Ialat," he said. "I regret that your visit is less than voluntary."

"That's one way to put it." Kirk said, looking around. He saw that the interior of the train was better lit and maintained than its deceptively rundown exterior. One-way windows, appearing black from the outside, were transparent within. Upholstered couches, packed with supplies and provisions, lined the rear compartment. A sealed doorway at the other end of the car presumably led to other compartments. "I'm Captain James T. Kirk of the *Starship Enterprise,* and this is my first officer, Commander Spock."

"Your names and deeds are already known to us," Lasem said before turning toward Vlisora. Concern furrowed his brow. "Your courage and commitment to our cause honors us all, High Priestess, but you know, of course, that you can never return to the royal temple now. Jaenab will neither forget nor forgive what you have done today."

"Jaenab?" Kirk asked.

"The God-King," she explained. The sorrow in her voice required no translation. "My husband."

Husband? Kirk needed a moment to process that revelation.

Spock merely arched an eyebrow. "Fascinating."

"They have many questions," she informed Lasem. "Is there someplace where we can converse in comfort and privacy? And perhaps provide our guests with food and drink?"

"Of course." He indicated the doorway ahead. "The upper-caste carriage is at your disposal." He paused to address a female subordinate, who also sported civilian attire. "Let us be under way once more. Commence route dragon-corbel-quaternion."

"Yes, Lasem." She repeated the command into a blinking turquoise bracelet. "Get us moving."

A moment later, the train lurched to life, briefly throwing Kirk off balance. The curved gray walls of the tunnel seemed to rush past the windows as the train smoothly accelerated toward . . . where?

"We going somewhere?" Kirk asked.

"Always," Lasem said wryly. "To everywhere and nowhere."

"A mobile command center," Spock deduced. "Constantly in motion to elude detection."

Lasem nodded. "And to protect our treasures."

"Treasures?" Kirk asked.

Lasem smiled proudly. The interior doorway opened at his approach. "Come and see."

Along with Vlisora, he led them through a string of compartments, all of which appeared to be packed with art, literature, and historical artifacts. Transparent bins held stacks of books, scrolls, and data storage devices. Fossils, both humanoid and otherwise, had been carefully wrapped and organized. Other items had been piled together more haphazardly. A granite cartouche inscribed with alien hieroglyphics was propped up against a jade bust of some ancient Ialatl priestess. An illuminated manuscript lay open atop what appeared to be an ornately decorated sarcophagus. Rolled-up tapestries and canvases were tucked awkwardly into corners. Prehistoric bone tools shared shelf space with modern-looking erotic artwork. It was like navigating through the overstuffed basement of a library or museum.

"A most impressive collection." Spock paused briefly to admire a beautifully rendered map of the planet. "If there is time, I would appreciate the opportunity to examine the contents more carefully."

"All this art and knowledge has been condemned by the Crusade," Vlisora explained, "for not adhering to the strictest, most literal interpretations of our ancestors' teachings. Indeed, much of it is officially listed as 'purged.' Countless scholars and curators and even a few sympathetic Crusaders have risked much to save these precious relics from destruction and preserve them for future generations." A sweeping gesture encompassed the cluttered stockpile. "The train is but one of several moving repositories, forever keeping one step ahead of the Crusade."

"Like an old-fashioned shell game," Kirk said.

Vlisora did not get the reference. She gave him a puzzled look. "Forgive me?"

"Never mind," he assured her. "Just a human figure of speech." He took a rough count of the Ialatl in sight. There appeared to be only a handful of rebels occupying the train. "I take it this is not your entire resistance movement?"

"Not at all," Lasem said. "But we find it wiser not to concentrate in large numbers, or even to share our identities too widely. Each small enclave functions independently for the most part, with contact between separate enclaves kept to a minimum."

Kirk nodded. "So that if one group is captured,

they can't be forced to inform on the others." He was familiar with the concept from Earth's own history, as well those of numerous other worlds. "Isolated resistance cells, with members knowing only their own immediate comrades and superiors."

"Precisely," Vlisora said. "It is the only way. The Crusade's informers are everywhere, sniffing out heretics and radicals."

"And now fugitives from another universe," Lasem said, guiding them through another doorway into the compartment beyond. "But you may take shelter here, if only for a time."

They found themselves in what looked as if it had once been a luxury coach for VIP travelers. Plush chairs and couches, with plenty of leg room, faced elegant coffee tables inlaid with jade and turquoise. A muted blue carpet covered the floor. Books, bins, and boxes were piled on every available surface, but Lasem cleared off one couch to make room for his guests. The displaced treasures were relocated to an out-of-the way corner of the carriage.

"Please, make yourselves comfortable," Lasem said. He procured several bottles of an amber liquid from an overhead luggage rack and placed them on the cluttered table before Kirk and Spock. "Drink this. It will restore you."

Kirk hesitated before consuming the unknown liquid. Ideally, he would want to analyze the drink first, but the Crusaders had confiscated Spock's tricorder back on Ephrata IV. And he *was* damn thirsty.

"Thanks," he said. "Bottoms up."

The drink was cool and refreshing, with a distinctly nutty aftertaste. Spock observed Kirk's reaction before helping himself. Kirk gulped down the whole bottle and opened another before getting down to business. He needed to be sharp now, not groggy and dehydrated.

"I'm grateful for your hospitality, but I still need answers," he said. "What are we doing here, and why did you rescue us from the Crusaders?"

"It's quite simple," Vlisora said. "We desperately need your help to free our world from the madness that is crushing our civilization—and which now threatens your own universe."

"But we know little about your world," Kirk protested, "let alone the nature of the threat."

"Perhaps you can elaborate on how this present situation came to pass," Spock suggested. "More data on your world and the Crusade's objectives would be of great value at this point."

"Of course." She chuckled ruefully. "You must understand that it is easy to forget that our ways and history are unknown to you. We have little experience with foreigners, or 'aliens' as you call them. Indeed, the words are obscure in our language."

She took a deep breath before launching into her explanation.

"Know then that Ialat is unlike your own worlds and Federation, which, so I understand, are populated by a bewildering variety of races, species, and cultures. There is but a single continent and kingdom on our world, a single civilization stretching back for untold millennia, our true origins lost in the mists of myth and legend.

"Moreover, there are no other planets orbiting our sun, and no evidence of life in the starry void beyond, so we have always assumed that we were the only sentient beings in creation, and that Ialat was the unquestioned center of all things, created by our divine ancestors at the dawn of this present cycle of existence. Jaenab, my king and husband, is believed to be the direct descendant of our ancient creators, carrying on a lineage that extends all the way back to the previous creation and the infinite cycles before that. As you saw, he can communicate with all our people by means of a crown, which has been passed down from ruler to ruler for generations."

"A telepathic amplifier," Spock theorized, "based on forgotten technology."

"That is what some of our own scientists and archaeologists believed," she said, "before their theories ran afoul of the Crusade. It is now forbidden to regard the Crown as anything but a sacred gift from our creators and the divine birthright of the God-King."

"Your husband?" Kirk said.

A sad smile hinted at conflicted feelings. "Am I not the High Priestess?"

Apparently that was meant to be self-explanatory.

Spock had a more urgent concern. "But how did the Crusade come to wield such power?"

"It was not always so," she said. "Until recently, all was well and our world thrived. Because we were unified in our ways, there was little dissent and thus no cause for oppression. The God-King attended primarily to spiritual matters, performing the traditional rites and ceremonies while allowing the civil authorities to govern with little interference from the priestly caste. The arts and sciences flourished during a golden age of peace and prosperity. The mastery of gravity, over a generation ago, caused an explosion of new innovations and applications, making our lives even easier."

Kirk recalled the highly advanced metropolis he had glimpsed before. "So what went wrong?"

"An unexpected scientific breakthrough," she said. "Experiments in applied gravity accidentally pierced the fabric of space-time . . . and revealed the existence of an entirely new universe. *Your* universe."

"A remarkable accomplishment," Spock said.

"But with dire consequences," she said gravely. "You must understand, we thought we were entirely alone and unique. We had never even conceived of the notion of other worlds or beings. The shock of discovering that literally billions of other species and civilizations existed was more than our society could absorb overnight. The result was a backlash that captured even the heart and mind of my own beloved husband and king. A wave of religious extremism, violently opposed to any new or unorthodox ideas, spread like a collective madness. The opening of the rifts was seen as the sign of an impending apocalypse . . . and the Crusade was born."

"In reaction to a severe cultural trauma which your homogeneous society was not equipped to cope with," Spock concluded. "An irrational response, but not without a certain dangerous logic."

"I don't know," Kirk said. "It seems a bit extreme to me. On Earth, First Contact led to a grand awakening that ultimately unified Earth and allowed humanity to takes its first steps toward joining a larger interplanetary community. We didn't go crazy . . . and set out to convert the rest of the universe to our ways."

"True," Spock conceded, "but recall that Earth, for all its troubled history, had been a world of myriad races and cultures almost since the time the first protohumans learned to walk erect. You had dealt, sometimes badly, sometimes nobly, with the challenge of conflicting ideologies and belief systems for many thousands of years, and, to give humanity its due, you had already begun to make progress in overcoming racial, religious, and other prejudices long before my own forebears introduced you to the reality of extraterrestrial life."

"You mean your forebears said hello to your *other* forebears," Kirk said, reminding Spock of his mixed heritage. "You don't need to refer to humanity in the third—or second—person."

"But I generally prefer to do so," Spock said, with a

slightly pained expression. "In any event, put yourself in the place of the Ialatl, who had never even dealt with diversity among their own kind before discovering a separate universe teeming with strange new worlds and civilizations. Is it any wonder that they reacted by clinging even more tightly to the timeless verities that were all they had ever known?"

I suppose, Kirk thought. In all fairness, there had been some xenophobic extremists back in Jonathan Archer's time, when Earth and Starfleet were just beginning to encounter the various alien species that would someday come together as the United Federation of Planets. But thankfully those reactionary elements had ended up on the wrong side of history. Humanity had ultimately rejected fear of the unknown and had chosen to seek out new ideas and worlds instead.

Unlike the Ialatl, it seemed.

"Just so," Vlisora confirmed. "My people cannot accept that your people can exist without our Truth. They are determined to enlighten you . . . for your own sakes."

Kirk recalled Sokis's intolerant attitude back on Ephrata. "I'm getting the picture, but I still don't understand what your God-King wants with Spock and me. Why bring us here to your world?"

A guilty look came over Vlisora's face.

"In truth, that was my doing, not my husband's. I led the Crusaders to believe that it was the God-King's will that you be sent through the portal, so that I could secure your aid."

Kirk could not contain his anger. "*You* had us dragged here against our will, away from my ship and my crew?"

"I had no choice! You were our only hope!"

"Why?" he demanded. "Why me?"

"Because you are the God-Slayer," she said, as though the answer were manifestly obvious. "The Freedom-Bringer."

Kirk blinked in surprise. "Excuse me?"

"I have laid eyes on the forbidden knowledge captured from the world you call Ephrata IV. My comrades and I," she said, gesturing at Lasem, "have carefully perused the records of your voyages and exploits. We know of the many worlds you have liberated from the weight of oppression, of the many tyrants and false gods you have overthrown: Landru, Vaal, the Oracle of Yonada, the Controller of Sigma Draconis VI, the Providers of Triskelion, the Platonians, the heartless elites of Stratos, Apollo of Olympus, the all-powerful Squire of Gothos . . ."

"Well, yes," Kirk said, slightly embarrassed by the litany. "You've obviously done your homework. . . ."

"Imagine our excitement when we discovered the existence of one such as you, and that the Crusade meant to lure your vessel to Ephrata IV," Lasem stated. "Never in our history has anyone opposed the God-King, yet you have often waged such battles."

"It would appear, Captain," Spock said with a trace of amusement, "that your reputation precedes you."

"We do not mean to discount your own vital role in such victories, Mister Spock," Lasem added hastily. "The Starfleet chronicles make it clear that you and Captain Kirk have achieved your mighty feats in tandem. Together you have accomplished many times what our struggling rebellion has only dreamed of."

"Surely it is not by chance," Vlisora said, "that the ancestors brought you within the Crusade's grasp. I truly believe that you were sent to restore freedom of thought to Ialat."

"Hang on there," Kirk said. His earlier anger at being shanghaied by Vlisora and her cronies gave way to an acute awareness of just how much they expected of him—and how severely he was likely to disappoint them. "I'm afraid there's been a serious misunderstanding here. Our Prime Directive expressly forbids us from interfering in the affairs of other worlds, not to mention other universes."

Her brow wrinkled in confusion. "But your many victories over the alien gods . . . ?"

"Those were special cases," he insisted, "usually where the safety of my ship was at stake, or where it was necessary to correct some previous influence that was distorting the natural evolution of a civilization. I never set out to overthrow any existing governments or religions. Your internal affairs are your own business."

"But it was the discovery of *your* universe that

drove my people mad," she argued. "So is it not your responsibility to undo the damage, to 'correct' the insanity that your very existence brought about?"

"A clever bit of sophistry," Spock said, "but your logic is flawed. It was not our scientists that created the rift and exposed your people to the fact of our existence, nor did we induce you to react to that discovery by retreating into fanaticism and fundamentalism. We cannot be held accountable for your own cultural inability to cope with an unexpected truth."

"But we were not ready!" she insisted. "We had no Prime Directive to guide us. You cannot blame us for not knowing where to turn."

"It's not about blame," Kirk said. "Believe me, I'm not judging you. My own planet has survived similar crusades and inquisitions. I think I understand what you're going through here, and I admire your determination to set things right, but you can't look to us to fight your battles for you. This is none of our business. We don't have the *right* to take sides here."

"It that so?" she said bitterly. "Then think of your own worlds . . . and what the God-King means to do to them. Or have you forgotten that the Crusade is no longer merely our 'business'?"

She had a point. Kirk remained concerned about his ship—and the security of the Federation.

"Tell me more," he said. "What exactly is the Crusade doing on Ephrata IV? Just how big a threat do they pose?"

"Bigger than you can imagine." She leaned forward, intent on getting her message across. The intensity of her tone imbued every word with dire import. "The world you call Ephrata is only the beginning."

Kirk gave her his full attention. "I'm listening."

"Under the right circumstances," she began, "when the planes are in alignment, we can open a portal between realities big enough for small cadres of Crusaders to pass through, but our warrior-priests cannot teleport across vast gulfs of interplanetary space—and my people never developed space travel. The Crusade needs starships like your *Enterprise* to spread from world to world."

"So that distress signal was a trap," Kirk realized.

"Just so. And even now, Sokis and his Crusaders are no doubt attempting to take possession of your ship, using every resource at their disposal."

Kirk was troubled, but not terribly surprised, by this news. Sokis had obviously been up to no good.

"He may find that harder than he anticipated," he said, "if I know a certain Scotsman."

"Scotsman?" Lasem echoed.

"Let's just say my crew is not going to give up the *Enterprise* without a fight."

"But it is a fight they may not win," Vlisora said. "And there is more. The energy and equipment required to keep the rift open is considerable. Another portal needs to be built on the other side, to stabilize the passage. Thankfully, Ephrata lacks the resources and infrastructure to construct more than a small portal on that side, just enough to allow a small cadre to pass back and forth, but should the Crusade reach a major industrialized planet, with greater manufacturing capabilities and a larger population to convert, they will be able to open more and larger portals, allowing them to conquer yet more worlds, and spread like a chain reaction throughout your entire Federation."

"A disturbing scenario," Spock said, "but not entirely implausible."

Kirk took the threat seriously as well. He recalled how only a handful of Crusaders had conquered Ephrata IV and turned many of the quadrant's brightest minds into faceless, unthinking zealots. If the Crusade seized control of the *Enterprise* and used it to spread their insidious Truth from planet to planet, building portals large enough to bring entire armies through . . .

"All right," he said. "Let's talk."

He was still deeply uncomfortable with the idea of leading a revolution here on Ialat, but clearly he needed to stop the Crusade and protect the Federation, no matter what.

"So how do we close that rift?"

EIGHT

"Put the intruder in the brig," Uhura ordered. "And keep him under close guard."

Maxah remained sprawled on the floor of the bridge where she had decked him with the slate. He did not appear to be playing possum, but a pair of grim-faced security officers took no chances as they dragged him off the bridge. Uhura was relieved to see him go.

She had enough to deal with now.

The captain's chair was empty, waiting for her. She experienced an understandable moment of trepidation, wishing for all sorts of reasons that Scotty had not gotten himself injured, but she did her best not to let her nerves show. She was in charge now. She needed to step up and do the job, just as Starfleet had trained her to do.

But who was going to do her job in the meantime?

She sat down in the chair and hit the intercom button. "Lieutenant Palmer, report to the bridge immediately."

Elizabeth Palmer was the relief communications officer. She could take over Uhura's post until things got back to normal.

If things got back to normal.

The doors to the bridge slid open and Doctor McCoy rushed onto the bridge, clutching his medkit. The sight of Uhura in the captain's seat provoked a momentary double take that passed as soon as the doctor caught sight of Scotty lying wounded on the floor. The unconscious engineer was losing color beneath the burns on his face and hands. Even out cold, his scarred face was twisted in pain. Low moans escaped his lips. His breathing was shallow and erratic. He looked as though he was going into shock, if he hadn't already.

"Good Lord!" McCoy rushed to his patient's side. "What in God's name happened here?"

"He was caught in an explosion," Charlene Masters explained. She flinched at the memory. "He got a bad shock, and was flung across the bridge."

Making room for the doctor, she returned to her own post at engineering. A repair crew was already working to bring the station back on line, swapping out fused and cracked components for replacement units. Stabilizers were placed on fractured or severed conduits. Masters joined in the repairs, still holding on to the alien baton she had captured from the intruder. Uhura made a mental note to have the baton examined at the first opportunity.

She watched anxiously as McCoy examined Scotty with a handheld medical scanner. The compact device whirred and hummed as it passed over the unconscious engineer, emitting worrisome beeps far too often for Uhura's liking.

"How is he, Doctor?"

McCoy did not look up from his patient. His worried expression warned Uhura not to expect an encouraging diagnosis.

"Electrical burns, internal bleeding, a fractured skull." McCoy placed a portable respirator over Scotty's nose and mouth, then administered a hypospray to his shoulder. Uhura didn't ask what it was for. "You and you," he said, commandeering two hefty crewmen. "Step lively. We need to get this man to sickbay, stat!"

His voice sounded raspier than usual. He looked flushed and feverish. A dry, hacking cough rattled his body and he tottered slightly as though dizzy. He sneezed loudly.

"As if my sickbay wasn't full enough already," he muttered.

Uhura remembered the Therbian fever outbreak that had knocked so many crew members off their feet. Plus, she had to imagine that Scotty wasn't the only casualty of the *Enterprise*'s violent battle with the gravity beam. She was tempted to ask McCoy for a full report on the injured, but decided that could wait for later. Fixing Scotty took priority.

Striking a delicate balance between care and speed, McCoy and his newly deputized orderlies moved Scotty into the turbolift. McCoy lingered on the threshold, visibly torn between the immediate medical emergency and the larger crisis. Uhura assumed he had plenty of questions about the recent commotion.

"You done tossing the ship about?" the doctor asked. "Or should I expect more customers in sickbay?"

"I wish I knew," Uhura said honestly. "But this isn't over yet."

The turbolift doors started to close, but McCoy reached out and held them open for one more minute. "And the captain . . . and Spock and the others?"

"I'll keep you posted," she promised. "As soon as there's anything to report."

That was good enough for McCoy. He withdrew his hand and the turbolift whisked Scotty and him away to sickbay. Uhura took a moment to hope that Scotty would be okay. The usually hearty engineer had not looked good when he was being carried off the bridge.

Take care of him, Doctor, she thought. *The* Enterprise *wouldn't be the same without him.*

Moments later, the same doors opened and Lieutenant Palmer dashed onto the bridge. Her blond bun was slightly undone, as though she had put herself together in a hurry. A fresh bruise on her forehead and a slight limp suggested that she had taken a tumble during the recent turbulence. Her hazel eyes widened when she spotted Uhura in command.

"Reporting for duty . . . sir?"

"Mister Scott has been injured," Uhura explained quickly. "I'm going to need you to take over for me at communications."

Palmer grasped the situation at once. "Understood, sir."

She took her post, leaving Uhura one less thing to worry about. Settling into the big chair, Uhura tried to figure out what do next.

"Mister Ferrari," she said. "What is the status of the . . . gravity beam?"

"Still holding on to us," he reported from the science station, which was mercifully still intact. "They've got us on a tight leash."

"Can't we get out of the line of fire? Perhaps by moving to the other side of the planet?"

He shook his head. "Not as long as we're stuck in this geostationary orbit. We're orbiting in synch with the rotation of the planet, so whatever is projecting that beam is always going to be right beneath us."

So much for a strategic retreat, Uhura realized. "What about the ship's phasers? Can we target the source of the beam?"

"Not with any sort of precision, Lieutenant," Chekov said. "That unusual gravimetric distortion on the planet is still interfering with our long-range sensors. We'd have to target the entire Institute to be sure of hitting the target."

Which would mean killing hundreds of people, Uhura realized, *and probably the landing party as well.*

She wasn't willing to go there, not even to free the ship.

"Lieutenant Palmer," she instructed instead, "send an emergency transmission to Starfleet. Apprise them of our situation."

They were too far away from the rest of the fleet to expect any immediate reinforcements, but the sooner the brass knew about the crisis the better, if only to warn other ships to stay clear of the Ephrata system.

"No luck, sir," Palmer reported. "I can't contact Starfleet. Some sort of interference is blocking the signal." She scowled at the negative readings on her console. "I'm sorry, sir."

Uhura sympathized with Palmer's frustration. She'd been in the same position too many times before. It was an awful feeling.

"Just keep trying."

She briefly considered launching a recorder buoy containing all relevant data and logs up to this moment, but decided against it. Chances were, the buoy would get caught in the same gravity beam holding the *Enterprise*. At worst, it might get yanked down into the planet's atmosphere, where it would burn up on entry.

Besides, she thought, *we still have more questions than answers to report. We don't even know who we're dealing with, or what's become of the landing party.*

"Lieutenant Uhura!" Palmer announced. "We're being hailed from the planet."

"The captain?" Uhura asked, not letting herself

get her hopes up. She was still smarting from the way Maxah had tricked them before. She wasn't about to be fooled again.

Palmer shook her head. "I don't think so. I believe it's the commander of the aliens."

Uhura remembered the "they" Maxah had ranted about. Could this be them?

"Put it on-screen," she ordered. The familiar command sounded strange coming from her lips. "Let's get acquainted."

"Yes, sir."

Palmer patched through the transmission, as Uhura had many times before, and the high-altitude view of Ephrata IV's northern hemisphere was replaced by the head and shoulders of a somber-looking humanoid that clearly belonged to the same species as Maxah. Uhura noted that his "beard" was much fuller and more impressive than the younger alien's, while his garments appeared fancier as well. The top floor of an observatory, complete with a towering subspace telescope, could be glimpsed behind him. Uhura assumed that it was part of the Institute.

"This is Lieutenant Nyota Uhura of the *Starship Enterprise*," she identified herself. "To whom am I speaking?"

"*I am Sokis of Ialat, warrior-priest of the Crusade.*" His deep voice gave him an undeniable gravitas. "*And I speak for the Truth.*"

"And what truth is that?" she asked.

"*The Truth that has brought our Crusade across the veil of reality to liberate you from falsehood and annihilation.*"

She had no idea what that meant.

"Can you be more specific? Why are you holding our ship?"

"*Your vessel belongs to the Crusade now. Lower your shields so that we may take possession of it . . . and spread the Truth to all your worlds.*"

All right, she conceded. *That's more to the point.*

"And if we don't comply?"

"*Our mighty gravity cannon will drag you down from the heavens!*"

Uhura feared that wasn't an idle threat. An image of the *Enterprise* plunging into the planet's atmosphere, burning up like a falling star, flashed before her mind's eye. The prospect chilled her to the bone.

But she knew what Captain Kirk would say.

"No dice. We're not turning over the *Enterprise* to you or anybody else. You can forget boarding us."

This was not the answer Sokis wanted. His spines bristled.

"*You dare risk our wrath?*"

"Risk is our business. Haven't you heard?"

Angry black eyes glared balefully from the screen. "*Perhaps a further taste of our power is in order.*" He gestured to an off-screen subordinate. "*Let the weight of the Truth pull you down from your arrogant perch!*"

The ship's prow dipped sharply forward, diving

toward the planet below. Uhura didn't need Ferrari to tell her that the gravity beam had been ramped up in a big way. A flashing red light between the helm and nav controls signaled danger.

"Sir!" Fisher reported. "We're going down!"

"Show me!" Uhura ordered.

An orbital view of Ephrata IV took over most of the screen, consigning Sokis to a small window in the upper left-hand corner. Was it just her imagination, or did the planet already look larger and closer than before? Uhura grabbed onto her armrests to keep from tumbling from her seat. She braced her heels against the chair's elevated footrest.

"Maintain shields!" she ordered. "Full reverse!"

Straining engines thrummed loudly as the *Enterprise* fought the gravity beam like a fish on a line, being drawn inexorably to its doom. Ordinarily, the bridge always felt to be on an even keel, no matter its orientation in space, but now Uhura was staring down at the viewscreen while her usual station was above and behind her. The tilted deck was vertigo-inducing.

"It's no good!" Fisher hollered back, shouting over the din of the engines. "I'm barely slowing us down!"

"Can we survive atmospheric entry?" she asked.

"At this angle and velocity? Unlikely," Masters predicted. The engineering station was still under repair, so she hastily performed the necessary calculations on a handheld data slate. "If we're lucky, the shields might hold . . . until we slam into the planet."

Ephrata's upper atmosphere loomed larger on the viewer. Uhura tugged on her collar. Was it already getting hotter on the bridge or was that just her? *Just my luck,* she thought. *I'm in command of the ship for all of fifteen minutes before it crashes.*

It was not exactly the note on which she hoped to end her Starfleet career.

"Hull temperature at two thousand one hundred seventy degrees!" Masters reported. "Structural integrity at risk!"

"You can still save yourselves!" Sokis boomed from his section of the screen. *"Surrender your vessel to the Crusade. The Truth demands it!"*

He sure seemed to want the ship. Uhura wondered why.

"Mister Ferrari, are there any other vessels in the vicinity?"

He peered into his scanner. A blue glow tinted the planes of his face.

"Not that we can detect, no."

I thought as much, Uhura mused. Could it be, then, that the "Crusade" was stranded on Ephrata IV? If that was the case, would they really risk destroying their only way off the planet? Certainly this wouldn't be the first time some planetbound adversaries wanted to hijack the *Enterprise* for their own purposes. Maybe this Sokis was like the Kelvans, or those androids on Mudd's world.

She decided to call his bluff.

"Save your breath, mister. Starfleet doesn't take well to ultimatums." Uhura put on her best poker face, the one that had once broken the bank at that casino on Ishtar Station. "You want to crash this ship, be my guest."

She heard a few startled gasps around her. Glancing about the bridge, she recognized the anxious looks on her fellow crew members' faces. It was the same one she'd worn whenever Captain Kirk had played chicken with some seemingly intractable foe, like that racist duochrome cop from Cheron. In the past, the bad guys had always blinked first.

She hoped that history would repeat itself.

"Are you mad as well as ignorant?" Sokis said, with a definite edge of frustration in his voice. His mane flared outward. *"Do not test me!"*

Uhura stuck to her guns. "Consider yourself tested."

By now, Ephrata IV filled practically the entire viewer. Roiling plum and magenta clouds waited to envelop the *Enterprise,* which was on a collision course with the planet. Its single continent could be glimpsed through the cloud cover. Vast plains, mountain ranges, and rivers could be made out below them, which meant the ship was much closer to the planet than it ought to be. It would be a hard landing, if they didn't burn up in the atmosphere first.

"Hull temperature twenty-five hundred degrees and climbing!" Masters reported.

"Four minutes to impact!" Chekov announced.

How far was Sokis going to push this? Uhura sweated out the seconds, in more ways than one. Had she misjudged the enemy's resolve?

Did I make the right call?

"Maximum shields!" She used her intercom to alert the entire ship. "All hands, brace for impact!"

So much for my short stint in the captain's chair, she thought. Her biggest regret was that Chekov and Palmer and the others were going to perish as well, but she wasn't sure what else she could have done. Surrendering the *Enterprise* had never been an option.

"Lieutenant!" Ferrari yelled. "The gravity beam! It's slacking off!"

Hope flared inside her. Maybe Sokis had blinked after all.

"You hear that, Mister Fisher?" she called out to the helm. "Pull us out if you can!"

"Aye, aye!"

To her relief, the planet began to recede slightly. Within moments, she could glimpse open space beyond its circumference. Ephrata IV's sole moon could be spotted in the distance, out beyond the *Enterprise*'s orbit. The system's sun was still shining on the cloud-covered continent in the foreground. Uhura estimated that it was still daylight at the Institute, where the landing party was.

"That's better." She signaled Palmer to mute the audio so that Sokis couldn't listen in as she conferred with Fisher. "Can you get us out of orbit, too?"

Fisher tried to steer the ship around, away from

Ephrata, but the view on the screen remained the same. The engines thrummed unhappily.

"Sorry, sir," he said. "This is as far as we go, at least without ripping the ship in half."

"The gravity beam is still there," Ferrari verified. "It's just stabilized at its previous intensity." He lifted his gaze from the scanner. "We're back where we started, stuck in place above the Institute."

Beats crashing into the planet, Uhura thought, *or being boarded by hostile aliens.*

"I can live with that . . . for now." She turned toward Palmer. "Put Sokis back on."

The alien commander reclaimed the better part of the viewer, as well as his voice.

"Behold our mercy," he said grandly. *"We have given you more time to recognize the error of your ways."*

"Uh-huh," Uhura said skeptically. "I have your number now. You want this ship too much to destroy it."

Sokis did not deny it.

"That may be, but there are other avenues of persuasion available to me." A cruel smile exposed gleaming black incisors. *"Or have you forgotten that I hold your comrades hostage?"*

Her heart sank.

You're not about to let us forget, are you? she thought.

"Hang in there, Scotty! Don't you even think of dying on me!"

Assisted by the two security officers he had conscripted on the bridge, McCoy rushed Scotty into sickbay. The unconscious engineer was laid out on an antigrav stretcher, the better to keep him from being bumped or jostled. An olive green thermal blanket was draped over him to combat shock. A respirator was in place over his face, which looked alarmingly pale and clammy. McCoy was worried; Scotty hadn't looked this bad since Nomad had "killed" him a few years ago, and this time there was no renegade space probe to resurrect him if his injuries proved too severe. Scotty's fate was in the hands of plain old twenty-third-century medicine.

Let's hope that's enough, McCoy thought.

Unfortunately, sickbay was even more crowded and overburdened than he remembered. Nurse Christine Chapel was already performing triage on crew members injured during the recent ruckus, although, at a glance, McCoy didn't spy anything more serious than some minor burns, sprains, and fractures. Nothing comparable to Scotty's critical condition. There were also still some Therbian fever sufferers in the recovery ward who were not quite ready to be discharged to their own quarters. A few of the sick crew members had actually gotten out of bed to assist Chapel in processing the newly injured. McCoy was grateful for their help and initiative. Starfleet churned out good people.

Like Scotty.

"Oh my!" Chapel exclaimed as the men hustled the stretcher through the automatic doors. She looked up in dismay while applying a fast-setting splint to Yeoman Greenberg's right arm. "Is that Mister Scott? What happened to him?"

"What didn't?" McCoy rasped impatiently. There was no time to give her a full rundown on Scotty's accident. "We need to get him into surgery right away." He glowered at the overrun facilities. "Clear a biobed, stat!"

The primary biobed, located in the main examination room, was presently occupied by a red-robed technician with a freshly bandaged head. McCoy guessed that Chapel had been scanning the man's brain for any deeper traumas, just to be safe. The patient hopped off the bed without prompting, surrendering it to Scotty, who was deftly transferred from the stretcher to the bed. Despite their care, the motion still pained Scotty, who moaned feebly beneath the respirator.

"Those burns—" Chapel murmured.

"We can treat those later," McCoy said. "Right now I'm more worried about his insides."

The biofunction display panel mounted above the bed immediately reset itself. Illuminated graphics charted Scotty's pulse, respiration, blood pressure, neural activity, and other vital signs. McCoy frowned at the readings, which only confirmed what the portable med scanner had told him on the bridge. Scotty's vital signs were ebbing fast.

"He's bleeding internally from the liver and spleen," he diagnosed. "We need to open him up."

Chapel was already prepping for surgery. While McCoy cut away Scotty's scorched uniform, she slipped on a pair of sterile gloves before laying out a tray with all the usual apparatus: laser scalpels, hypos, a trilaser connector, reader tubes, and so on. Then she guided a surgical support frame into place above Scotty's torso. Activating the frame generated a sterile field to keep the surgical area free of infection. Her transparent gloves were merely an extra safety precaution, but McCoy approved of the measure; they'd learned the hard way that standard decontamination procedures were not always effective against unknown alien bacteria and viruses. Better to play it safe and go the extra mile to keep their patients disease-free.

She applied an anesthetic to ensure that Scotty remained out cold during the procedure; the drug would also help relieve his pain. The security team cleared any unnecessary personnel from the examination room. McCoy regretted displacing the other patients, but there was nothing to be done about it; he needed to give Scotty his full attention.

Too bad M'Benga is still attending that xenopathology conference on Samaritan Station, McCoy thought. *We could use another MD at the moment.*

"He's ready for you, Doctor."

"Thank you, Nurse." McCoy stepped toward the biobed, only to experience an inconvenient bout of dizziness. Fever and fatigue caught up with him at the worst possible moment. He reached to steady himself against the wall, his head swimming. A ragged cough tore itself from his lungs. He clasped a hand over his mouth to keep the effluvia from spraying.

Chapel eyed him with concern. "Doctor?"

Damn it, he swore silently. *I need to be a doctor now, not a patient!*

"Get me a hypo. Point-five cc's of cordrazine."

She gave him a puzzled look. "For Mister Scott?"

"No, for me!" He needed something to keep him alert and on his feet long enough to get through the operation. "And get me one of those old-time surgical masks from the medkits." He felt another cough coming on. "Steri-field or no steri-field, the hell if I'm going to cough and sneeze into Scotty's chest cavity!"

Chapel responded immediately to his unorthodox requests. She pressed the hypospray against his shoulder. The hypo hissed as it injected the powerful stimulant right through the fabric into his bloodstream. His foggy head cleared at once and he felt an instant burst of chemically induced energy. The inevitable crash would hit him hard later on, but, in theory, not until after he had saved Scotty's life.

"Is there any word of the landing party?" Chapel asked as she helped him don the surgical mask. The fabric masks were kept on hand primarily for landing missions to planets where advanced medical technology might be unavailable and/or overly conspicuous.

Her voice caught briefly in her throat. "What about the captain . . . and Mister Spock?"

He shared her concern for Jim and the others, but they couldn't think about that now. Their patient deserved their full concentration.

"That's out of our hands, Nurse." His hoarse voice was slightly muffled by the mask. "Unlike Mister Scott."

Despite his admonition, he couldn't help worrying about the ship's prospects as well. Uhura looked as though she had a lot on her plate, and the invaders on the planet weren't making things any easier for her. He prayed he wouldn't have more casualties soon—and that the landing party could take care of themselves.

I knew I should have beamed down with them, he thought irritably. *Or maybe it's a good thing that I didn't.*

The steri-field cast an orangish glow on McCoy's worried features. He glanced up at the biofunction display. Arrows were sinking all across the board. Scotty didn't have much longer, unless they could stanch that internal bleeding at the source.

He held out his palm. "Scalpel."

She slapped the tool into his hand.

Funny, he thought. *It feels heavier than usual.*

NINE

At the moment, Sulu felt more like the Man in the Iron Mask than d'Artagnan.

"Praise the Truth," he murmured, trying to sound convincingly brainwashed. He racked his brain for the right words. "I was blind, but now I see."

"The Truth and nothing but the Truth," Yaseen chimed in beside him. A silver mask hid her true feelings. "So help me."

Their Crusader escorts led them across the conquered campus, which was also undergoing a conversion of sorts. Masked converts, chanting in unison, were hard at work, using the accumulated rubble to construct a large, multitiered pyramid around the shimmering triangular rift. Other zealots were dismantling damaged buildings to provide more raw materials for the pyramid. Gravity rays, wielded by Crusader overseers, rendered massive steel beams and cornerstones all but weightless, so that they could be readily moved into place. Sulu was startled by how much progress had been made since the last time he had crossed Pearl Square.

Scoping out the scene from behind his mask, he

failed to spot any Starfleet uniforms among the work crew. If Captain Kirk and Mister Spock had been converted, there was no evidence of it . . . yet.

He chose to take this as a good sign.

"Work on the new temple proceeds apace," the lead Crusader observed to his companion. "Our adopted kin are tireless in their efforts."

"Indeed, Brother Tabus," the other Ialatl said. "The Truth lends strength to both body and spirit."

A solid meal wouldn't hurt either, Sulu thought. He wondered if he and Yaseen were destined to join the labor crew. That might not be a bad thing, especially if it gave them an opportunity to slip away and search for the rest of the landing party, or maybe even find a way to contact the *Enterprise.* He regretted that Maxah had not had time to tell them where the captain and Spock were. *And where did Maxah head off to anyway?*

The construction project dominated the center of the square. To Sulu's surprise, and slight disappointment, their guides veered away from the pyramid-in-progress and led them instead to a tall domed building on the outskirts of the campus. Purple ivy covered the structure's walls. A mammoth subspace telescope, which was big enough to hold a full-sized turbolift, projected from the roof of the dome. Unfamiliar hardware, of alien design, was grafted to the outer casing of the scope, spreading across it like an invasive creeper. A steady emerald beam, over five meters in diameter, shot from the top of the scope toward the heavens. The beam, which was the same green hue as the enemy's gravity weapons, widened as it ascended into the sky for as far as the eye could see—and beyond.

That can't be normal, Sulu thought. The Crusaders seemed to be putting their own stamp on the Institute and its facilities. *I'm guessing that's not just a telescope anymore.*

But what exactly was the gravity beam aimed at?

The *Enterprise*?

He hoped the ship's shields were holding.

An elevator brought them to the top floor of the observatory, which had also undergone a serious makeover. Ialatl technicians fussed over an array of exotic new equipment at the base of the converted subspace telescope. The alien add-ons had been married to the telescope's original controls in what Sulu suspected had been a shotgun wedding. Humming cables crisscrossed the floor, feeding power to the modified scope. A wall-sized viewscreen, intended to display distant quasars, nebulas, and space-time anomalies, currently held an image of the *Enterprise*. An emerald beam enveloped the trapped starship.

Yep, Sulu thought. *Definitely not just a telescope anymore.*

He wished he could confer with Yaseen, and pick her brain on what they were seeing, but they had to appear devout and complacent for the time being. Too much curiosity could raise unwanted suspicions on the part of their newfound "brothers."

"More power!" an imperious Crusader demanded. His cape and lance marked him as the commander of the aliens. Sulu recognized him from Yaseen's description. "Divert more power to the gravity cannon!"

"But we have already tapped into the Institute's main generators, High Brother," a technician replied. "Be assured that the cannon has more than enough power to hold the infidels' vessel in place . . . or bring it crashing down from the heavens, should you desire."

Sulu's mask concealed his dismay. Things were worse than he thought. He and Yaseen exchanged a worried look, which went unnoticed in the general hubbub. The *Enterprise* was possibly in more trouble than they were.

"High Brother Sokis," Tabus addressed his commander. He led Sulu and Yaseen forward. "We have brought the new adoptees as you requested."

Sokis turned away from the technician to inspect the masked newcomers. Sulu's gaze was drawn to the warrior-priest's obsidian lance. Yaseen had told him all about how Sokis had employed the lance to subdue the landing party after Sulu had been stunned.

I'd like to get my hands on that, Sulu thought, and not just because he was an enthusiastic collector of archaic weapons. *And maybe do something about that "gravity cannon," too.*

"And have you both embraced the Truth?" Sokis asked.

"Yes, High Brother," Sulu said, imitating Tabus. "The Truth has set us free."

"Amen," Yaseen added. "Hallelujah."

Sokis nodded in approval. "It is well. I welcome you both to the Crusade." He gazed up toward the purple sky, which could be seen around the edges of the colossal telescope-turned-cannon. "Sadly, your crewmates stubbornly reject the Truth, but we shall deliver them from ignorance regardless." He lowered his gaze toward the "adopted" Starfleet officers. "Perhaps concern for your well-being will cause them to rethink their foolish defiance."

Oh, hell, Sulu thought. *He's going to use us as hostages to try to force the* Enterprise *to surrender.* His jaw set behind his mask. *Forget it. That's not happening.*

"Restore contact with the captured vessel," Sokis commanded his underlings. "Let that arrogant female look upon our latest adoptees."

Female? Sulu was puzzled by the remark. *Who has Sokis been dealing with? What happened to Mister Scott?*

In any event, he couldn't let the Crusaders turn him and Yaseen into bargaining chips. They needed to do something.

His gaze zeroed in again on Sokis's lance. He risked a peek at Yaseen, who nodded at him subtly. "Wait for it," she whispered.

A heavy-duty duranium wrench rested on a counter nearby, ignored by the Crusaders tending to the alien machinery. Yaseen sidled toward it, then "accidentally" tripped over one of the many cables snaking across the floor. Stumbling forward, she snatched the wrench from the counter.

"One for all and all for one!" she shouted before hurling the wrench at the viewer with all her strength. The heavy tool shattered the screen. Sparks burst from the ruptured circuitry. Broken shards flew like shrapnel. Startled Crusaders ducked for cover. She yanked off her silver mask, exposing the defiant brown face beneath it. She flung the mask away from her. "Take your Truth and shove it!"

"Heretic!" A furious technician lunged at Yaseen, underestimating her Starfleet training. She deftly flipped him over her shoulder into his dumbfounded colleagues. A Crusader swung his baton at her, but she cartwheeled out of the way, landing at the base of the cannon, where she swept a dumbstruck Ialatl's legs out from under him with a scissor kick that demonstrated exactly why she had been assigned to security. He tried to scramble to his feet, but she stomped on his ankle to keep him down. Bones crunched. The man let out a high-pitched screech.

"No!" Sokis gasped. "How is this possible?"

Recovering from surprise, Tabus and the other Crusaders drew their batons and aimed them at Yaseen.

"Stop her!" Tabus ordered. "Weigh her down!"

"Wait! Hold your fire!" A frantic technician rushed between the Crusaders and their target. His eyes widened in alarm. Agitated tentacles wriggled around his panicked face. "You'll disrupt the cannon!"

Sulu guessed that would be bad. With all eyes on Yaseen, and Sokis still frozen in shock, unable to comprehend how Yaseen had unTruthed herself, Sulu took advantage of the distraction to make his own move. Lunging at Sokis from behind, he grabbed the High Brother's lance arm, twisting it savagely, and wrenched the weapon from the Ialatl's grasp. Sokis spun around in fury, only to find the tip of his own spear at his throat.

"You dare?" he thundered.

"And then some," Sulu said. The length of the lance made up for the height difference between them. He cast a warning look at the other Crusaders. "Stay back . . . or I'll see just how sharp this spear is!"

"Come on, d'Artagnan!" Yaseen called out to him. She scrambled up the side of the cannon as nimbly as a Rukiltosi lizard-monkey, using the alien encrustations as hand and foot holds. She tried to yank some of the modifications free, no doubt hoping to sabotage the cannon, but they were welded too securely to the original apparatus to dislodge. Nearing the top of the cannon, she hung to its side, her lithe figure silhouetted against the purple sky and the emerald beam above her. "Let's get the hell out of here!"

"You go!" he shouted back. "I'm not done here!"

She hesitated atop the cannon, then nodded and reluctantly sprang from the cannon onto the rooftop, vanishing from sight.

Tabus and his fellow Crusaders paused as well, uncertain whether to pursue Yaseen or rescue their leader. Sulu held the soldiers at bay by keeping the point of the lance lodged against the High Brother's throat.

"Surrender my weapon!" Sokis demanded. For the first time, his stentorian voice quavered. "You know not the power you wield!"

That's for sure, Sulu admitted silently. As an old-time weapons enthusiast, he had handled spears and lances before, but not one that could control gravity as aggressively as Yaseen had described. His fingers cautiously explored the control rings girding the shaft. Judging from Sokis's reaction, and the worried expressions of the other Crusaders, the lance packed plenty of firepower.

Maybe he should put that to good use?

He nodded at the gravity cannon. "That thing is locked on the *Enterprise*?"

"Your vessel is meant to serve the Crusade!" Sokis insisted. "It can have no greater purpose than spreading the Truth throughout this forsaken universe!"

"I'm going to take that as a yes," Sulu said. Spotting a certain technician in the crowd, he recalled the alien's panicky reaction when the Crusaders had targeted the cannon with their batons. "And I'm thinking maybe the best thing I can do right now is eliminate a threat to the *Enterprise*."

"No!" Sokis exclaimed. "In the name of the Truth, I command you to leave our mighty cannon alone!"

"Not a chance."

Stepping away from Sokis, Sulu swung around and aimed the head of the lance at the looming cannon. There was no sign of Yaseen; he had to hope that she was already well clear of the observatory. He fumbled with what he prayed were the firing controls.

His prayers went unanswered.

He had hoped that a powerful gravity beam would "disrupt" the cannon, or at least tear the huge weapon from its moorings, freeing the *Enterprise*. Instead the head of the lance suddenly became a thousand times heavier. A bright green glow rippled up and down its length, while it keened like a Senturan banshee. The spear crashed through the floor, dragging Sulu behind it.

Guess I pushed the wrong button, he thought.

The lance tore through floor after floor. Only the fact that its point was smashing through the floors ahead of Sulu kept him from colliding with the building's sturdy construction. Reacting quickly, he let go of the lance and twisted in midair. His fingers grabbed onto the ragged edge of the pit carved out by the super-heavy lance. For a second, the damaged floor threatened to come loose beneath his grip, but he managed to get hold of an exposed steel joist that supported his weight. Dangling above the newly created chasm, he glanced down in time to see the lance smash through the ground floor of the observatory and keep plunging down toward the heart of Ephrata IV. A bottomless pit opened up beneath Sulu. He wondered how far the lance would fall before the heat and pressure of the planet's core destroyed it.

Oops.

The severed joist began to give way. Grunting, he clambered up onto the floor above and scrambled away from the tattered hole. Loose bits of tile and insulation tumbled into the waiting pit. Taking care not to join them, he jumped to his feet. Ironically, the silver mask had protected his face from any serious cuts or scratches, but his hands and uniform had seen better days. His shirt and trousers were ripped in places, along with some of his skin. Blood leaked from various scrapes and lacerations, which stung like the devil. His ears were ringing.

Could be worse, he figured.

Glancing around, he found himself in what appeared to be an abandoned planetarium about three stories below the cannon's control room. Confused shouts and exclamations came from the floors above and below him. Sparks and flames erupted where the falling lance had torn through random power conduits. Smoke billowed up from the lower levels.

"Find the heretics!" Sokis bellowed from above. "Do not let them escape!"

Sulu judged that he had worn out his welcome, not to mention pretty much blown his cover as a faithful "adoptee." He was tempted to discard his mask, but decided that it might come in handy later on. Heavy steps pounded up and down the stairs outside the planetarium. He figured that he had less than a minute before the Crusaders found him. Glancing around, he spotted a window hidden behind Venetian blinds.

Please don't let it be locked, he thought.

Racing to the window, he shoved aside the blinds and yanked on a pane of transparent aluminum. To his relief, the window slid open easily and he climbed out on the narrow ledge outside, which faced a drop of at least seventeen stories. There wasn't much in the way of footing, so he flattened his back against the outer wall of the observatory as he cautiously inched his way along the ledge, trying not to look down.

"Where's an antigrav lifter when you need one?" he muttered.

He had just managed to get to the left of the open window when he heard Crusaders barging into the planetarium. He held his breath and prayed that the frantic soldiers wouldn't notice the disturbed blinds amid the greater destruction caused by the lance. There was, after all, a large, gaping pit in the middle of the floor.

"Do you see the heretic?" a furious voice demanded. "Is he here?"

Crusaders noisily searched the room, turning over

seats and displays. "There is no sign of him," another soldier reported, proving himself more devout than observant. "Perhaps he has plunged to his death."

"We cannot take that chance! Keep looking!"

Sulu sighed in relief as the men moved on to search the rest of the building. Now he just needed to figure out how to get down from the ledge without breaking his neck.

A conspicuous lack of fire escapes made him question the planet's building codes, but a growth of thick purple ivy covered the observatory's venerable walls. He tugged experimentally on the vines. They felt like they *might* support his weight . . . maybe.

Beats waiting for somebody to spot me up here, he decided. He could hear more footsteps and shouting drawing nearer. It sounded like the entire campus was up in arms—and possibly out for his blood. He was pretty sure he didn't want to find out how exactly the Crusade dealt with turncoats. *Time to find someplace a little less exposed. . . .*

As he cautiously started down the wall, he couldn't help wondering what had become of Yaseen. He wanted to think that she had made a clean escape and was just waiting for him to catch up with her.

Otherwise, he was on his own.

TEN

"Please, eat. Restore yourselves."

The underground train sped through the abandoned tunnels. In the luxury car, Kirk helped himself to a plate of fresh fruits, vegetables, and alien antipasto provided by Vlisora and her fellow freethinkers. The exotic morsels were tangy but refreshing. Kirk hadn't realized how hungry he was until now.

Native attire had been supplied as well. A pair of hooded ponchos, made of a metallic bronze fabric, were draped over a nearby stack of relics, for him and Spock to wear when they had to venture out into the open again. Kirk assumed local garb would be less conspicuous than their battered Starfleet uniforms.

"I appreciate your hospitality," he told Vlisora, who was seated opposite him. Lasem had left to check on his people, leaving the High Priestess alone with the fugitives. "And my compliments to your chef."

"Indeed," Spock said. Being a vegetarian, he refrained from sampling the meatier tidbits. "It is logical that we take advantage of this opportunity to replenish our energies."

"Especially if we're going to take out that portal,"

Kirk said. "The way I see it, that's our first priority. We need to stop the Crusade from spreading further into our universe, no matter what."

Spock did not disagree, but raised an important caveat. "You realize, of course, that destroying the portal might trap both of us here permanently?"

"If that's what it takes," Kirk said grimly. "Ideally, we'll time matters so that one or both of us make it back through the rift before the portal is closed, possibly with the help of our friend here." He looked hopefully at Vlisora. "But, one way or another, we need to shut down that portal for good."

"And what of our world?" she protested. "Surely you don't intend to abandon us?"

Kirk sighed. "I explained before. The Prime Directive—"

"—is no excuse for leaving Ialat under the oppressive weight of the Crusade," she insisted, her golden spines bristling along the top of her head. "I did not risk all to bring you across the rift simply to have you flee back to your own universe before confronting the God-King!"

"Your husband," Kirk clarified. "I admit I'm still a bit puzzled by that. How is it that you've ended up on opposite sides?"

Her indignant tentacles sagged, falling flat against her bare scalp.

"Strange as it may seem, we were once very much in love. Our union was ordained by our roles in society, but we were happy together . . . until the discovery of your universe turned our understanding of reality upside down, throwing timeless beliefs into question. Jaenab took this shock deeply to heart, perhaps because of his profound connection to our people, perhaps because this new revelation struck at the very roots of his identity and authority. In any event, I could only watch in dismay as the husband-king I loved slipped away from me, seizing upon a militantly absolutist interpretation of the ancient texts, until even I dared not speak against the Crusade."

Her black eyes moistened. A golden tear trickled down the elegant planes of her face. She dabbed at it with a napkin.

"You must understand," she continued. "Jaenab means well. He truly believes that he is protecting our people by holding fast to the old ways and waging war on dangerous new ideas. And that he is rescuing your varied peoples from ignorance and oblivion. But the Crusade is crushing our culture . . . and now endangers your worlds as well."

It was easy to tell that she still had feelings for her husband, even if she was urging Kirk to overthrow him. He could sympathize; he knew the pain and frustration of watching a loved one turn into someone you barely recognized. He had once cared very deeply for Janice Lester, before bitterness and self-loathing consumed her. But at least Janice had never attempted to conquer the Federation.

"So you want me to fight your husband, maybe even destroy him?"

"I pray it will not come to that," she confessed, "but the Crusade must be stopped. Better that Jaenab be destroyed than let his present madness infect both our universes."

Kirk admired her determination to place the freedom of her people over her own personal anguish. But that didn't change the Prime Directive.

"First things first," he hedged, not wanting to alienate their only ally at this point. "I need to make certain my universe is safe before we can even discuss saving yours. We have to quarantine the Crusade before it spreads any further."

She mulled it over.

"There is wisdom in your words," she conceded. "Very well. Let us strike our first blow against the portal, before taking the battle to the God-King himself."

"That could be difficult," Spock pointed out. "The portal rests atop a levitating pyramid, making it rather inaccessible, and it is guarded by a force field as well. Achieving our objective presents definite challenges, to say the least."

"I may be able to assist you there," Vlisora said, lowering her voice to a hush. "As it happens, there is a technician at the Temple of Passage who is sympathetic to our cause. He may be willing to allow us access to the facility."

Kirk grinned. "You have an inside man."

"Perhaps," she said cautiously. "A former archaeologist whose computer models tracing the migrations of our earliest ancestors were suppressed by the Crusade. He had to renounce his own work in order to remain in favor with the regime."

Spock asked the obvious question. "If you already have a contact within the pyramid, why cannot *he* simply sabotage the portal?"

"He dares not. It will be risky enough to ease our entry. To lower the force field, confront the guards, and actually destroy the portal is too much to ask of any Ialatl." She offered an apologetic shrug. "Please remember, rebellion does not come easily to us. It is against our very nature to defy the God-King." She massaged her temple, wincing slightly. "Truly, I hear his commandments echoing inside my brain even as we plot against him."

Kirk didn't know whether it was a good or a bad thing that he couldn't hear Jaenab's telepathic communications himself. "What's he saying?"

"The same," she reported soberly. "That you are to be hunted down and brought before him for judgment. And that I have been condemned as a heretic, adulteress, and traitor."

"I'm sorry," Kirk said. Still, it was probably just as well that he and Spock dispose of the portal in person. It was their best chance of ever seeing the *Enterprise* again. "This can't be easy for you."

"I made my choice." She dried her eyes. "I will see it through."

The captain noticed Spock frowning. The expression was subtle enough that most people might miss it. "Something bothering you, Mister Spock?"

"I confess that this outbreak of extreme religious mania makes me uncomfortable," he replied. "It is most illogical."

"I don't know," Kirk said. He couldn't resist the temptation to tweak Spock a bit in McCoy's absence. "Vulcans have their own esoteric practices and rituals that can seem positively strange and mystical to outsiders. Mind-melds, the *Kal-if-fee,* and so on."

"All based on centuries of rigorous logic and science," Spock insisted, perhaps a trifle defensively. "It is true that my people can sometimes be a bit . . . inflexible . . . where our traditions are concerned, but I must categorically reject any comparison to the Crusade. Certainly, Vulcan has never seen fit to impose its ways on other species and cultures . . . as Earth can attest."

"Fair enough," Kirk said. "And don't think we're not grateful that your Vulcan ancestors didn't try to conquer or convert us, despite our shameless propensity for emotion."

"Humans are not Vulcans. Converting you to Vulcan ways would be as illogical as attempting to turn a *sehlat* into a tribble, or a Klingon into an Organian." A wry smile dispelled his frown. "And we are wise enough to recognize a hopeless cause when we see one."

"Like freeing humans from emotions and illogic?"

"Precisely," Spock said. "Nevertheless, I fear that I may be out of my element, and of limited use to you, on this particular mission. Religious revivals and doomsday prophecies are hardly my fields of expertise."

"Perhaps not," Vlisora said. "But who knows? It may be that your celebrated logic and rationality will prove to be our best weapon against the unthinking zealotry that has consumed my people."

"We can only hope—" Kirk began.

An explosion, somewhere up ahead, shook the train. The floor of the carriage rocked beneath them, spilling uneaten food and drink onto the carpet. The train listed to one side, scraping against the curved wall of the tunnel. Sparks flared outside the porthole.

"What the devil?" Kirk exclaimed.

"The Crusade!" Vlisora blurted. Anxious tentacles writhed atop her head. She jumped to her feet. "They're closing in on us!"

"That would be the most logical conclusion," Spock agreed as the train leveled out again. "It seems the conflict has come to us."

The train braked abruptly, toppling heaps of boxes and loose artifacts. Vlisora lost her balance and started to fall. Kirk lunged forward to catch her before she hit the floor.

"Careful," he said. "That was a sudden stop."

"A mere jolt is the least of our worries," she replied. "The enemy is upon us, even sooner than I anticipated!"

A moment later, Lasem burst into the carriage to confirm their dire suppositions.

"We're under attack!" he announced redundantly. "They've closed off the tunnel ahead of us, cutting off our escape!"

"But how did they find us?" Vlisora asked.

"The Crusade is sparing no effort to recapture our guests," he said. "They are swarming the tunnels in full force, using every resource at their disposal . . . including entire flocks of *scrilatyl*."

"*Scrilatyl?*" Kirk asked.

"A winged serpent native to our world," she explained, "famed for its tracking abilities."

Kirk recalled the creature embossed on the hull of Vlisora's flyer. *In other words, they've called out the bloodhounds.*

"So what now?" he asked.

"Going forward is impossible," Lasem said. "And the Crusade is close behind us. Our only choices are surrender or resistance." He reeled slightly, clutching his head. "The God-King demands that we give ourselves up. He promises absolution for all who return to the Truth . . . and hand over the foreign infidels."

"How generous," Kirk said drily.

He hoped Lasem and his cohorts weren't planning to take their ruler up on his offer.

"We cannot surrender," Vlisora said. "Nor allow the Crusade to capture the God-Slayer."

"I know." Lasem swept his ebony gaze over them. "So only one recourse presents itself. We must jettison this car, leaving you behind, while the rest of us race back along the tracks to face the enemy. If the ancestors are with us, we shall buy you enough time to slip away while the Crusaders and their trackers are otherwise engaged."

Kirk felt guilty for ever doubting the man's conviction. He was reluctant to abandon the rebels, even though this wasn't really his fight.

"But your people . . . your treasures?"

Lasem was philosophical. "In bygone days, our people often faced trial by ordeal, letting their departed ancestors determine their fate. So must it be now. Our destinies are in the hands of the ancestors. We can only follow our consciences . . . and have faith that they will not lead us astray."

"I appreciate your courage," Kirk said, impressed. "And your willingness to sacrifice yourself for your cause."

"Lasem was once a priest," Vlisora explained, "before the Crusade."

A siren squealed, followed by a frantic voice over the train's public address system:

"Lasem! The Crusaders are advancing on us, led by a swarm of scrilatyl! By the ancestors, I've never seen so many wings and fangs in one place!"

Both fear and awe could be heard in the nameless rebel's voice. Lasem replied into the bracelet on his wrist.

"Reverse course! Full speed! Let's ram this train right down the Crusaders' throats!"

"Yes, Lasem! With pleasure!"

Lasem turned urgently toward Kirk and the others. "Time eludes us! As soon as this carriage is uncoupled, you must make your escape. My comrades and I shall keep your pursuers occupied for as long as we can endure." He paused long enough to offer them the same four-fingered salute Vlisora had employed before. "May your ancestors watch over you!"

Spock replied by parting his own fingers in a traditional Vulcan sign. "Live long and prosper, Lasem."

"Unlikely," the rebel leader said. "But I value the sentiment." He moved briskly toward the rear exit, even as the train lurched into motion, zooming back the way it had come. "Now . . . make haste!"

He disappeared out the exit, which slid shut behind him. Moments later, a jarring rattle signaled that the luxury car had been jettisoned from the train. Rushing to the exit to confirm this, Kirk peered out a porthole at the back of the train as it sped away from them, straight into the oncoming Crusaders. Ominous green lights flashed farther down the tunnel, where the train was heading. Kirk heard shouts and explosions.

Good luck, he thought.

Detached from the departing train, the carriage soon skidded to a halt. Vlisora snatched up the waiting ponchos and hurled them at Spock and Kirk. "Hurry! We must depart!"

"So I gather," Kirk said.

He and Spock hastily donned the hooded garments, pulling them on over their uniforms, while Vlisora opened an emergency escape hatch in the side of the carriage. She beckoned anxiously to them. "This way! Quickly!"

"We're coming!" Kirk promised. He glanced back at his first officer. "Spock?"

"Just a moment, Captain." Spock procured a fossilized wooden staff from a pile of artifacts that had spilled onto the floor. He held the staff up for Vlisora's inspection. "I trust this is not a relic of exceptional rarity or significance?"

"Merely an archaeological exhibit," she stated, looking it over quickly. "A hunting staff from the early protodynastic period. Of historic interest, but hardly unique or irreplaceable. Why?"

"Under the circumstances, I would prefer not to be completely unarmed." Spock hefted the staff, which was similar in length to a Vulcan *lirpa*. "Not quite as effective as a phaser, but with your permission . . . ?"

"Yes! Take it!" she said. "Now let us go . . . while we still can!"

"After you," Kirk said. "Ladies first."

They scrambled out of the abandoned carriage,

dropping onto the curved floor of the tunnel, which had clearly not been designed for pedestrian traffic. There was only a narrow gap between the car and the tunnel wall, making for a tight squeeze, but they slipped past a short string of discarded carriages, including the bullet-shaped lead car at the end, to reach an empty stretch of track beyond. Vlisora led the way once more, brandishing her handy palm-light. A luminous white beam lit up the murky tunnel. Dust and smoke, stirred up by the recent explosion, muddied the beam.

A violent din, coming from the opposite end of the tunnel, added urgency to their retreat. Emerald gravity beams flashed in the distance, along with brilliant orange flames and geysers of yellow sparks. Crashing metal competed with furious shouts, cries of pain, ear-piercing screeches, and a frenzied flapping that sent a primordial chill down Kirk's spine.

What was that about winged serpents again?

Spock glanced back at the flashing green lights. "Ironically," he observed, "gravity is actually the *weakest* of the four fundamental forces."

"You wouldn't know it from those weapons," Kirk said grimly. "Or from how they clobbered us back on Ephrata IV."

Hurrying away from the fighting behind them, they didn't get far before coming to a dead end. The beam from the palm-light exposed a fresh cave-in ahead. Heaped debris shifted worryingly as it settled.

Loose scree trickled between fallen slabs and chunks of masonry. Dust wafted down from cracks in the ceiling.

Kirk saw no easy way past the obstacle. His phaser might be able to carve a way through eventually, but only at the risk of causing an even greater collapse. And who knew what forces might be waiting on the other side of the cave-in? *Somebody* had to have set off that explosion. Kirk was in no hurry to run into them.

"Where now?" he asked.

"There are service corridors and emergency exits through the network," Vlisora said. She swept the dusty air with the beam from her light, coughing on the floating particulates. "There must be one . . . There!"

The glowing beam found a sealed doorway marked by an indecipherable alien rune. Actual cobwebs, unlike the camouflage webbing on the rebel's train, shrouded the long-forgotten exit. Kirk tried the door, which resisted his efforts to open it. He tugged strenuously.

"Mister Spock?"

"Do you require assistance, Captain?"

"If you don't mind. . . ."

He surrendered the stubborn door to Spock, who took hold of the latch with one hand. As on the flyer earlier, his Vulcan strength proved sufficient to the task. Decrepit hinges groaned as the door came unstuck, swinging open to reveal an unlit stairwell beyond. Startled rodents or lizards—or some exotic combination thereof—with silver skin, black eyes, and golden whiskers, scurried away in fright.

"Nicely done, Mister Spock," Kirk said. "You see, you're already proving of great use on this mission, despite your earlier concerns."

"I am gratified that you think so."

Vlisora had no patience for their banter. Glancing fearfully at the commotion farther down the tracks, she darted into the stairwell, taking their only light source with her. "Please! We must be away from here. Lasem and his forces cannot hold out for long!"

Kirk nodded, not wanting the rebels' valiant efforts to go to waste. He and Spock followed Vlisora up the stairway toward the upper levels of the subway system and, in theory, the surface. The tumult of battle gradually died away as they climbed, but Lasem's sacrifice still haunted Kirk's conscience. He wasn't sure how he could live up to the rebels' desperate hopes and expectations—or even if he should.

Are they asking too much of us?

The stairway led to another doorway, which opened onto an underground loading station running parallel to a length of tracks a meter below. Kirk could easily imagine hordes of commuters crowding the platform, back when the rail system was still a going concern. Now the empty platform was as dark and desolate as the tomb of some forgotten Romulan emperor. Faded graffiti and cobwebs obscured obsolete signs and markings. Something slithered across the tunnel below.

A hot, muggy draft carried the promise of a route to the surface, somewhere at the other end of the station. They walked briskly across the platform, brushing aside the hanging cobwebs, which clung to Kirk's face and hands. He grimaced in distaste. Despite the risk of exposure, he'd be glad to get out of these musty catacombs.

"Captain." Spock cocked his head, as though listening to something. "Do you hear that?"

Not at first, but then Kirk's merely human ears picked up what Spock had already detected: an ominous rustling overhead, along with angry hissing.

"*Scrilatyl!*" Vlisora exclaimed.

She tried to catch the flying predator in the beam of her palm-light, but caught only quick, momentary glimpses of wildly flapping silver wings. Kirk was reminded of a frantic bat that had once invaded his attic back when he was growing up in Iowa. He drew his phaser, but the creature's erratic flight pattern made it impossible to get a bead on it. Spock struck a defensive stance with his staff.

Vlisora spun about on the platform, unable to keep the *scrilatyl* in view. Something hissed above and behind her. She whirled around, aiming her palm-light, just in time to reveal a serpentine creature, boasting scalloped silver wings, segmented coils, and two vicious foreclaws, swooping down at her. Black eyes and fangs gleamed like polished ebony. Golden spines bristled like whiskers above its gaping jaws. A savage hiss evolved into a nerve-jangling screech. Startled, Vlisora screeched almost as loudly.

A heartbeat later, she was knocked to the floor. Her palm-light flew from her hand, skittering off the platform onto the tracks below. Blackness descended on the abandoned station, hiding both Vlisora and her attacker. Frantic cries, shrieks, and screeches echoed confusingly off the tunnel walls. Spock's staff clattered to the ground. Kirk heard Vlisora fighting and screaming, but wasn't sure where to fire his phaser. He didn't want to risk stunning her when they might need to flee on foot at any moment.

Damn it, he thought. *I need to see what's happening!*

An unconventional tactic occurred to him. Switching his phaser from stun to heat, he fired at the ceiling, energizing the ceramic tiles until they glowed red. A dim, ruddy radiance illuminated the platform, revealing . . .

Spock locked in combat with an enraged *scrilatyl.* He had the thrashing creature by the throat, holding it away from his body, as the animal snapped and hissed at him. Flapping wings stirred up the air. Clawed forelimbs slashed at Spock's chest, drawing dark green blood. A serpentine tail whipped about madly.

"Kill it!" Vlisora cried out, sprawled on the platform a few paces away. The back of her tunic was shredded, barely holding together. Delicate silver scales could be glimpsed through the rents in her garment, along with long, shallow scratches. The incarnadine glow from the ceiling made the scratches look gorier than they were. She shouted urgently. "Before it summons others!"

A pained look came over Spock's face. A sharp crack cut off the creature's wild screeching, and it went limp in his grip. He released the *scrilatyl,* which fell lifeless at his feet.

"A pity," he said with obvious regret. "It seemed a remarkable life-form."

Kirk recalled that *tal-shaya* was considered a merciful form of execution by the ancient Vulcans. "You did what you had to."

"I know," Spock said. "But it is a waste of life regardless."

Kirk helped Vlisora to her feet. "Are you all right?"

"Well enough," she assured him, despite her torn flesh and clothing. "The *scrilatyl* are trained not to kill their prey, merely hold them for the hunting party. And to call out when the prey is cornered."

Like a mastiff pinning a poacher until the gamekeeper arrives, Kirk thought, relieved that the renegade priestess had not been seriously harmed by the creature. "What about you, Mister Spock?"

"Mere scratches, Captain." He inspected the slashed poncho over his chest. Wet green stains glistened on the torn fabric. "Assuming the creature's claws are not envenomed?"

Vlisora shook her head. "Praise the ancestors, no."

The light from the cooling roof was already fading. Kirk jumped down onto the tracks and recovered Vlisora's palm-light. Climbing back onto the platform, he turned the beam on the dead *scrilatyl,* taking a moment to examine the alien creature more closely.

A scaly silver hide, glossy black eyes, a beaked nose, golden tentacles in place of whiskers . . . it was hard to miss the resemblance to the Ialatl.

"One of your divine ancestors?" he asked.

"More like a distant cousin, evolutionarily speaking." She contemplated the lifeless carcass. "Legend has it that the first God-King was suckled by a female *scrilatyl* in a cavern beneath what is now the royal temple. They have been the symbol and totem of the kingship ever since." She looked gravely at Spock. "To kill one is a mortal sin, punishable by death."

"Regrettable," Spock said. He recovered his staff. "My apologies."

Vlisora did not seem inclined to hold his transgression against him. "And my thanks," she answered. "I would have done the same if I could."

Kirk doubted that the Crusaders would be as forgiving.

"We'd better destroy the evidence then."

A brilliant pulse from his phaser incinerated the *scrilatyl*'s remains, leaving nothing but a blackened scorch mark on the platform. The smell of burnt flesh hung in the air.

Kirk worried briefly about the phaser's charge. The weapon was designed to function for extended landing missions, but its power packs were not infinite in capacity. They could be in trouble if he used the phaser indiscriminately.

"That is well," she said. "But we cannot linger. The *scrilatyl*'s cries will draw its kin . . . and the Crusaders close behind them. We must seek higher ground."

Reclaiming her light, she guided them to another stairwell that led them up out of the tunnels to the city above. Spock used his staff like a machete to clear away the cobwebs clotting the way out. Vlisora cautiously stuck her head out of the subway entrance before urging them onward.

"The way appears clear. Come!"

Night had fallen on Ialat, bringing with it a warm drizzle that Kirk found preferable to the sweltering heat of day—and which gave him and Spock a good excuse to pull their hoods over their heads.

Seems we lucked out with the weather, Kirk thought. *So to speak.*

They found themselves on the ground level of the city, in what struck Kirk as a less than salubrious district. Graffiti and litter contrasted sharply with the gleaming metropolis he had earlier glimpsed from above. Run-down storefronts showed obvious signs of disrepair. Weeds sprouted through cracks in the pavement. The streets and sidewalks were empty, as though the city's citizens knew better than to venture here after dark. Flying vehicles zipped by high over-head, displaying no interest in descending to this level. The lights of the upper towers barely filtered down from above. Kirk glanced around at the relative squalor.

"Not exactly a good neighborhood, I take it?"

"Hardly," Vlisora confirmed, glancing about warily. She tucked her pendant beneath the collar of her tunic, whether out of fear of theft or simply to conceal her status as High Priestess, Kirk could only guess. She gestured at their grubby surroundings. "As I mentioned before, my people took to the air after the Gravity Revolution, leaving the ground to wither in neglect. Today the lower levels of the city are often abandoned to crime and vice. Few come here without shameful intent."

"I have to admit that I'm somewhat relieved to find out that vice is still an issue here," Kirk said with a smile. "What with the Crusade and all."

"We are still but flesh and blood," she admitted. "As were even our divine ancestors, although many of the Crusade's most strident adherents often prefer to overlook that fact." She shrugged. "Even in the midst of the present craving for purity and deliverance, a so-ciety of total righteousness is not possible . . . or even desirable."

"I know what you mean," Kirk said. Most of the "perfect" societies he had encountered in the past, from Eminiar VII to Gamma Trianguli VI, had usually turned out to have a fly in the ointment—and to be distinctly less than human. "Too much of anything, even righteousness, can be a bad thing."

She gave him a knowing look. "Now *that* is the God-Slayer I was praying for."

"That's not what I meant," he said, still uncomfortable with the idea that Vlisora expected him to overthrow her God-King. "I'm just saying that such frailties make your people seem a little less . . . alien."

The rain began to fall more heavily.

"Might I suggest we continue this discussion elsewhere," Spock said, "perhaps somewhere less exposed?"

"Practical as ever, Mister Spock." Kirk looked to Vlisora for direction. "Any ideas on that score?"

She scanned the shadowy, rain-swept streets and alleys. Her gaze lighted on a solitary flyer parked at the curb. The aircraft, which was noticeably smaller and less elegant than the royal flyer she had crashed earlier, appeared unoccupied. It would be a tight fit, but it looked as though it might hold three. Kirk wondered how hard it would be to hot-wire.

"The ancestors have seen to our needs," she declared, clearly thinking along the same lines. Abandoning the shelter of the tunnel entrance, they dashed over to the flyer, where she directed Kirk to fire a narrow phaser beam at a locking mechanism. A hatch opened . . . and a siren sounded. "Misbegotten spawn!" she swore. "The alarm!"

Reaching into the cockpit, she muted the alarm, but the damage was already done. A door swung open on the ground floor of one of the surrounding buildings. Raucous music and laughter spilled onto the sidewalk, followed by a portly Ialatl who staggered out of the inauspicious-looking edifice. The man's tunic was disheveled. His four-toed feet were bare. Viscous orange syrup or jelly smeared his mouth and beard. He stared belligerently at Kirk and the others.

"You there! What are you doing with my flyer?"

Kirk lowered his face, but it was too late. The light from the doorway fell upon his and Spock's conspicuously alien countenances. A look of shocked recognition came over the Ialatl's messy face.

"It's you!" he gasped. "The infidels from beyond!" He backed away, shouting at the top of his lungs. "Over here! It's the infidels! They're here!"

Damn, Kirk thought. *I should've known this was too easy.*

He stunned the man with a phaser beam, dropping him to the pavement, but the stranger's frantic cries had not gone unheeded. Male and female Ialatl, in various stages of undress, poured out of the building, clutching weapons both genuine and improvised. Canes, bottles, ropes, chains, forks, skewers, and actual knives and hammers had been drafted into the holy cause of defending Ialat from the dreaded infidels. Even here in the depths, it seemed, the word of the God-King still held weight.

"There they are!" a woman shrieked. The spines across her head stood up like the quills of a porcupine. She waved a dripping steel ladle at the fugitives. "Get them . . . as the God-King wills!"

Shouting furiously, the mob surged toward Kirk and the others. A collective frenzy contorted their silver faces. Pounding feet trampled over the stunned Ialatl in their haste to capture the infidels.

"Get in!" Vlisora shouted. She slid into the pilot's seat and fired up the control panel. Kirk and Spock dived into the passenger seats behind her. Spock wedged his staff into the compact space. Vlisora spun a knob and the hatch sealed behind them, right before the mob swarmed over the flyer. "By the ancestors, they're worse than rabid *scrilatyl!*"

The frenzied crowd hammered on the hull of the flyer, trying to smash their way in. A metal trash bin was hurled at the tinted cockpit window, causing spidery cracks to spread across the transparent material. Bricks, rocks, and naked fists banged against the closed hatch, the ferocious blows reverberating inside the besieged flyer. Kirk felt like they were being buffeted by photon torpedoes.

"Maybe we should get a move on," he suggested.

"Allow me a moment to disable the tracking system," Vlisora said, flinching as a flung vase shattered against the windshield. She hurriedly fiddled with the controls. "So that the Crusade cannot remotely shut off our engines again!"

Probably a good idea, Kirk acknowledged. Provided that the determined mob were willing to grant her that moment. Their bellicose shouts penetrated the abused hull of the flyer.

"Seize the infidels! The God-King demands it!"

The dashboard controls went dark, then reignited.

"Done!" Vlisora declared. Antigrav engines keened to life as the flyer began to lift off from the curb. "Hang on!"

The crowd threw themselves on top of the flyer to weigh it down. Their fingers scrabbled for purchase on the dented hull. They climbed over each other, kicking and scratching, to get onto the flyer.

"I gather," Spock observed calmly, "that ordinary citizens such as these are not equipped with the gravity weapons employed by the Crusaders?"

"That is correct," Vlisora confirmed. "Such arms are granted only to the priesthood and the military, which are now one and the same."

The flyer sagged briefly under the weight of its unwanted passengers, but Vlisora revved up the engines and the flyer angled up from the street. Unlucky Ialatl slid off the hull, falling to the pavement below. One determined member of the lynch mob hung on to the roof with wild-eyed persistence, but Vlisora banked sharply to the right, throwing him off the flyer. He called out to his ancestors as he fell.

"That antigrav safety net you mentioned before,"

Kirk said. "Is it in effect even in a neighborhood like this?"

"I'm not sure," she confessed.

Kirk looked down, but the flyer was rising too fast. They had already left the unsavory area behind.

Troubled, he turned his gaze ahead. Their ultimate destination, the huge floating pyramid, loomed in the distance, hovering over the city like an immense mirage.

"Straight ahead," he told her. They couldn't take the chance of being apprehended before they shut down the rift.

Next stop, the portal.

ELEVEN

Captain's Log. Stardate 6013.0. Lieutenant Uhura reporting.

I remain in temporary command of the Enterprise. We've had no word from Captain Kirk and the landing party for hours now, and Mister Scott is still incapacitated. My concern for our missing captain and crewmates grows, even as our own situation has taken a new turn for the worse. . . .

Back in the days before artificial gravity, Earth astronauts returning from extended tours of duty in space often had trouble adjusting to standard gravity again. Uhura now knew how they felt. She could have sworn she had gained over fifty kilograms during the last few hours. Just sitting was exhausting.

"We're not imagining it," Charlene Masters reported. Her battered engineering station wasn't pretty, but it was up and running again. "The environmental gravity on all levels is steadily increasing. We're currently at two hundred percent standard gravity . . . and rising."

"No wonder I feel so heavy," Chekov said. "It's like I've got a *mugato* sitting on my shoulders."

"You're not alone," Uhura said, hoping that was the right thing to say. "We're all feeling it."

Sokis was trying a more subtle approach, she realized. Instead of threatening to crash the *Enterprise,* he intended to wear them down by gradually increasing the gravity aboard the ship.

"This is a siege tactic," she explained. "Sokis is trying to break down our resistance."

"Like the Muunian sand torture," Chekov said, getting the idea. "Slow, but effective."

"Let's hope not." She turned toward Masters. "What about our own artificial gravity systems? Can you compensate?"

"Already on it," Masters said, "but I'm afraid that I'm fighting a losing battle. They're raising our gravity faster than I can lower it." She shook her head. "They've got the technological edge here. It's like I'm trying to outrace a warp-capable starship on impulse."

Uhura trusted that Masters was doing her best. "Understood."

The intercom whistled for attention. Palmer took the call.

"It's sickbay," she reported. "Doctor McCoy."

Uhura braced herself for more bad news. "Pipe him through."

The doctor's raspy voice issued from the speakers:

"McCoy here. What's wrong with the blasted gravity?"

He sounded even more cantankerous than usual.

Uhura guessed that the extra gravity had not improved his temper any.

"Just our friends on the planet making life a little more uncomfortable for us." She quickly explained the situation to the doctor. *I probably need to address the entire crew at the first opportunity,* she decided. *Inform them of the nature of the problem . . . without making the situation sound too hopeless.*

It was a tricky balancing act. She marveled at how often Captain Kirk must have walked the same tightrope.

"*Well, can't you do anything about it?*" McCoy groused. "*The strain is taking a toll on my patients, especially Scotty.*"

She remembered the engineer's burnt and blasted body being carried off the bridge. "How is he, Doctor?"

"*Not good,*" he said bluntly. "*He came through surgery well enough, no thanks to that roller-coaster ride we took, but he's still in a coma. He needs a chance to heal, but this extra gravity is putting even more strain on his body. He needs some relief . . . or we could lose him.*"

The weight on Uhura felt even heavier than before.

"I understand, Doctor. Uhura out."

She shut off the transmission and consulted Masters again. "About the gravity . . . prioritize sickbay as much as feasible. Forget the rec rooms and gym and personal quarters. Try to normalize the gravity on only the most crucial decks, including the medical facilities."

To be honest, she wasn't sure how much flexibility the shipboard gravity system allowed, but at least she could give engineering some general priorities. The rest was up to them.

"Gravity triage," Masters said, nodding. "I'll do what I can, sir, for as long as I can." A weary sigh escaped her lips. "I won't lie to you, though. I really wish Mister Scott could lend us a hand right now."

Don't we all, Uhura thought, but kept it to herself. She knew she had to keep up a brave front, despite the growing weight, both real and figurative, trying to beat her down. She lifted her chin and gazed at the stationary planet on the viewer. Her voice summoned up all the strength and authority it could muster.

"I'm worried about Scotty, too," she admitted, "but I know you can handle it, Charlene. Just stay focused on the big picture." It was clear by now that more than the ship or the landing party was in danger. "We can't allow the Crusade to escape Ephrata IV and menace the rest of the Federation with their gravity cannons."

Nobody disagreed. She knew the entire bridge crew had families and loved ones scattered across the quadrant.

"I hate to say it," Chekov said, "but maybe we need to start planning for some worst-case scenarios." He paused briefly before finding the nerve to continue. "Perhaps even General Order Twenty-four?"

The suggestion provoked gasps around the bridge. Everyone knew what Chekov was proposing: using every weapon at their disposal, from the ship's phasers to photon torpedoes, to "sterilize" the planet below, eliminating the threat completely.

Just like a Russian to expect the worst, Uhura thought, then dismissed the thought as unworthy of her. Truth to tell, the same ghastly option had already occurred to her.

"I hope it doesn't come to that," she said.

Especially since they still didn't know what had become of Captain Kirk and the rest of the landing party. She hated being cut off from both the captain and Starfleet. The lack of communication was maddening.

But there was still one possible source of information available to her.

"The prisoner," she stated. "Bring him back to the bridge. Under heavy guard."

Palmer looked at her in surprise. "Sir?"

"You heard me," Uhura said. "I think it's past time I had a talk with our uninvited visitor."

"Yes, sir," Palmer said.

Ideally, she would conduct the interview in the brig, but Uhura wasn't about to leave the bridge at a time like this. Besides, why should she have to hike all the way down to the brig in this gravity?

Maxah would have to come to her.

"Lieutenant Masters, do you still have the intruder's weapon?"

"Yes, sir." She retrieved the polished black baton from a force-shielded compartment under her console. "I'm afraid I haven't had a chance to examine it yet."

Well, it's not like we haven't been busy, Uhura thought. "Hang on to it, but keep it out of sight."

The last thing they needed was the prisoner somehow getting hold of his weapon again, but maybe there was a way to turn the Crusaders' technology against them?

She could only hope.

"Gravity at two hundred fifteen percent," Masters reported. "And rising."

Despite the oppressive weight, security made good time escorting their prisoner to the bridge. Within minutes, the tall, silver-skinned alien was standing before Uhura, watched carefully by four scowling security guards who didn't appear inclined to cut the intruder much slack after his earlier rampage through the *Enterprise*. Maxah's hands were cuffed behind his back. Uhura assumed he had been thoroughly (and uncomfortably) searched for any hidden weapons or communicators. He did not appear to be putting up a fight. If anything, he struck Uhura as more defeated than hostile. His spines drooped limply.

"You asked to see me?" he said.

"I don't think we were properly introduced before," she said. "I'm Lieutenant Uhura, currently in command of this starship." She didn't volunteer that she was the one who had walloped him with the data slate; that probably wouldn't be conducive to a civilized discussion. "And you are?"

"Maxah, formerly of the Crusade." He cracked a rueful smile. "I suspect I am no longer in the good graces of my esteemed brothers."

Uhura recalled that he had urged Scotty to flee Ephrata right before the gravity cannon snagged the ship. Could it be that he was actually on their side?

"Why would you go to such lengths to keep your 'brothers' from capturing the *Enterprise*? Why choose us over your own kind?"

He chuckled to himself. "Your comrades down on the planet asked me much the same questions, before I did what I could to protect them."

Uhura leaned forward eagerly, excess gravity be damned. "Our landing party? You've been in touch with them?"

"Briefly. Before I tricked my way aboard your vessel."

"What do you know?" She kicked herself for not interrogating him earlier. "What's happened to them?"

"Your captain and first officer were sent on to our own universe, where my allies hope to make common cause with them. The two others, the ones you call Sulu and Yaseen, were still on Ephrata IV when last I saw them. Their minds were then their own, but I know not how they have fared since."

Uhura was relieved to find out that the captain

and the others were still alive, at least as far as Maxah knew, but the rest confused her.

"Hold on," she said. "What was that about your 'own universe'?"

"There is much to explain."

"Then keep talking, mister, and make it snappy." She slumped back into her chair, feeling as though she had gained five kilograms in as many minutes. "We're not getting any lighter."

She listened intently as Maxah explained that the Crusade had invaded this universe by means of some sort of dimensional rift, but that he was actually affiliated with a resistance movement opposed to the apocalyptic religious mania that had consumed his people, the Ialatl.

"Not long ago, we were a peaceful, enlightened people," he insisted. "Our spiritual beliefs enhanced and deepened our lives, imbuing them with meaning, but they did not drive us to convert others—or to lash out at anything that did not readily fit into our Truth. We believed in the future as well as the past, progress as well as tradition, reason in concert with religion. Nor did we eagerly anticipate the destruction of everything we had built."

"I would hope not," Uhura said. The *Enterprise* had prevented doomsday on occasion. "I'm kind of fond of survival myself."

"As am I," he insisted. "Trust me, unlike my more fervid brothers and sisters, I am in no hurry to witness the end of creation. Reality may indeed die and be reborn someday, as our oldest legends maintain, but, for my part, the end of the universe can take its time. There is still too much to see and explore in our universe—and in yours as well."

His passion was convincing. Uhura found herself inclined to believe him. It was a risk, but she was running out of alternatives. She could practically feel herself getting heavier by the minute, gaining weight without gaining mass. She was sweating like a *targ* just sitting in the captain's chair. *I must be at least 120 kilograms by now,* she estimated. *A far cry from my usual forty-eight or so.*

"Gravity at two hundred fifty percent," Masters reported. "I'm losing ground here."

Uhura decided that they had discussed philosophy and religion long enough. It was time to get down to brass tacks.

"You hear that?" she said to Maxah. "You feel that? Your Crusade won't be happy until we're all too heavy to move—or until we let them board this ship."

"No!" he protested. "You must not do that. If the Crusade spreads beyond this meager world, into the heart of your civilization, you will have no chance!"

"Then help us," Uhura said. "If you're serious about saving us from your own people, then show us how to combat that gravity cannon. We have that weapon you used before. Can we use that to break free?"

He laughed bitterly at the notion. "Might as well

deploy a rowboat against a battleship. My mace is a hand weapon, intended for personal defense, but it lacks even the power of the High Brother's spear. To pit it against a mighty gravity cannon . . ."

"Is like pitting a hand phaser against the *Enterprise*'s phaser banks," Uhura finished for him. "Yes, I get it." She should have known it wouldn't be that easy. "But you still understand this technology better than we do. That has to count for something." She indicated Masters at engineering. "Our own people are doing their best to fight back, using our own artificial gravity systems, but your people have the edge on us. Can't you do anything to help us hold our own?"

He looked down at the deck, unable to meet her eyes.

"Maybe for a time," he hedged. "But it's no use. You cannot overcome the gravity cannon forever. Better that you crash your ship into the planet than let your minds and worlds be enslaved by the Crusade!"

That wasn't what Uhura wanted to hear.

TWELVE

"Find the heretic!"

All work on the temple in the square had ceased as the masked Ephratans conducted a house-by-house, building-by-building search of the campus. Hours had passed since Sulu had escaped the observatory, but the hunt continued. The search parties were armed with sticks, bricks, knives, ropes, and other ad hoc weaponry, the better to subdue their elusive prey.

All that's missing is pitchforks and torches, Sulu thought.

He marched along with the crowd, shouting just as vociferously as the others. He had exchanged his telltale Starfleet uniform for a conservative gray suit he had "borrowed" from a locker in the gymnasium, while his silver mask made it possible to blend in with the mob. He was glad he had decided to hang on to it.

Unfortunately, he was still lacking a phaser or communicator. His only weapon was a fencing foil he had also lifted from the gym. While it felt good to have a sword in his hand, he would have preferred a phaser, especially considering the odds against him.

The foil's safety cap had been removed, baring its point.

Beggars can't be choosers, I guess.

He had been keeping one step ahead of the Crusade and its overzealous converts ever since escaping the observatory. A lynch mob had almost caught up with him at the locker rooms, but he'd managed to slip into the mob's ranks undetected . . . at least so far.

"Find the heretic!"

Sulu was amused to note that he'd apparently been promoted from "infidel" to "heretic," presumably because he had rebelled *after* professing to accept the Truth, as Yaseen had.

Fawzia . . .

He frowned, concerned about his missing crewmate. He had not laid eyes on Yaseen since that dustup at the observatory. Had she gotten away as well, or had the Crusade caught up with her? He could only hope that she was still on the loose and that they would somehow succeed in linking up again. If only there was a way to contact her without giving himself away . . . !

"All clear!"

The leader of the search party pronounced the science building free of heretics. Sulu followed the mob back out onto the lawn outside, the pockets of his borrowed suit bulging slightly. One good thing about taking part in the manhunt: it had given him an opportunity to reconnoiter, do a little foraging, and plot his next move. Just evading capture wasn't enough. If he was stuck here on Ephrata IV, behind enemy lines, he was damn well going to *do* something.

Namely, a little old-fashioned sabotage.

As the search party moved on to a vandalized art gallery, he discreetly broke away from the crowd and slipped off down a narrow side passage. Sticking to the shadows and avoiding the more frequented paths, he made his way across the sprawling campus and adjoining woods to his chosen target: the Institute's main fusion generator complex.

He'd picked out his target carefully. Both the gravity cannon and the dimensional rift were well guarded by Crusaders, but the gravity cannon was obviously drawing a lot of power from the Institute's generators. If he could knock the power out, maybe he could weaken the gravity beam long enough for the *Enterprise* to break free.

Which would strand him here on Ephrata, naturally, but that was a sacrifice he was willing to make. He figured Yaseen would feel the same way—as would the captain and Mister Spock, wherever they were.

Unlike the more elegant academic buildings and museums, the generator complex was a blocky, utilitarian facility painted a dull olive green. The unsightly complex was conveniently located at the far end of the valley, out of view of the rest of the campus. A chain-link fence, festooned with warning signs, guarded the generators, as did a pair of bored-looking Crusaders posted at the front gate. The soldiers hummed an Ialatl hymn as they paced back and forth before the entrance. Getting past them was job one.

Sulu crept up on the complex, hiding behind leafy trees and bushes. He took pains to stay downwind of the guards, having no idea what their olfactory abilities were. People said that Klingons could smell an enemy from kilometers away, although Sulu suspected that was just a myth. The Ialatl were even more mysterious.

So why take chances?

The guards stood between him and the generators. He knew his fencing foil was no match for their gravity batons, but he had allowed for that. . . .

The explosion went off right on schedule, back at the campus. A thick plume of black smoke rose up behind him. Fire alarms could be heard in the distance.

Thank you, chemistry labs, Sulu thought. He'd assembled the bomb, as well as the timing mechanism, from materials scavenged from the Institute's abandoned laboratories. He felt bad about inflicting yet more damage on the ravaged campus, but figured they could spare one empty lecture hall. At least he prayed it was still empty; it had been when he'd planted the bomb.

The explosion got the guards' attention.

"By the God-King's holy lineage!" a Crusader exclaimed. "It must be the work of the heretic!"

His partner agreed. "Such perfidy must not go unpunished!"

Sulu hoped the attack would draw the guards away from the generator complex, but he'd underestimated their discipline. To his frustration, the guards remained at their posts.

Guess we're going to have to do this the hard way.

Stepping out from behind a tree, he rushed toward the gate, waving his foil in the air. His mask made him look like just another "adopted" human.

"Brothers! The new temple is under attack! Defend the Truth!"

The guards went on alert. "Halt! Identify yourself!"

Ignoring the command, Sulu kept running. He thrust his free hand into the heavy pocket of his jacket. His fingers closed on a smooth glass canister.

"I serve the Truth," he called out, evading the question. "To arms, brothers! The temple must be defended!"

The guards stubbornly stuck to protocol. Their hands found their batons.

"Identify yourself . . . or feel the weight of the Truth!"

"Identify this!"

He plucked the canister from his pocket and hurled it at the guards. The clear container shattered at their feet, releasing a cloud of billowing white fumes that rose up to choke them. The men gasped and clutched their throats. Tears streamed from their dark eyes. They coughed violently.

Yes, Sulu reflected. He had made good use of that chem lab.

The formula was actually an old family recipe, supposedly devised by a distant relative back in the twentieth century. He was supposed to have developed it as a humane alternative to bullets when dealing with the vicious crooks and racketeers who infested that era . . . or so family legend had it. Sulu had no idea how exaggerated the stories might have grown over the generations since. In any event, the formula itself was just basic chemistry these days.

He slowed to a stop, anxious to see if the improvised knockout gas had the desired effect on the Ialatl. The invaders appeared to breathe oxygen, but who knew exactly how their body chemistry worked. Without an adequate knowledge of their biology, he couldn't be certain that that the gas would do the trick. What if the Crusaders proved resistant to its effect?

"Traitor!" a guard coughed. "Heretic!"

Sulu started to worry. In theory, the gas would have knocked out a Gorn by now, but the Crusaders were still on their feet. Tottering unsteadily, a wheezing guard drew his baton. Angry tears flooded his silver face.

"Heretic! Infidel!"

"Make up your mind," Sulu said.

Playing it safe, he reached into his other pocket and retrieved another gas bomb. It shattered against the Crusader's chest, distracting him. A second white cloud enveloped the men, adding to the fumes.

So much for my last bomb, Sulu thought.

To his relief, the second dose of gas got the job done. One after the other, the two Crusaders sagged to the ground in front of the open gate. Sulu waited a few seconds for the fumes to disperse before cautiously advancing toward the gate. He hated using both his gas bombs on the duo, but at least they hadn't gone to waste. Holding a hand over his nostrils and mouth, he prodded the guards with the tip of his foil to make sure they weren't playing possum. Broken glass crunched beneath his boots. The last lingering traces of the gas made his eyes water. He fanned the air to clear it.

Satisfied that the guards were genuinely down for the count, he stepped over their unconscious bodies. The men's fallen batons caught his eye. After his mix-up with Sokis's lance, which had nearly taken him on a one-way trip to the planet's core, he was reluctant to mess with the Ialatl's alien weapons again, but . . . waste not, want not. Handling them gingerly, he tucked the inert batons into his belt before leaving the gassed guards behind.

Black smoke still rose from the campus behind him, so he assumed the other Crusaders still had their hands full dealing with the blown-up lecture hall. Rushing past the gate, he headed for the main generator building. A sign was posted at the entrance: OFF LIMITS! AUTHORIZED PERSONNEL ONLY.

Sulu ignored it.

He sprinted into the building. As expected, the complex was largely automated. He raced down an empty corridor. With any luck, he wouldn't encounter anyone besides a few brainwashed technicians, assuming they weren't all out hunting for heretics.

Powerful fusion generators thrummed in the background. From the sound of them, he guessed that the Crusade had them running at full capacity to power the gravity cannon and their other hardware. Sulu hastily reviewed his plan as he searched for the primary control room. Ideally, he hoped to avoid a full-scale overload and explosion; too many lives, including those of the brainwashed Ephratans, would be lost in such a disaster. But maybe a catastrophic shutdown would cause a blackout that would knock out the gravity cannon.

Granted, the Institute surely had some backup generators and batteries elsewhere, but would those be enough to sustain the voracious demands of the gravity cannon? He was gambling that wasn't the case.

Worth a try, he thought. *If I have to, I can always go after the backups later.*

Directional signs, in multiple languages, guided him to the central control room, which reminded him of engineering back on the *Enterprise.* A galleried mezzanine, complete with safety rails, overlooked a vast chamber lined with blinking consoles and computer banks. Wall monitors tracked the energy flow and operation of the fusion generators. They were all within safety margins, but creeping toward the red zone. The Crusade was going all out to keep the *Enterprise* snared.

But not for much longer, Sulu vowed.

He crept out cautiously onto the mezzanine, wishing that Scotty were along on this mission. The redoubtable engineer would be right at home in this complex and would know exactly how best to foul up the works. Sulu wouldn't have minded Yaseen's assistance either. He could probably use some of her Za'Huli prayers right now. . . .

Peering down at the main floor of the control room, he was thrilled to see that Yaseen had beaten him to the punch. A familiar figure in a regulation red skirt stood over a control panel, her back to Sulu. A three-bladed *kligat,* a Capellan throwing weapon native to that planet's fierce warrior tribes, hung at her hip. In addition, a length of oxidized metal rebar, roughly as long as Sulu's foil, rested on the console within easy reach. Clearly, he hadn't been the only one foraging for weapons.

"Hey there!" His heart leaped at the sight of her. "Looks like we both had the same idea."

"I knew you'd come here," she replied. "Tactically, it was the obvious target."

"Now you're sounding like Mister Spock," he quipped. He dashed down a short flight of steps to the ground floor. "Still, you know what they say about great minds thinking alike. . . ."

She turned away from the controls, revealing the silver face masking her true features. A fervid gleam in her eyes gave him a bad feeling. His heart sank.

Oh, no, he thought. *Please let that just be a disguise.*

"My mind has been opened to the Truth," she said with the conviction of a true believer. "But all is well, Hikaru. You too can be rescued from oblivion."

Sulu felt sick to his stomach.

Not her, too. Not Fawzia. . . .

"Sorry," he said. "No thanks."

"It is not for you to decide. None can refuse the Truth."

Her finger stabbed a button on the control panel. Sirens blared and crimson warning lights flashed on and off. Sulu glanced anxiously at the nearest exit, where a force field crackled into existence, trapping him in the control room. He knew that reinforcements had to be on the way.

"Don't do this!" He couldn't resist trying to get through to the real Yaseen, somewhere beneath the Crusade's programming. He took off his own counterfeit mask and flung it away from him. "Take off that awful mask and let's get the hell out of here!"

She shook her head.

"You can't escape the Truth, Hikaru."

"I think I liked it better when you called me d'Artagnan." He approached her warily. "Remember that? 'One for all and all for one'?"

The motto left her unmoved.

"The Truth is one. The Truth is all."

Sulu realized time was running out. More Crusaders would be here soon and the only way out was through that control panel, which was also his best shot at shutting down the generators while he still had a chance.

He just had to get past Yaseen first.

"You have no idea how much I hate doing this." He brandished his foil, wishing to heaven that he had one more knockout bomb. "Step away from those controls . . . please."

She did not step aside.

"You *will* be delivered to the Truth . . . or at least most of you!"

She plucked the *kligat* from her belt and flung it at him. The razor-sharp weapon spun through the air with potentially lethal accuracy; an identical weapon had once killed a friend of Sulu's, Lieutenant Bob Grant, back on Capella IV. This one was on track to take Sulu's sword arm off.

Yaseen was playing for keeps.

Keen reflexes, honed by countless hours of fencing practice, barely saved Sulu from dismemberment. His foil flicked out, deflecting the *kligat,* which struck an auxiliary display panel instead. Plasma erupted as the deadly blades lodged in the console, causing a short circuit. Sulu threw up a hand to protect his face from the surge. The close call sent adrenaline shooting through his veins.

"Are you out of your mind?" he shouted. "You almost took my arm off!"

She shrugged. "The Truth demands sacrifices of us all."

Not done yet, she snatched up the length of rusty rebar and held it like a sword. She lunged at him, swinging the bar.

"En garde!"

He parried the blow just in time. Rusty metal rang against a tempered steel blade. Sparks flew where the swords met, like a deflector field flashing when struck by a phaser beam. He attempted a riposte, thrusting at her shoulder, but she expertly danced away from the attack, keeping her guard up. Obviously, she was no slouch at sword fighting.

Just my luck, he thought. *Another thing we have in common.*

They dueled across the floor of the control room, trading thrusts, feints, and parries. Under other circumstances, he might have enjoyed the bout, but at the moment, he found himself wishing that Yaseen were a bookish historian or linguist, not a seasoned security officer.

"Surrender to the Truth!" she demanded. She swung the rebar like a cutlass, trying to batter her way past his defense, but his sturdy modern foil withstood the jarring blows. "Do not wallow in ignorance!"

"Take off that mask!" he countered. "Then we'll talk!"

A flying kick knocked her backward into a bank of consoles. Her sword arm drooped, and for an instant, he had a clear shot at her chest. He hesitated, unwilling to run her through, and the moment was lost. She rebounded from the console, going for the kill, but he batted the thrust away with his own sword and counterattacked.

"Abandon your rebellion and you will be spared!"

She exhorted him through crossed swords, their faces only inches apart. Her eyes were wide with fervor. Sulu glimpsed his own reflection—and future?—in the polished silver surface of her mask. Her breath was incongruously sweet. She forced him backward across the chamber, toward the steps leading to the mezzanine. The rebar skated across the guard of the grip, sparing his fingers. A forceful cross almost tore his sword from his grasp.

I'm holding back, he realized. *And she's not.*

A skillful feint failed to penetrate her defense. She charged at him head-on, driving him partway up the steps. The rebar stabbed at his face, but he spun around, dodging the strike, and punched her in the face with the hilt of his sword. The blow dented the silver mask, giving her metal lips a permanent sneer. She staggered backward, momentarily stunned.

"Stop this!" he begged. "Don't make me fight you!"

"The fault is yours! The Truth brings only harmony and peace!"

The rebar came whistling through the air. He

parried in time, but the impact sent a numbing jolt through his arm. Sensing an opening, she lunged again, but he ducked beneath the attack and dived out of the way.

We're too evenly matched, he thought. *I need an edge.*

Desperate, he grabbed one of the batons in his belt and aimed it at her. "Don't make me use this!" he bluffed.

"I do not fear the weight of Truth!"

Taking hold of the rebar with both hands, turning it from a sword to a spear, she charged forward, intent on impaling him. His hand forced, he twisted the control rings on the baton, praying that this time he got it right. Otherwise, he might be smashing through the floor once more.

Let's try this again. . . .

The baton lit up. An emerald beam struck Yaseen, halting her charge. Crashing to the floor, she skidded to a stop less than a meter away from him. She let go of the rebar before its heightened weight crushed her fingers. It sank into the floor, carving out a deep depression in the tiles.

"How about that," Sulu said. "It worked."

Her fall did nothing to shake her artificially imposed convictions. "Sacrilege! That weapon is meant to serve the Crusade!"

He still couldn't believe those words were coming from Yaseen. Worse yet, that she actually believed them. He couldn't bear to see her like this one minute more.

"Let's get that mask off you," he declared. "I miss your real face."

"That *is* her real face," a deep, stentorian voice intruded. "Now."

Sulu looked up to see Sokis, along with an honor guard of Crusaders, gazing down at him from the mezzanine. In the heat of the duel, he hadn't even heard the soldiers arrive. More Crusaders appeared at the lower exits. The force field evaporated. The sirens fell silent.

"Stay back!" Sulu pointed his glowing baton at Sokis and his entourage while edging toward the unattended control panel. If he hurried, maybe he could still shut down the generators long enough for the *Enterprise* to break orbit. "I'm not sure that gallery will support your weight . . . if I zap you with a little supergravity!"

Sokis chuckled scornfully. "Do you truly think you are in control here?" A new lance had taken the place of the one Sulu had inadvertently banished to the center of the planet. Its polished head spun like a top. A jade radiance burned along the length of the spear. "Have you forgotten I am a High Brother?"

Uh-oh, Sulu thought. *He's up to something.*

Acting quickly, he fired the baton at the smirking warrior-priest, but nothing happened. The glow within his own weapon sputtered and died, going black and lifeless in his grip.

"Great," Sulu said sarcastically. Apparently the

commander's lance had the ability to override the lesser Crusaders' batons. Not a bad way to enforce discipline, he conceded. "Rank has its privileges, I see."

"Indeed," the High Brother said. "As is only fitting."

Sulu tossed the defanged baton aside. He still had his fencing foil, of course, but somehow he doubted that would be enough to overcome a host of Crusaders. He was seriously outgunned here.

Sure enough, a barrage of gravity beams dropped him to the floor, even as Sokis used his own lance to lift the weight from Yaseen. The triumphant warrior-priest strode down the steps to personally help her up.

"Rise, my adopted sister. You have truly redeemed yourself for your earlier disobedience."

"Thank you, High Brother." Yaseen took his hand and climbed to her feet. "I was blind, but now I see."

Sulu was sickened by her declaration. The unquestioning devotion in her eyes and voice was a hundred times worse than the weight grinding him into the floor. He let go of his useless foil.

"What now?" he asked bitterly. "Are you going to brainwash me, too?"

A malicious smile lifted the High Brother's lips. Sulu got the distinct impression that Sokis had not yet forgiven him for taking him hostage in the observatory and stealing his original lance.

"I think not," Sokis said. "The Crusade may have a better use for you."

THIRTEEN

"Lieutenant Uhura," Palmer said. "It's Sokis again. He's hailing you."

Uhura frowned. This couldn't be good. Despite the rising gravity levels aboard the ship and the threat to the people now directly under her command, she had not forgotten Sokis's veiled threats against the landing party. She glanced at Maxah, who was leaning against the safety rail for support. Nothing about his doleful expression encouraged her.

"Put him through," she ordered, with an aside to Maxah. "Don't go anywhere."

She wanted his input on this.

"I can scarcely lift my feet," he said wryly. "You may trust me to remain at your side."

Palmer forwarded the transmission from the planet. "On-screen."

Sokis reappeared on the main viewer. His spines flared as he spotted Maxah upon the bridge.

"Apostate! Traitor! How dare you show your duplicitous visage in the company of the infidels!"

To his credit, Maxah did not flinch from his leader's rebuke. He defied gravity by lifting his chin boldly.

"It is you—and your barbaric Crusade—who have betrayed millennia of progress and civilization by enforcing dogma at the expense of liberty . . . and exporting our self-inflicted madness on this blameless universe."

"*Blameless?*" Sokis scoffed. "*Ignorant, you mean. We are here to deliver this confused and deluded realm from falsehood. Would you rather it be consigned to oblivion when Creation begins anew?*"

Uhura observed the heated exchanged with interest. She had half expected Maxah to apologize or try to justify his actions to his commander, but instead he seemed eager to express his true feelings now that his cover had finally been blown. He must have wanted to tell Sokis off for who knows how long.

More evidence that they could trust the defector?

"That's enough," she interrupted. Unfortunately, Uhura didn't have time to indulge Maxah in this respect. "I believe your business is with me, High Brother Sokis."

The irate warrior-priest was not quite ready to change the subject.

"*Is it not woeful enough that you willfully resist the Truth, even in the face of its overwhelming weight? Must you harbor this despicable apostate as well?*"

"Brother Maxah is currently in our custody," Uhura stated. "And last time I checked, the Federation was not party to any transdimensional extradition treaties. We will take any requests for asylum under review." She tried not to let her gravity fatigue show. "What else do you want?"

"Your vessel, of course, to spread the Truth through-out alien stars."

She gave him points for consistency.

"We've already discussed that. Our answer hasn't changed, despite your unwarranted interference with our internal gravity systems."

"Which shall only grow more severe the longer you resist," Sokis promised. *"But that is not the only means of inducement at my disposal."*

Uhura braced herself. *Here it comes.*

The view on the screen pulled back to reveal Sulu in captivity, surrounded by unsmiling Crusaders. The helmsman, who had inexplicably exchanged his uniform for gray civvies, appeared in one piece, but was obviously in enemy hands. His face held a stoic expression, betraying no sign of fear or surrender, as he maintained his dignity despite his precarious situation.

"Sulu!" Chekov exclaimed, unable to hold in his feelings. "They've got Sulu!"

Uhura kept her cool. "I see that, Ensign."

Intent on Sulu, it took her a moment to note that Sulu's captors included a masked woman in a red Starfleet uniform. Uhura's head tilted back in surprise.

Ensign Yaseen?

"As you see," Sokis declared, *"we have two of your*

kin among us. Sister Fawzia has accepted the Truth, but this one"—he indicated Sulu—"has committed wanton acts of sabotage against the Crusade and even assaulted my own person."

"Good for you, *tovarich*," Chekov muttered darkly. "I hope you made them pay dearly."

If Sokis heard the young Russian's caustic remark, he paid it no heed. He continued addressing Uhura: "*By all rights, his crimes against the Truth cry out for the most severe punishment. . . .*"

Uhura knew where this was going. "But?"

"*His fate is in your hands,*" Sokis said. "*If you relinquish your vessel, as well as the traitor in your 'custody,' Hikaru will be permitted to embrace the Truth as Sister Fawzia has. But if you continue your self-destructive rebellion, I shall have him publicly executed as an example of what befalls those who defy the Crusade. The choice is yours.*"

"No!" Sulu shouted. "Don't listen to him! You can't surrender the ship, not for my sake!"

Sokis's spines darkened. "*Silence the heretic!*"

To Uhura's horror, it was Yaseen who carried out the High Brother's order. The masked security officer clasped her fists together and swung them against the back of Sulu's neck, knocking him to his knees. She stuffed a gag into his mouth.

Uhura gaped in dismay, unable to fathom the young officer's actions.

What in the world have they done to her?

"Well done, Sister Fawzia." Sokis turned away from Sulu to face Uhura. His stern expression held no hope of compromise. *"Well, what is his fate?"*

Uhura forced herself to look at Sulu. The gag muffled his voice, but his desperate eyes appealed to her. She didn't need an open frequency to receive his message loud and clear:

Save yourself. Save the ship.

The hell of it was, she knew he was right. Her heart felt like it was being ripped in two. Sulu was more than just a longtime crewmate; he was one of her best friends. Poignant memories, of good times in the rec room and shared dangers on dozens of worlds, flashed through her anguished brain. She knew she would never forgive herself if she let him die.

But that didn't matter. She was in command now. Her first responsibility was to the ship and the rest of the crew. There could be only one possible choice.

"No," she said irrevocably. "You can't have the *Enterprise,* no matter what ultimatums you issue." Her voice took on an even steelier tone. "But don't think for a minute that Starfleet is going to take this lightly. We believe in peace, but we have teeth, too. If I were you, I'd think long and hard before you push us too far."

She glanced briefly at Chekov. General Order 24 was still on the table.

"It is you who need to think hard on this," Sokis retorted. Confident in the righteousness of his cause,

he appeared unconcerned about Starfleet reprisals. *"Unless you rethink your foolishness, the heretic will die at sunset, only one hour from now. You have that long to reconsider and save Hikaru . . . or you will watch the Truth crush the life from him!"*

Uhura knew he wasn't bluffing.

FOURTEEN

The pyramid hovered above a huge circular reflecting pool, which was dozens of meters below. Floating disks ascended like stepping-stones to a circular platform above the pool. Tranquil water reflected the subdued glow radiating from the base of the pyramid. A light rain continued to fall, clearing the manicured park surrounding the pool. Along with the lateness of the hour, the damp weather appeared to have driven Ialat's teeming population indoors.

Lucky for us, Kirk thought. *We're overdue for a break.*

Their stolen flyer descended toward the park. Vlisora landed it in an open field a short distance from the pool.

"This is as close as we can approach by air," she explained. "We dare not land any nearer to our objective."

Kirk recalled the no-fly zone she had mentioned before. The last thing they wanted was to attract unwanted attention by violating the pyramid's controlled airspace.

"Understood." He unbuckled his seat belt. "Let's take out that portal."

Exiting the cramped flyer, whose battered hull bore the scars of their violent encounter with the slum-dwelling mob, they sprinted across the park and up the levitating stepping-stones until they reached the top disk, which bore a distinct resemblance to the elevator they had ridden down from the pyramid before. The immense temple hung high above them, shielding them from the rain. Kirk and Spock kept their hoods on anyway. They didn't want to get pegged as infidels again.

Once was enough, Kirk thought.

He craned back his head to view the base of the pyramid. As he understood it, Vlisora's nameless operative inside the temple was going to discreetly lower the antigrav disk to this platform, where they could hitch a ride back up into the bowels of the pyramid. Once inside, they would tackle the harder task: sabotaging the portal itself, while trying to make it home at the same time.

"You sure your person knows what to do?" Kirk asked.

Vlisora nodded. "I sent him a coded message from the flyer. He is awaiting our signal."

"All right." Kirk hoped the rebels' encryption protocols were up to snuff. He glanced around, feeling uncomfortably exposed atop the open disk. "Ring the doorbell."

"Very well." She rescued her pendant from beneath her collar, where she had hidden it earlier, and spun its concentric rings like dials. The pendant flashed and whined for a moment. "It is done."

Kirk wondered if the nested rings symbolized successive cycles of creation, emanating outward from some prime origin. Or were they merely decorative? No doubt a qualified xenoanthropologist would have a field day trying to explore and interpret every nuance of the Ialatl's culture and religion. At the moment, however, he had a more urgent mission.

I need to cut the Crusade off from my universe, at any cost.

Spock gripped his borrowed staff as he peered up at the pyramid. "How soon might we expect a response?"

"As soon as it is deemed safe," she said. "But it should not be—"

The base of the temple suddenly lit up like a searchlight, exposing the fugitives to a harsh white glare. Sirens screeched like enraged *scrilatyl*. Hatchways opened across the base, and a cadre of Crusaders descended feetfirst, clutching glowing green batons and lances. Luminous gravity fields controlled their descent. An electronically amplified voice boomed from above:

"*Surrender, infidels! You cannot escape!*"

"By the ancestors," Vlisora gasped. "We are betrayed!"

But by whom? Kirk wondered.

The rebel priestess resorted to her royal pendant

once more. Spinning its control rings, she deactivated the Crusaders' gravity weapons. Radiant batons and lances went dark, and the startled soldiers plummeted toward the shallow pool and hovering disks. Kirk braced himself for the ugly spectacle of men crashing to their deaths, but Ialat's vaunted safety net proved as effective as advertised, slowing the men's fall so that they merely splashed harmlessly into the water. A few Crusaders bounced off the floating stepping-stones first, taking some hard knocks, but none were killed or seriously injured.

That's good, Kirk thought, *I guess.*

The problem with the safety net was that it left the fallen Crusaders able to regroup. The sodden warriors scrambled out of the water and fanned out around the pool, surrounding Kirk and the others. A lance-wielding officer directed his men.

"Take the infidels . . . and the heretic priestess as well! By force of arms if necessary!"

Crusaders charged up the stepping-stones toward the uppermost disk, where the fugitives found themselves under attack from three separate pathways. Kirk stunned man after man with his phaser, sending them plunging back into the pool, while Spock took a more physical approach, expertly wielding the fossilized staff to parry the soldiers' inert batons and lances. Both ends of the staff were employed as weapons, striking Crusaders with enough force to knock them off the hovering disks, even as reinforcements raced up the disks to avenge their humiliated comrades. The pathways were laid out in such a way that the Crusaders could only charge the top disk a few at a time, but Kirk knew that his group's strategic position was untenable in the long run, even if his phaser didn't run out of power eventually. The Crusaders would keep on coming until he and the others were overwhelmed . . . or additional troops arrived.

"Where the hell is that elevator?" he demanded.

"That campaign is lost," Vlisora said, throwing herself into the fray. She kicked an oncoming Crusader in the jaw. Her spines flared along her scalp like an archaic Mohawk haircut. She smiled grimly. "It seems you have no choice, God-Slayer. You must wage war against the Crusade before the eyes of the world!"

Something about her tone, and a crafty glint in her eyes, fired Kirk's suspicions. A brutal possibility struck with the force of a Klingon disruptor.

"This was a setup. You wanted this fight!" He glared at her while picking off charging Crusaders with pinpoint accuracy. "Did you even have a man inside the pyramid?"

"Does it matter?" Her black mesh glove flared green, and a gravity beam sent a Crusader crashing down into the pool. She reached out with her other hand and tugged on Kirk's hood, exposing his very human profile. "The battle is upon us, Kirk. Strike for freedom of thought! Show my people that the God-King's will is not absolute!"

Spock's keen ears picked up the exchange. "It seems we have been manipulated, Captain."

"I'm getting that impression," Kirk agreed.

Vlisora was unapologetic. "Saving your universe is not good enough. Your Prime Directive be damned; you will either free us, as you have so many others, or you will become a martyr to freedom, inspiring others to oppose the Crusade."

"You've got it all figured out, don't you?" Kirk was tempted to turn his phaser on her. "You used us!"

"Forgive me," she said, "but there is nothing I would not do to lift the onerous weight of the Crusade from my people!"

Clearly, she could no longer be trusted. Looking past her, Kirk saw Spock's right hand let go of his whirling staff. Fighting with one hand, Spock backed up toward Vlisora. His free hand reached out to administer a nerve pinch. . . .

"I'm sorry, Mister Spock. I cannot allow that."

Spotting his reflection in the shimmering waters below, she spun toward him and extended a glowing emerald finger. A gravity beam struck Spock squarely in the chest, propelling him upward at an angle. Kirk watched in horror as his friend rose into the sky, barely missing the base of the pyramid, before disappearing into the clouds.

"Damn you!" He wheeled angrily toward Vlisora. "What did you just do?"

"Sent him into orbit, where he cannot obstruct

your destiny." Her silver face hardened. "Just as he feared, he was of limited use after all."

Kirk found it hard to accept that Spock was gone, just like that. He turned his phaser on Vlisora, briefly ignoring the next wave of Crusaders advancing up the steps.

"Bring him back down!" Kirk ordered. "Before he suffocates in the upper atmosphere!"

She shook her head. "It is too late for him."

"Bring him back, damn it!"

A Crusader came at him from the side, swinging a baton. Kirk ducked beneath the blow, then elbowed the soldier in the gut. The inconvenient distraction gave Vlisora a chance to adjust the settings on her pendant. Her black mesh glove keened again.

An irresistible pull latched onto Kirk's phaser like a tractor beam. He tried to hold on to the weapon, but it was yanked from his grip, flying across the platform into Vlisora's waiting hand.

She obligingly stunned a wave of Crusaders.

"I am not your true enemy," she insisted. "But the God-Slayer must face the God-King."

By now, a crowd of spectators had begun streaming into the park, drawn by the commotion, the God-King's telepathic commands, or both. Additional Crusaders descended on ropes from the pyramid above. Wailing vehicles raced toward the park. The growing throng began shouting in unison:

"Seize the infidel! Seize the infidel!"

Kirk guessed that Jaenab himself was speaking through the mob. He found himself surrounded and unarmed. He stared at Vlisora.

"Why?"

"Ialat is watching," she said. "You cannot be seen to flee the Crusade. You must stand and fight." A flicker of guilt crossed her face. "Farewell."

Deftly shifting the phaser to her other hand, she dived off the disk and swam for the edge of the pool. Clambering up onto land, she used both the stolen phaser and her gravity-glove to clear a path through the Crusaders and civilians to her waiting flyer. Determined Ialatl attempted to capture her, but green and sapphire rays shot forth from her mismatched weapons, stunning and/or dropping any would-be pursuers. Kirk watched her hijacked flyer take off into the sky without him.

But he had only a moment to do so.

More Crusaders charged onto the top disk, tackling Kirk and knocking him off his feet. Unarmed, he fought back with his fists, boots, and elbows, all the while wondering how long it would be before the Crusaders would be able to reactivate their weapons now that Vlisora was gone. How far did the override effect of her royal pendant extend?

As it turned out, it didn't matter. Angry and humiliated, the sodden soldiers were perfectly happy to subdue Kirk the hard way. The captain fought back as vigorously as he could, fueled by his fury over

Spock's death and Vlisora's treachery, but in the end, it was not artificial gravity that defeated him but sheer weight of numbers. A host of Crusaders pounded him with their batons until he couldn't have stood if he wanted to. Darkness encroached on his vision.

"Enough!" an officer shouted, calling the men off. He strode over to where Kirk lay, bruised and bleeding on the floor of the platform. A bearded silver face sneered down at Kirk. "See to it that he lives." He nudged Kirk with the toe of his boot, eliciting a gasp of pain.

"This one has an appointment with the God-King."

Just like Vlisora planned, Kirk realized.

He passed out.

FIFTEEN

"Fifteen minutes to sunset," Chekov reported.

Uhura watched nightfall creep across the hemisphere, approaching the location of the Institute. The day-lit side of Ephrata IV was rotating away from its sun, bringing Sulu ever closer to his scheduled execution.

"Gravity at three hundred percent," Masters said. "And—"

"And rising," Uhura finished impatiently. "I know."

She instantly regretted her snappish tone, but figured she could be forgiven for feeling a little stressed. The slow-motion gravity torture was wearing hard on all of them. Her back and joints ached from the extra weight. She was starting to feel out of breath and light-headed. Her heart labored to pump her blood to her head.

"Sorry to bark at you, Charlene. Keep me informed."

Masters didn't seem to take it personally. "Aye, sir."

Uhura studied the bridge. Nobody was standing anymore. Even the security officers on duty had collapsed into seats around the outer perimeter of the bridge. People were winded, gasping for breath from even the smallest exertion. Hearts and muscles strained against the unrelenting gravity. Uhura wondered how much longer they'd be capable of running the ship.

Nor was Maxah immune to the insidious effect of the gravity barrage. He leaned against the back of her chair, letting it help support his weight. His smoky aroma kept fooling her, making her think a fire had broken out on the bridge. His spines sagged toward the floor.

"If you will allow me my mace," he suggested, "I may be able to relieve your discomfort, if only for a time."

She hesitated. After observing his heated debate with Sokis, she was more inclined than ever to trust the younger Ialatl. Still, returning his weapon to him would be a real leap of faith—and she was feeling way too heavy to leap at the moment.

Then again, she thought, *maybe defying gravity is* exactly *what we need to do right now.*

"All right." She turned slowly toward Masters, feeling like she was weighed down by neutronium shackles. "Please return our guest's property, Lieutenant."

Masters paused as well. "Sir?"

"Are you sure that's a good idea, Lieutenant?" Chekov asked. The brash young ensign was more comfortable questioning Uhura than Masters was.

"Remember what he did with that wand of his before?"

She didn't blame him for being wary. For all she knew, she was making a big mistake.

"I haven't forgotten, Ensign." She nodded at Masters. "Do it."

"Yes, sir. "

Masters produced the baton, which was obviously much heavier than before. She needed both hands to lift it. Grunting with effort, she struggled to rise from her seat.

"Stay where you are," Maxah urged her. Letting go of the captain's chair, he lurched across the bridge, shuffling feet that were almost too heavy to move. Watching him fight the supergravity, grabbing onto consoles and railings for support, Uhura wasn't sure he was going to make it all the way to Masters's post at the engineering station, but, gasping for breath, he finally dropped into an empty seat beside Charlene. The chair sagged noticeably beneath his weight. He reached for his mace. "Thank you for holding this for me."

The apprehensive engineer handed over the baton. "Don't make me regret this, mister."

"I would not dream of it."

Like Masters, he needed both hands to support the baton's augmented weight. Grimacing, he twisted a ring on its shaft and an effulgent green light radiated from the baton.

The effect was immediate. Sighs of relief broke out across the bridge as the debilitating weight slackened to a noticeable degree. Uhura suddenly felt more comfortable than she had in hours. It still wasn't standard gravity, but it was more bearable than before. She actually felt like she might be able to stand up if she had to.

"That *is* a relief," she told Maxah. "Thank you."

"Bridge gravity at one hundred sixty percent," Masters confirmed. "Compared to three hundred and five percent elsewhere on the ship." She eyed the glowing baton speculatively. "I don't suppose we can patch that into the ship's main gravity generators?"

He shook his head. "The technologies are not readily compatible. Moreover, the range of the baton is distinctly limited. As I explained before, it is intended for personal defense, nothing more. Nor is it capable of counteracting gravity artillery on such a scale." He gave Uhura an apologetic look. "At best, I can only partially protect a small area for a time."

She took his word for it. An urgent notion struck her.

"Get that baton to sickbay," she ordered. "On crutches if necessary."

Maxah understood at once. "Your injured."

"Doctor McCoy's patients need relief more than we do," she said. It made sense; if a single baton wasn't enough to save the ship, maybe it could at least give Scotty a fighting chance.

Chekov rose to his feet. "I'll do it, Lieutenant. For Mister Scott."

"I appreciate the thought, Mister Chekov, but I need you here on the bridge." She beckoned to a security officer, Lieutenant Paul Alvarez, instead. A runner, Alvarez had placed in the Plutonian marathon last year. She figured if anybody could make it to sickbay, he could. "Get this to sickbay right away. Take the turbolift as far as you can."

"Yes, sir."

Maxah surrendered the baton without complaint. "Careful," he warned Alvarez. "Do not adjust the settings. There could be negative consequences."

"Understood," Alvarez said.

Uhura was impressed by Maxah's willingness to lend his only weapon to the cause of helping their sick and injured. She was trusting him more and more. *Maybe I shouldn't have clocked him with that data slate before.*

"Get a move on, Lieutenant," she instructed Alvarez, before swinging her head toward Palmer at communications. "Inform sickbay that relief is on the way. Explain the situation to them."

Palmer nodded. "I'm on it."

Bearing the glowing baton easily in one hand, Alvarez exited the bridge, taking its benign influence with it. Uhura groaned as the heavy gravity reasserted itself, crushing her back into her seat. She wasn't the only one. Chekov let out an "oomph" as he plopped back down behind the nav console.

Well, she thought, *it was nice while it lasted.*

She had no regrets, though.

"You made the right call, Lieutenant," Chekov said. "I'm sure the captain would have done the same."

"I'm glad you think so, Ensign."

Break time's over, she thought. On the screen, darkness continued to eclipse the solitary continent. "What's our status, Mister Chekov?"

He looked glumly at his readouts. "Ten minutes to sunset." Frustration overwhelmed him, and he pounded his fist against the control panel. "We have to *do* something. We can't let those Cossacks murder Sulu!"

Uhura sympathized. She felt the same way.

"What about Yaseen?" Fisher asked from the helm station. "Did you see her there, wearing that creepy silver mask? It's like she's one of them now!"

Uhura shuddered at the memory of Yaseen brutally striking Sulu down. She didn't know Fawzia well, but she couldn't imagine that the decorated security officer had willingly joined the Crusade.

"The Crusade has adopted her," Maxah explained. "As they did those other innocents on Ephrata IV."

"But I still don't quite understand," Uhura said. "How did the Crusade convert the people on Ephrata so easily?"

"The masks," he explained. "They do more than just make your faces copies of our own, hiding your unique and unsettling differences. They emit a signal that overcomes the wearers' ability to think freely, making them more susceptible to conversion. It beams the Truth directly into an adoptee's mind."

"A signal?"

Uhura's eyes narrowed. Signals were her specialty.

"What if we can jam or interfere with that signal?"

Maxah seized on the idea. "It's possible, if we can generate a countersignal on the right frequency."

Uhura grinned. "Now you're talking my language."

Masters provided him with a data slate. Ironically, it was the same one Uhura had used to brain him before. He hastily scribbled the relevant data onto the heavy slate. Rather than physically carry the object back across the bridge to Uhura, Masters obligingly transmitted the information to the data reader on the armrest of Uhura's chair.

She studied the data with a growing sense of excitement. In theory, it ought to be possible to generate a jamming frequency that would cancel out the signal emitted by the masks. The trick was going to be broadcasting it widely enough to affect the hundreds of brainwashed converts on the planet.

"Mister Ferrari," she said. "Can you rig the subsonic transmitter to blanket the entire Institute and the surrounding area?"

It should be doable, she thought. Mister Spock had once employed a similar technique to counteract the effect of those mind-altering spores on Omicron Ceti III. This was just a significantly more precise signal.

"I think so," Ferrari answered, a bit uncertainly. He was a competent officer and scientist, but he was no Mister Spock.

He'll have to do, she thought. Failure was not an option.

"Review the science logs relating to emergency measures taken during the *Enterprise*'s mission to Omicron Ceti III." She looked up the specific citation. "Stardate 3147.3."

His eyes lit up as he recalled the incident. He quickly called up the relevant logs. "Thank you, Lieutenant. That helps a lot!"

She assumed he had what he needed now.

"Lieutenant Palmer, patch communications into the subsonic transmitter. Prepare to transmit a signal on this precise frequency on my command."

She was tempted to reclaim her usual post and do it herself, but thought better of it. Now was no time to micromanage. Circumstances had placed the crew under her command. She had to trust them to do their jobs.

"Five minutes to sunset," Chekov counted down. "If we're going to do this, we need to do it soon."

"High Brother Sokis is hailing us from the planet," Palmer reported. "I think he wants us to watch."

"I'll just bet he does," Uhura said. "Ferrari, are we ready to go?"

He made some last-minute adjustments to the settings. "Almost."

"Palmer?"

"Awaiting your signal, Lieutenant."

Uhura experienced a sudden moment of doubt. Could she truly trust Maxah after all? What if that confrontation with Sokis had been staged for her benefit? Suppose this broadcast made things worse and only strengthened the Crusade's hold on the people below?

No, she thought, overcoming her fears. *I need to trust my gut, just like the captain would.*

"Prepare to open hailing frequencies."

SIXTEEN

Sulu was about to be stoned . . . literally.

The sun was setting in the east and he was flat on his back in Pearl Square, pinned to the ground by a scintillating green nimbus, while a floating heap of rubble hung weightless above him, slowly descending in synch with the sun. Massive chunks of marble, ceramic, steel, and thermoconcrete, plus jagged shards of transparent aluminum, hovered ominously, including twisted metal beams and pipes, slabs of shattered masonry, joists, railings, plumbing, and even the remains of various vandalized monuments and statuary. A mutilated bust of Galileo butted against the headless torso of what, judging from its sculpted robes, had once been some celebrated Vulcan philosopher. Broken stone and mortar added yet more mass to the accumulated debris. Its shadow stretched across Sulu, who was still clad in the civilian attire he had borrowed earlier. He wished he were in uniform.

"Behold, brothers and sisters, the price of willful ignorance and defiance." Sokis presided over the public execution. His replacement lance, presumably imported through the rift, held the debris aloft by means of a keening emerald beam. "This vile heretic was accepted into our fold, but chose to betray us even after being given the gift of Truth. Such flagrant ingratitude cannot go unpunished."

A sizable audience had turned out to witness Sulu's impending demise. Gathered Crusaders and masked converts looked on expectantly; from the size of the crowd, Sulu guessed that attendance was mandatory. Levitating video recorders captured the scene for posterity, and were no doubt transmitting the awful spectacle to the *Enterprise*.

"Don't do it, Uhura!" Sulu shouted, despite the supergravity weighing down his tongue. "Don't give in!"

"Silence!" Sokis ordered. "Or I will have you gagged . . . and deprive us of the valuable lesson of your final, agonized screams."

Sulu figured he'd gotten his message across. He had to trust that Uhura and the others would make the hard call and not surrender the ship for his sake. Still, he hated being used by the enemy like this. Uhura had to be going through hell right now.

Adding to his own ordeal was the fact that Yaseen was not just observing the proceedings, but had been assigned a position of honor. She stood at Sokis's right hand, her lovely face hidden behind a mask. The dented metal around her mouth had yet to be repaired, so that the frozen silver sneer remained. It didn't suit her.

"It seems," Sokis taunted Sulu, "that your comrades have abandoned you, choosing rebellion over your own well-being. A pity, but perhaps your dreadful fate will convince them of the error of their ways."

"High Brother?" Yaseen's voice held an unexpected quaver of doubt. "Forgive me, but I have to ask. Must we kill him? Can't he be given another chance to embrace the Truth, as I was?"

"But you redeemed yourself by foiling his heinous attack on the fusion generators. His myriad crimes are too great and too numerous. An example must be made."

Yeah, right, Sulu thought sarcastically. He knew this execution was mostly for Uhura's benefit, with the added bonus of giving Sokis a chance to get back at Sulu for personally attacking him at the observatory and destroying his fancy lance. For all his lofty rhetoric, the pious warrior-priest was not above holding a grudge.

Yaseen shifted uncomfortably. Her dark eyes implored Sokis.

"But surely he is not beyond saving?"

"The decision has been made, sister. His ending will serve the Truth, and bring countless others to deliverance." He handed his lance over to her. "Prove yourself once more, sister. Let him meet justice by your own hand."

She hesitated only for a moment before accepting the lance.

"Yes, High Brother."

So much for a last-minute appeal, Sulu thought. He appreciated Yaseen's failed efforts on his behalf, but honestly didn't know which prospect was less appealing: getting turned into a mind-controlled zombie again, as he'd been on Beta III and Pyris VII, or to be slowly crushed to death beneath a ton of rubble.

He was glad that Yaseen was not sharing his fate, however. At least she still had a chance to be saved. . . .

The sun sank toward the horizon. Bands of luminous violet and magenta streaked the sky; it was an ironically beautiful sight, given that it was also lowering the curtain on his life. He supposed he should be grateful to the universe for giving him one last sunset to enjoy before the end.

That's a blessing, I guess.

Yaseen had clearly been schooled in the lance's use. She expertly directed the gravity beam, lowering the hovering debris at a steady, inexorable rate. Watching the ponderous accumulation of junk sink toward him, centimeter by agonizing centimeter, Sulu felt as if he were trapped in a futuristic replay of "The Pit and the Pendulum." Despite his determination to die with dignity, as befitting a Starfleet officer, it was hard not to be terrified by the awful fate descending toward him. Sweat soaked his face, while his mouth was dry. His heart pounded in anxiety. An oppressive sense of claustrophobia ate corrosively at his nerves.

Hang on, he thought. *It will all be over soon.*

Or would it? The rubble was only centimeters above him, blocking out the fading sunlight and filling up his vision. He could practically taste the gritty texture of those concrete slabs, and yet the sinking debris was still taking its own sweet time. It was like watching a Romulan bird-of-prey bear down in slow motion.

Just how long and painful was this going to be? Were they planning to grind him slowly into the pavement? He found himself wishing that they would hurry up and just drop the whole load on him.

Get it over with, damn you!

"Sing, brothers and sisters!" Sokis exhorted his kindred. "Raise your voices in praise of the Truth!"

Crusaders and converts alike began chanting in unison. Even Yaseen joined in, lending her mellifluous voice to the alien hymn.

"Hey!" Sulu shouted over the singing. "Don't I get any last words?"

"UnTruth deserves no hearing!" Sokis said sharply. "Better you spend your final moments silently begging forgiveness from your worthless ancestors!"

I don't think so, Sulu thought. *I did my duty. I have nothing to apologize for . . . except maybe not saving Yaseen.*

The descending rubble began to press against his face and chest. Sulu twisted his head to one side to keep from being suffocated. He braced himself for the excruciating ordeal to come. This was not how he would have chosen to make his exit. A Klingon disruptor blast would be faster and more merciful. This was going to be ugly.

At least I got that sunset.

Then something odd happened. The chanting, which had been rising in volume and fervor, broke off abruptly. Peering out from beneath the rubble, Sulu saw the masked converts reel about, clutching their heads. Confused eyes peered out from behind a sea of silver masks. Fumbling fingers explored the alien contours of the false faces.

Wait a second, Sulu thought. *What's happening?*

Sokis was bewildered, too. "Brothers, sisters? What ails you?"

"Trust me," Yaseen said angrily. "You don't want to know." She ripped off her mask, freeing her face. Undisguised fury blazed openly. "Rock this, big brother!"

She swept the lance around and the gravity beam as well. The hovering rubble flew away from Sulu and crashed like a swarm of meteors into a nearby line of Crusaders, bowling them over. An avalanche of debris rained down on them. Spread out more thinly than it had been above Sulu, the barrage was still enough to put multiple soldiers down for the count. They moaned and whimpered on the pearly tiles. Slabs of concrete and chunks of marble pinned them as effectively as any gravity beam.

"No!" Sokis gaped in disbelief. "You belonged to the Truth!"

She turned the lance toward Sokis. "If I were you, I would shut up fast . . . before I do something that, frankly, I wouldn't really regret."

Sulu was impressed by her restraint. He would have been tempted to crush Sokis beneath his own debris, especially after the way the Crusade had hideously warped her mind.

"I don't understand," Sokis murmured. Backing away fearfully, he stumbled over a broken tile and toppled backward onto his rear end. "This cannot be happening!"

Sulu didn't understand either, but he assumed the *Enterprise* had something to do with his miraculous stay of execution.

Thanks, Uhura. I owe you one.

By now, the other converts were following Yaseen's lead and tossing away their own masks in revulsion. Sulu guessed that they had needed more time to recover since they had been brainwashed longer. Dozens of discarded masks hit the pavement. Rows of identical silver faces were replaced by a colorful panoply of diverse humanoid countenances. Confused and disoriented expressions gave way to various degrees of guilt, dismay, and anger.

"Oh my God." A handsome silver-haired human woman gazed at the ravaged campus in horror. "What have we done?"

"You mean what did they *make* us do," a middle-aged Andorian corrected her bitterly. His antennae twitched in rage. He unhitched a type-1 phaser from his belt. "Time to teach them a lesson or two!"

Tabus, who had escaped the barrage of rubble, tried to rally the remaining Crusaders, who were outnumbered at least seven to one. "To arms, brothers!" He drew his baton and targeted the rebellious mob. His comrades did the same. "Weigh down the heretics!"

The Crusaders moved to subdue the uprising.

Nothing happened. The unmasked mob remained upright.

"Sorry," Yaseen said, smirking. The teardrop-shaped head of the lance spun so quickly that it blurred. A jade radiance flashed along the length of the spear. "It's good to be the High Brother."

Within moments, the outnumbered Ialatl had a full-scale insurrection on their hands as the liberated Ephratans turned on their former brothers. The Crusaders fought back, wielding their inert batons like truncheons, but the odds and numbers were against them. Scientists, historians, artists, and administrators ganged up on the invaders who had violated their most precious commodities: their minds. An irate Tellarite, huffing and snorting, charged into battle like an Antarean devil-hog, swinging a shovel at a Crusader's head. A lithe green Orion woman pounced on Tabus from behind and twisted his tentacles until he screamed. A hissing Caitian slashed at the Ialatl with his claws. The Andorian security chief wielded his phaser with pinpoint accuracy, stunning Crusaders into unconsciousness.

"Silver bastards!" he snarled. "You're lucky we're civilized here!"

Video recorders darted about, capturing the melee. Fallen masks crunched beneath boots, hooves, and falling bodies. Still pinned to the ground, Sulu found himself in danger of being trampled as well.

"Excuse me!" he called out to Yaseen. "Over here?"

She spotted his predicament. "Oops," she said, blushing slightly. "Be right on that."

She swung the lance his way. It keened and flashed.

The emerald aura evaporated, taking the paralyzing weight with it. Sulu sprang to his feet, still mildly amazed that he wasn't just a pulped red smear on the pavement by now. "That's more like it."

"You done lying around, d'Artagnan?"

He gave her a courtly bow. "At your service, milady."

"Then make yourself handy," she said. "We've got some serious payback to dish out."

And then some, he thought.

A Crusader, grappling with a tripedal Edosian academic, bumped into him. A well-aimed karate chop took the distracted Ialatl out of the fight, and Sulu claimed the Crusader's baton. It wasn't a rapier or a cutlass, alas, but it would have to do. Another Crusader, armed with a truncheon of his own, faced off against Sulu. A black eye and a split lip indicated that some Ephratan had already gotten a few licks in. The alien soldier didn't seem happy about it.

"Yield, heretic!"

"You know," Sulu said, "I'm really getting tired of that word."

He tossed his baton back and forth between his right and left hands. The Crusader's black eyes tracked the weapon, trying to anticipate the direction of the attack.

"Think fast!" Sulu said.

He tossed the baton into the air above them. The Crusader's eyes instinctively turned upward, giving Sulu a chance to spring forward and deliver a solid elbow strike to the soldier's jaw while simultaneously pushing aside the arm holding the baton. The Crusader stumbled backward, dazed, and Sulu followed up with a rapid-fire combination of kicks and punches. He already had the man on the ropes as he reached out and caught his own baton on the way down. One last swing to the head was enough to lay the Crusader out cold. A staccato laugh escaped Sulu's lips.

That was a pretty smooth move, he thought, *if I do say so myself.*

He hoped Yaseen hadn't missed it.

Several meters away, an older woman, whom Sulu now recognized as Elena Collins, climbed onto an empty pedestal, taking the place of whatever statue had been torn down by the Crusaders. She waved her arms, shouting to be heard above the fracas.

"No killing!" she hollered. "Remember who we are! What we stand for!"

A stray Crusader rushed to dislodge her. "You stand for lies!"

She took advantage of her elevated position to kick him solidly in the jaw. He staggered backward into the melee, where a number of Dr. Collins's colleagues jumped him and dragged him to the ground.

"That's open to debate," she observed.

Yaseen, finding herself momentarily clear, scanned the square for a new target. Her dark eyes zoomed in on the dimensional rift, which shimmered at the center of the square, less than twenty meters away. She swung the lance toward it.

"Wait!" Sulu shouted. "What about the captain and Spock?"

According to Sokis, Captain Kirk and Mister Spock had been sent through the rift to the Ialatl's own dimension. It might become necessary, Sulu knew, to seal off the portal for the sake of the Federation, but for the time being he wanted to give Kirk and Spock every chance to make it back to the *Enterprise*, no matter what might have befallen them on the other side of the rift.

Lord knows the captain has beaten the odds before, Sulu thought. *Like that time in the Tholian web.*

"Right!" Yaseen agreed, lowering the lance. "Got a little carried away there." She joined up with him at the fringe of the battle. A screeching Crusader tackled her at the waist, but she took the fight out of him by steering his head down into her knee. She shoved him aside without a second glance. "So what now, Lieutenant?"

That was an easy one.

"The gravity cannon," he reminded her. "The *Enterprise* pulled our butts out of the fire. I think it's time we returned the favor."

Abandoning the lopsided battle in the square, which the Ephratans appeared to have well in hand, they raced across the campus to the observatory building. A small complement of guards, dutifully manning their posts despite the tumult in the square, were shocked to discover that their batons had lost their mojo. A wave of Yaseen's lance yanked the guards to the ground.

"Apostates! Turncoats!" a downed Ialatl cursed them. "We should have let your miserable universe perish! You don't deserve our Truth!"

"You're right," Yaseen said. "We don't."

She kicked him in the ribs as she rushed past him.

Sulu couldn't blame her.

They headed into the building. The bottomless pit carved out by Sulu's mishandling of the High Brother's lance had been roped off for safety's sake, but they could still hear the gravity cannon thrumming twenty stories above. Taking the fire stairs two steps at a time, they ran up to the observation deck on the top floor. Sulu was winded by the time they reached their target, but adrenaline and duty kept him going. Yaseen was breathing hard, too.

Only a handful of technicians were tending to the cannon. They gasped in surprise as the Starfleet duo burst into the chamber, especially when they spied Sokis's lance in Yaseen's grip.

"Clear out!" she ordered them. "Now!"

Her fierce tone and expression brooked no argument. Sulu backed her up, smacking his captured baton against his palm. He mimicked a surly Starfleet MP breaking up a gang of unruly cadets.

The techs beat a hasty escape, leaving Sulu and Yaseen alone on the observation deck. He glanced warily at the gaping chasm he'd accidentally created hours ago, then at Yaseen's newly acquired lance.

"You really know how to use that thing?"

"The virtues of a solid religious education," she quipped. "You should have tried it."

She took aim at the cannon.

"Hold on a second." He remembered how panicked that one tech had become when he'd tried this same stunt before. He wasn't sure exactly what the frantic Ialatl had been afraid of, but Sulu didn't want to trigger a gravitational "disruption" that might turn the Institute into a crater or a wormhole or God knows what. "Hitting a gravity cannon with a gravity beam sounds dicey to me." A better idea occurred to him. "How about you take out the floor beneath it instead?"

She shrugged. "Works for me."

The spinning head of the lance dipped. An emerald beam targeted the floor, which collapsed under its own weight, taking the massive cannon with it. The corrupted subspace telescope tore loose from its moorings and crashed over twenty stories to the basement. A near-seismic tremor shook the building to its foundations, throwing Sulu and Yaseen off balance. The cannon's emerald gravity beam vanished from the night sky. Sulu assumed that meant the *Enterprise* was no longer in danger.

You're welcome, he thought.

Unfortunately, the cannon's spectacular collapse proved too much for the already damaged building. The walls shook as the entire building began to give way beneath them. Alien machinery plunged through the crumbling floor. The restored viewer shattered once more. Jagged chasms opened up across the floor, zigzagging toward Sulu and Yaseen and cutting off their escape routes. Sparks erupted from severed cables. Noxious vapors billowed from broken pipes.

"A little bit of overkill, don't you think?" A tremor threw Sulu against Yaseen. "I thought you said you knew how to work that lance."

"It was a crash course," she replied. "Sue me."

The floor disintegrated around them. Cascades of falling tile and masonry ate away at whatever shrinking footing still remained. Sulu and Yaseen backed away from the expanding chasms. With nowhere else to go, they climbed up onto the console facing the viewscreen. Strobing warning lights and spinning gauges indicated that the control panel was having a cybernetic breakdown. Sulu's boots trampled over random switches, buttons, and dials, none of which were likely to do any good at the moment. He fought to keep his balance atop the quaking workstation, while peering down at the mangled remains of the gravity cannon several stories below. The trembling observatory felt as if it was only moments away from coming apart altogether. A deafening roar nearly drowned Sulu out.

"Nice knowing you!"

"Not so fast!" She grabbed him, wrapping her arm around his waist. "Hold on tight!"

She aimed the lance at the doomed console, and a beam of negative gravity propelled them upward through the open gap in the roof of the observatory, only seconds before the devastated building collapsed beneath them. Twenty stories pancaked on top of each other, burying what was left of the gravity cannon and the exotic alien equipment. A billowing cloud of dust and debris rose from the wreckage. Frightened Ialatl soldiers and technicians ran for cover. The booming crash echoed like thunder off the surrounding hills.

That's the second time I've escaped being pulped today, Sulu realized. *Maybe somebody* is *looking out for me.*

Hundreds of meters above the smoke and dust, hanging in the cool night air, Sulu and Yaseen drifted above the campus. From their sky-high vantage point, he saw that the Ephratans had already reclaimed their Institute. Sokis and his Crusaders were lined up on the ground, at the mercy of their former converts, while campus security, armed with phasers, stood guard over the portal, watching out for reinforcements from Ialat. Looking closer, he saw that there were still a few pockets of fighting going on here and there around the campus, but the outcome was hardly in doubt. The Crusade no longer controlled Ephrata IV.

Sulu hoped the folks on the *Enterprise* were enjoying the show.

"What was that you were saying about overkill?" Yaseen asked.

He gazed down at the collapsed observatory. He guessed that all of the mysterious Ialatl technology had been crushed beneath the weight of the fallen building. Chances were, Starfleet engineers would find very little to salvage or study—which was possibly just as well. The last thing the quadrant needed right now was a gravitational arms race.

"I take it back," he said.

He held on to her for dear life as an autumn breeze wafted them above the campus. They clung together tightly, slow dancing through the sky.

"You know," he said, "I could get used to this."

She turned her face toward him. He decided he liked it much better than the silver one. She smirked at him with her own, natural lips.

"Watch the hands, d'Artagnan."

SEVENTEEN

The revolution was being televised.

Live images, conveniently provided by the Crusade, gave Uhura a front-row view of the uprising on Ephrata IV. Cheers erupted spontaneously on the bridge as Sulu escaped execution—and Yaseen sent the arrogant "High Brother" tumbling onto his holy derriere.

"Yes!" Chekov exclaimed. He high-fived Fisher. "That'll teach those Cossacks to try to flatten our friend!"

Uhura didn't begrudge him his outburst. She felt like cheering as well.

"Well done, people," she praised the bridge crew. The jamming signal had obviously turned the tide on Ephrata, just as they had hoped. She turned toward Maxah, who was still seated beside Charlene Masters at engineering. "Thank you so much for your help."

"I did what I could," he replied. "What had to be done."

His own reaction to the images on the screen was notably more subdued than Chekov's or the rest of the crew's. His silver face bore a somber expression as he quietly watched the Ephratans take back their home. Uhura thought she understood; despite his passionate opposition to the Crusade, he had to have profoundly complicated feelings about betraying his own kind. Those were his former comrades being assaulted on the viewer.

"No regrets?" she asked.

"Only that my people forced my hand, and may not soon understand why I did what I did."

"Well, *my* people will not forget," she promised. "And neither will I."

Then, without warning, the excess gravity went away. Her spirits lightened, along with her flesh and bones, as the gravity on the bridge abruptly reverted to normal. Excited chatter and gasps of relief, coming from all around her, suggested that she wasn't the only one who felt a whole lot lighter all of a sudden.

"The gravity beam has been shut off!" Ferrari confirmed. "It's gone completely!"

"Music to my ears," Uhura said. Although she couldn't be sure, she suspected that they had Sulu and Yaseen to thank for this highly welcome development. "The *Enterprise* is not being held in place anymore?"

"No," Ferrari said. "We're free."

Uhura resisted the urge to jump for joy now that she finally could. It seemed that she had brought the ship safely through the crisis after all.

"Shall I break orbit, Lieutenant?" Fisher asked from the helm.

Probably a good idea, she thought. From the looks of it, the Crusade was being routed down on the planet, but it couldn't hurt to put some distance between the *Enterprise* and Ephrata IV until they knew it was safe to return for Sulu and the others.

"Roger that, helmsman. Take us out of orbit, but not out of the system." She leaned toward Maxah. "What exactly is the range of that gravity cannon?"

Before he could reply, Palmer called out from communications.

"Lieutenant! We're being hailed from the planet." A grin broke out across her face. "It's Mister Sulu!"

"Are we certain?" Uhura wanted to believe it, but she remembered how Maxah had tricked them before. "Do we have visual and/or verbal confirmation?"

Palmer dispelled any doubts. "It's really him, sir. I'd stake my stripes on it."

"Not necessary," Uhura said, satisfied. "Just pipe him through."

The hopeful mood on the bridge went up another notch as Sulu appeared on the main viewer, replacing their view of the fighting down on the planet. He looked a bit the worse for wear, but he was beaming jubilantly, as was Ensign Yaseen, whose bright smile was no longer masked by a face not her own. The interior of an office could be seen in the background; Uhura assumed that the landing party (or what remained of it) had commandeered the Institute's communications system. She only wished that Captain Kirk and Mister Spock were with them.

Just be thankful that Sulu and Yaseen are all right, Uhura thought. *One upset victory at a time.*

"Good to see you, Lieutenant, Ensign," she addressed the screen. "Looks like you're having some excitement down there."

"You could say that," Sulu responded. *"What about the ship? We destroyed the gravity cannon, but—"*

"We're fine," she assured him, "but I'm pleased to hear that the cannon's been taken care of. Is it really no longer a factor?"

"Trust me." Sulu exchanged what seemed like a private joke with Yaseen. *"It's out of the picture. You don't need to worry about it anymore."*

That was just what she wanted to hear.

"Belay that last command, Mister Fisher," she instructed the helm. "Return to standard orbit."

"Aye, aye, sir."

He began to turn the *Enterprise* around.

"Any chance of a pickup?" Sulu asked. He plucked at his incongruous gray suit. "I'm eager to get back in uniform."

"And kick the dust of this planet off us," Yaseen added. "No offense to the locals."

"I think we can manage that," Uhura replied. She trusted Sulu's assessment of the situation on the ground. "Lower deflector shields, Mister Chekov." She activated the intercom on her armrest. "Uhura to transporter room. Lock onto the signal from the planet and prepare to beam Lieutenant Sulu and Ensign Yaseen aboard."

"*Yes, sir!*" Lieutenant Kyle acknowledged via the comm. "*Will do.*"

Uhura took her finger off the comm button. "Anything else I can do for you, Mister Sulu?"

"*Well, I am curious about one thing,*" he admitted. "*How is that you're in the captain's chair?*"

She recalled that he didn't know about Scotty's accident, and that the injured engineer had still been in a bad way the last she'd heard. Had Alvarez managed to get that gravity mace to sickbay in time? And had it made any difference?

"Mister Scott is in sickbay," she explained briefly. "You can get the full story later. . . ."

Once I find out whether Scotty is still alive, she thought.

"Reentering standard orbit," Fisher reported. "Now within transporter range."

Lieutenant Kyle didn't waste any time. On-screen, Sulu and Yaseen dissolved into twin pillars of energized matter that swiftly faded from view, leaving only a sparkling afterimage behind. Palmer shut down the transmission once the two officers had completely dematerialized. An orbital view of Ephrata IV reoccupied the screen.

Confident that they had been safely beamed aboard, Uhura accessed the intercom again.

"Uhura to sickbay. Requesting an update on Mister Scott."

McCoy personally responded over the comm:

"Looks like he's going to pull through, thanks to that glowing green lifesaver you sent our way. Not having to fight that blasted weight made all the difference." The irascible doctor sounded slightly more chipper than before. *"Plus, it turns out that a certain stubborn Scotsman can take almost as much abuse as his precious engines."*

She could believe it. The hard part was going to be keeping Scotty away from engineering long enough to recover. He wasn't one to readily accept being cooped up in sickbay, especially when there were repairs to be made to the ship and its systems. McCoy was probably going to have to put Scotty under restraint.

"And the rest of your patients, Doctor?"

"Enough to keep us hopping, but nothing critical." He coughed loudly. *"Now if I could just shake this damn fever . . . !"*

"Physician, heal thyself," she advised. "Uhura out."

Another weight lifted from her shoulders. At least she didn't have to worry about Scotty anymore.

"I knew Mister Scott was going to make it," Chekov blustered. "He's as sturdy as the *Enterprise* herself."

"So it seems," she agreed.

Palmer adjusted her earpiece. "Transporter room reports that Sulu and Yaseen are aboard, sir."

"Thank you, Lieutenant," Uhura replied. She momentarily considered having them report to sickbay to be checked out, but decided that McCoy and his staff already had their hands full. Sulu or Yaseen could decide for themselves if they needed medical attention. "Have them report to the bridge as soon as they're able."

She wanted to debrief them on what had transpired on Ephrata IV—and what had become of the captain and Mister Spock.

"I have a request of my own," Maxah said, crossing the bridge to join her in the command circle. "When convenient, I would like to be returned to Ephrata so that I can accompany my fellow Ialatl back to our native universe."

"Are you sure you want to do that?" she asked. "I can't imagine you're going to get a warm reception from Sokis and the others." She took his hand, which was smooth and cool to the touch. His smoky aroma teased her nostrils; she was getting used to it. "I'm certain the Federation would be willing to grant you asylum, considering your actions today."

"Your hospitality is most generous," he answered, "but I am still Ialatl. My place is with my people, back where I belong. They may judge me a traitor and apostate now, but I have faith that someday, perhaps soon, they will come to understand why I sided against the Crusade."

"I hope you're right," she said. "But it's your decision."

She didn't attempt to talk him out of it. To be honest, she wasn't sure if she would be willing to abandon Earth and the Federation forever, even if she somehow found herself facing a court-martial.

I'd probably want to go home and face the music, too.

"There is another matter that needs to be attended to," he reminded her. "Once my kin and I have been sent back through the rift to Ialat, you must destroy the portal . . . to prevent the Crusade from launching another campaign against this realm."

She knew he was right, but she was in no hurry to take that step.

"What about Captain Kirk," she asked, "and Mister Spock?"

He withdrew his hand and gazed down at her sadly.

"I fear they may be beyond rescuing."

EIGHTEEN

The throne room of the God-King was easily as impressive as his title. Towering obsidian columns, carved in the heroic likenesses of his regal ancestors, supported a high, vaulted ceiling that made the Sistine Chapel back on Earth seem like a utility closet. Incense flavored the air. Lilting alien melodies emanated from concealed speakers or musicians. Huge bas-reliefs, covering entire walls, depicted the mythic history of the dynasty, beginning with a massive panel that portrayed the first God-King being suckled by a maternal *scrilatyl*, just as Vlisora had mentioned. Carved marble wings, edged with hammered silver, enfolded the divine infant, whose serene countenance lacked the spiny beard of an adult Ialatl. Kirk recalled that this legendary scenario had supposedly played out in a cavern beneath this very temple-slash-palace. He decided it was probably best not to mention that *scrilatyl* Spock had killed in the subway tunnels.

Spock. . . .

His friend's apparent death back at the reflecting pool ached like a raw wound, more painful than any of the bumps and bruises inflicted by the pyramid's guards. Granted, he had not actually seen Spock die, but Vlisora had sent him soaring toward the stratosphere and beyond. It was hard to imagine that Spock could have survived.

She didn't need to do that, he thought angrily. *Spock didn't need to die.*

But mourning his friend, and bringing Vlisora to justice, would have to wait. Kirk forced himself to focus on his current surroundings. Another colossal bas-relief immortalized two shirtless male Ialatl competing against each other in a contest that appeared to involve batting a severed Ialatl head through a hoop. A subsequent panel had the loser being relieved of his own head as well, while the winner offered praise and glory to his ancestors, who were shown beaming down at him from the heavens. Cheering throngs rejoiced in the background.

Gruesome, Kirk thought, *but interesting.* The decorative panels jogged his memory. *Didn't Lasem say something about "trial by ordeal"?*

The throne room was dominated, appropriately enough, by an imposing black throne, inlaid with jade and turquoise, resting atop a tiered dais at the far end of the palatial chamber. Polished stone steps led up to the throne, which was presently unoccupied. A slightly smaller throne, off to the side and one tier below, was possibly intended for the God-King's spouse. It, too, was empty. Kirk guessed it was going to stay that way, unless Jaenab had already acquired a new, less treasonous High Priestess.

Where is Vlisora now, he wondered, *and what is she up to?*

"Prepare yourself, infidel, to face the judgment of the God-King!"

A cadre of Crusaders, decked out in their palace best, shoved Kirk forward toward the throne. The sharpened tip of a gravity-lance prodded him in the back. He could feel its point even through the rumpled native poncho he was still wearing over his Starfleet uniform. Drying brown stains testified to his rough treatment at the hands of the guards. A split lip smarted. His face was bruised and scratched.

Temple guards, along with assorted priestesses and miscellaneous functionaries, watched avidly from the sidelines. A smaller, wingless version of a *scrilatyl* perched on the shoulder of a priestess-in-waiting. It screeched at Kirk as he passed by. He wondered when Jaenab himself was going to make his grand entrance.

"Are we expecting the God-King soon?" he asked.

"Patience, infidel!" the leader of his escorts said sharply. He poked Kirk with the lance again. "All must wait on the God-King's pleasure."

Kirk didn't put up a fight. Unarmed and severely outnumbered, there wasn't much point aside from the possible satisfaction of getting a few licks in before a gravity beam decided things. Besides, as Spock had pointed out earlier, there was something to be said for finally getting a chance to speak face-to-face with the God-King instead of just his minions. If Jaenab was anything like his fanatical worshippers, talking sense to him was not going to be easy, but Kirk needed to make the effort. Maybe words would prove more effective than phasers, fists, or force.

It's worth a try, he thought. *For diplomacy's sake.*

Trumpets blared. An amplified female voice boomed from above:

"All kneel before the God-King!"

The assemblage dropped to their knees save for the guards, who remained alert and at attention. All present, with the exception of Kirk, began chanting a hymn of praise. A spear landed heavily on his shoulders, and Kirk got the message. He knelt down on one knee, sacrificing a degree of dignity in the interest of etiquette. A starship captain often had to show proper respect to alien royalty and dignitaries.

A luminous green spotlight fell upon the empty throne, which began to rise from the dais. Glancing upward, Kirk saw a shining silver figure descending to meet the throne, much as the Crusaders had floated down from the pyramid before. The emerald effulgence poured down from the ceiling through a circular hatch. The base of the ascending throne glowed green as well, as did the obsidian scepter in the figure's hand.

Lifting his gaze further, Kirk got his first good look at the God-King.

Jaenab was a tall, muscular Ialatl who was clearly in the prime of life. Disdaining the severe black tunics that attired his warrior-priests and priestesses, he wore a pleated black kilt with rich green trim. A voluminous cloak was draped over his broad shoulders, and his scaly hide had been buffed and polished until it practically shone. His spiny mane was an even brighter shade of gold than those of his subjects.

As God-Kings went, he certainly looked the part.

And, then of course, there was his crown. A jade circlet, studded with reflective black mirrors, girded his brow. Kirk recalled that, according to Vlisora, it was this very crown that permitted Jaenab to communicate telepathically with every other Ialatl. One of the looming bas-reliefs showed the first God-King, now grown into manhood, forging the crown from his own flesh and bones. Kirk suspected that its true origins had more to do with the long-forgotten science of some vanished civilization.

Like the Oracle on Yonada, he thought. *Or the Controller on Sigma Draconis VI. One culture's advanced technology becoming its descendants' holy relic. . . .*

Descending as from heaven, the God-King met his rising throne about three meters above the dais. The spotlight faded away as he took his place upon the throne, high above his subjects. He held out his scepter and the chanting ceased.

"Rise, my faithful sons and daughters. Your devotion is duly noted."

His retinue climbed to their feet. Kirk took advantage of the opportunity to do the same. His bruised body protested the exertion. Biting down on his lip, he managed to avoid swearing in the God-King's presence.

That might go over poorly, he guessed.

Jaenab gazed down at Kirk from his levitating throne. "This is the infidel from the false universe?"

"It is, Divinity," the commander of the guard stated. "Captured according to your will."

Jaenab nodded. "Show me."

None too gently, the guards tore the blood-stained poncho from Kirk's body, exposing his equally soiled Starfleet uniform. Onlookers gaped at the alien being on display. Jaenab's lip curled in distaste.

If I'd known I was going to be presented to royalty, Kirk thought wryly, *I would've worn my full dress uniform.*

"And his companion?" Jaenab asked. "He was indeed lost to the sky?"

Kirk gathered that the God-King had already been briefed on the night's events. He assumed that the official account was fairly damning where he was concerned. *All the more reason to try to present my side of the story.*

"As reported, Divinity."

Jaenab turned his gaze toward the empty throne below. His brilliant mane darkened noticeably.

"And the *former* High Priestess, whose name shall no longer be spoken?"

"She remains at large, Divinity," the commander

said, shifting his weight uncomfortably. This was clearly a touchy subject. "But the search continues apace. We have already located her stolen flyer, which was found abandoned in an empty garage in the old arts district, and we have reason to believe that she has not gone far. Every *scrilatyl* in the realm is hunting her."

Kirk wasn't sure whether to root for the serpentine trackers or not.

"Redouble your efforts, Crusader. The harlot antipriestess must be brought to judgment, even if it means gazing upon her deceitful countenance once more." A heavy scowl indicated that he was not looking forward to his next encounter with his errant wife. He gladly turned his attention back to Kirk. "So you are the God-Slayer?"

Kirk cringed. *There's that name again. . . .*

"With respect, Divinity, I'm no 'God-Slayer.'"

He took a step toward the throne, earning a warning growl from the nameless commander. "Watch yourself, infidel!"

"The stranger may approach," Jaenab declared. "I confess myself intrigued. I have never met a being from another universe before, let alone so infamous a creature."

"My 'infamy' may have been overstated," Kirk said, being careful not to contradict Jaenab directly. Chances were, the God-King was considered infallible. "I'm simply James T. Kirk, a representative of the United Federation of Planets. We are a peaceful people who pose no threat to Ialat or its ways. Our Prime Directive expressly forbids us from interfering with your culture or religion."

"Is that so?" Jaenab scoffed. "Then how do you explain this?"

He gestured with his scepter at a mammoth bas-relief depicting a former God-King being crowned. The panel revolved in its setting to reveal a large circular viewscreen on the opposite side. The mechanism operated smoothly, without any noise or friction, not unlike the automatic doors back on the *Enterprise.*

Kirk expected images to appear immediately upon the screen, but instead the literally king-sized disk detached itself from the wall and floated above the throne room, where it began spinning like a top. The speed of its rotation caused the disk to blur into a large floating orb, hovering more than three meters overhead. The orb was eye-level with the God-King. Everyone down on the floor had to tilt their heads back to look upon it.

Holographic images appeared within the spinning orb. Recorded earlier, they caught Kirk in the act of fighting back against the Crusaders during the battle beneath the floating pyramid. Caught in the white-hot glare of the searchlight, Kirk fired his phaser at the oncoming guards before resorting to flailing punches and kicks. He had to admit that it didn't look good.

"I can explain—" he began.

"Are you not seen here in open defiance of the

Crusade?" Jaenab interrupted. "Brazenly attempting to trespass upon the Temple of Passage in order to strike at the portal bringing Truth to your worlds?" He pointed his scepter accusingly at Kirk. "Word of your rebellion is already spreading throughout Ialat, encouraging those among us who have recklessly turned away from the Truth."

Just as Vlisora hoped, Kirk realized. It dawned on him that Jaenab could not afford to go easy on him, not after Kirk's very public tussle with the Crusaders. If Vlisora had successfully positioned Kirk as a hero to her fellow dissidents and freethinkers, the God-King needed to crack down on him without delay. *Unless I can convince him otherwise.*

"I was simply acting in self-defense," Kirk insisted. "After being brought to your world against my will."

"Yes, by the devious machinations of the anti-priestess!" Jaenab thundered. "Do you deny that she and her perfidious associates sheltered you, fed you, fought on your behalf, even died for you?"

Kirk received the accusation like a blow to the gut. He remembered Lasem and his allies holding off the Crusade while he escaped from the tunnels. "Died?"

"Defending you from the Truth," Jaenab stated. "A few of my more deluded sons and daughters perished in your unholy cause, while many more await trial for their crimes."

Guilt stabbed Kirk, even though he knew it wasn't

truly his fault. He prayed that Lasem at least had survived the battle on the train tracks.

"None of that was my intention," he argued. "I have no quarrel with you or your people, except with regards to the safety of my own universe."

"Then you are willing to accept the Truth?"

There's the rub, Kirk thought. He knew they were venturing onto dangerous ground. He answered as honestly and cautiously as he could.

"Let me make myself clear. We respect your Truth, and we are open to learning more about it in a free exchange of ideas, but the Federation is home to many beliefs, peoples, planets, and philosophies. There's no guarantee that your Truth will be accepted above all others."

He hoped that would be good enough for the God-King.

He suspected it wouldn't be.

"It is not *our* Truth," Jaenab said vehemently. "It is the only Truth. There is none other."

Kirk went out on a limb. "Perhaps we have our own truths."

"Deceiver!" Jaenab accused him. "You say your Federation wants only peace, but word has only now come to me that, aided by your very starship, the newly adopted people of Ephrata IV have risen up in revolt and taken arms against the Crusade!"

Kirk felt a surge of hope, if not for himself, then for his ship and the imperiled world he had left behind.

"Wait. Are you saying that the Ephratans are no longer under your control?"

"For now, perhaps. But do not deceive yourself into believing that the Crusade can be halted so readily. Even if Ephrata IV is lost to us, we can always begin anew on another of your worlds." He shrugged beneath his royal cloak. "It is no small matter to open a portal between our realms, but with the End of this creation approaching rapidly, we need not put aside resources for the future. Now, in these final days, it is our sacred duty to bring the Truth to as many of your worlds as possible . . . even if we must bankrupt ourselves to do so!"

Kirk believed him. In his experience, the scary thing about people who truly believed that the End was near was that they felt they had nothing to lose. He could easily see Jaenab sparing no expense and effort to "save" the Federation in the name of his unshakable Truth. Whatever was happening on Ephrata IV was just a minor setback. The Crusade was going to keep on coming.

Vlisora was right, he realized. *He needs to be stopped.*

"Sorry. Starfleet isn't going to stand for that . . . and neither am I."

Scandalized gasps greeted Kirk's insolence. Jaenab merely nodded, however, as though he had expected nothing less.

"Your own words condemn you," he said, pronouncing

judgment. He raised his already rotund voice. "Have this 'God-Slayer' taken to a place of execution and have the Truth crush him before the eyes of the world!"

Kirk wasn't sure exactly what that entailed, but he guessed it wasn't going to be pretty. Luckily, he had a better idea.

"Not so fast!" he shouted before the Crusaders could drag him away. He pointed dramatically at the looming bas-relief depicting the ancient contest. "I demand trial by ordeal . . . against the God-King himself!"

The gasps from the court were even louder this time. Even Jaenab was taken aback. It took him a moment to formulate a response.

"That privilege is not for such as you! You are not even Ialatl!"

"But isn't the Crusade all about bringing your Truth and your ways to my people? If your hallowed traditions do not apply to us, then why bother? Why cross to my universe at all?"

Jaenab struggled visibly to find an answer. "Because, you see . . . because . . ."

"The Truth *must* apply to all peoples," Kirk declaimed, turning the God-King's own words against him. "Or it is only *your* Truth, not *the* Truth." He knew he had Jaenab on the spot, so he pressed his point home, making sure the whole throne room was listening. "You say you're all about the old ways and traditions. Prove it. Let your revered ancestors decide my fate . . . or are you afraid that you don't truly know their will as well as you think you do?"

"Divinity!" the captain of the guard cried out. "I volunteer to compete against the infidel in your name! Name me your champion!"

Forget it, Kirk thought. *That doesn't work for me.*

He kept the pressure squarely on the throne. "What's the matter? Is the God-King afraid to face the God-Slayer?"

The spines around Jaenab's face stiffened. They flared outward in fury. He glared down at Kirk from his lofty perch.

"You know not whom you challenge!"

"Then show me!" Kirk dared him. "Show your people that no mere infidel is a match for the true God-King!"

He needed to make it impossible for Jaenab to back down. He prayed he wasn't just tempting immediate retribution instead.

"Divinity," the guard began. "Do not let this foreign creature provoke—"

"Enough!" Jaenab roared. He placed his hands against the sides of his crown. "Let all Ialatl know that the God-King has accepted the infidel's challenge . . . in order to demonstrate now and for all time that the Truth cannot be defeated!"

He twisted a turquoise ring on his scepter, and his throne descended back onto the dais. Jaenab stood, shedding his cumbersome cloak, and handed his crown over to a waiting priestess, who placed it reverently on the seat of the throne. Kirk guessed that it was too precious to risk in any sort of strenuous challenge.

Probably one of a kind, he thought.

"So be it." The God-King posed before his throne with his hands on his hips. He strode down a short flight of steps to confront Kirk on the floor of the throne room. He was at least a foot taller than the captive Starfleet officer, not counting the spines framing his imperious visage. "You will have your trial, 'God-Slayer,' although I suspect the contest will be scarcely worth my time."

He could be right, Kirk thought. It occurred to him to that he might have bitten more than he could chew. Certainly, Jaenab didn't seem all that concerned about the outcome of the match. Kirk couldn't help peeking again at that grisly panel depicting the loser of the trial relinquishing his head. How could he expect to beat the God-King at his own game? He barely knew what he had let himself in for.

"To the arena!" Jaenab declared. "And the judgment of my divine ancestors!"

Kirk hoped he hadn't just outsmarted himself.

NINETEEN

The ball flew at Kirk's face.

He batted it away with his forearm, creating an equal and opposite motion that sent him flying backward into the glowing green bars of the cage. The impact momentarily knocked the breath out of him.

"What's the matter, God-Slayer?" Jaenab taunted. "Are you afraid of a mere ball?"

Kirk's trial by ordeal was under way in the arena, which was located only a few city blocks from the royal temple. He found himself inside a floating geodesic sphere, roughly twenty meters in diameter. The sphere consisted of a lattice of incandescent metal bars that generated a zero-g environment inside the sphere. A huge open-air stadium/amphitheater surrounded the levitating cage. Tens of thousands of cheering Ialatl were packed into the stands, while vigilant Crusaders, armed with lances, stood guard over the scene from elevated watchtowers. Kirk saw little chance of escaping the arena, even if he could somehow squeeze through the narrow gaps between the bars, a feat that would challenge even one of the boneless contortionists of Dloggia Prime.

He grabbed onto a bar to keep from bouncing off the cage back into the weightless interior of the sphere. Taking a moment to get his bearings, he tracked the errant ball as it ricocheted wildly inside the cage as though in an antique pinball machine. The ball was made of a translucent rubbery substance that was currently tinted silver. A polished humanoid skull formed the core of the ball, giving it heft while providing a stark reminder of the stakes. As Kirk understood it, the skull belonged to the last Ialatl who had lost such a trial.

"What does your skull look like, foreigner?" Jaenab kept his own eyes on the ball. "I look forward to seeing it preserved in rubber!"

The God-King clung to the bars on the other side of the arena. It was necessary to occasionally stop and hang on to something in order to control one's movements in zero g. Otherwise, you risked bouncing around as randomly as the ball.

"I prefer my skull with skin on it," Kirk replied. "If that's all right with you."

Both contestants were bare-chested, something Kirk appreciated, considering the sweltering heat of the morning. The match had barely begun and yet he was already dripping with sweat. A silver sash was tied around his waist to indicate that he was the defendant in the trial. Kirk noticed that Jaenab, who wore a satiny black sash, appeared perfectly comfortable in the heat, enjoying a serious hometown advantage. The

God-King was used to this environment, not to mention this challenge.

Shades of the Koon-ut-kal-if-fee, Kirk thought. He flashed back briefly to his life-or-death duel with Spock a few years back. He had been at a serious disadvantage there as well. Too bad McCoy wasn't on hand to whip up another sneaky potion this time around.

A circular copper hoop rotated slowly at the center of the arena, revolving on its axis at a rate of one rotation every two seconds. The levitating hoop also expanded and contracted like a pulsar, going from more than two meters to just forty centimeters in diameter. At its most compact, the ring was too small to permit the ball to pass through. That was not an accident.

The caroming ball came within reach of Kirk, and he redirected it with a backhanded swat. The ball flew toward the spinning hoop, but arrived a second too late; instead of passing through the hoop, it collided with the copper edge, which was now facing it. It bounced off the ring, going back into play.

"Damn," Kirk muttered. "Almost."

The rules of the contest had been explained to him. The object was very simple: bat the ball through the hoop, using any part of your body, while trying to prevent your opponent from doing the same. What made it tricky was the constant rotation and periodic contractions of the goal, along with the total absence of gravity, of course.

Could be worse, Kirk thought. At least there were no edged weapons or fire pits involved, and the lack of gravity did not intimidate him. Zero-g training exercises were mandatory back at the Academy, and he had always excelled at them. Maybe he had a chance at victory, despite the fact that he was playing the God-King's game.

At the moment, the ball was still tinted silver, matching Kirk's sash, but then Jaenab kicked off from the side of the cage to intercept the ball. As he struck it with the flat of his hand, the ball instantly turned as black as his sash, indicating that the next point would be assigned to him, unless Kirk came into contact with the ball first and turned it silver again. The darkened rubber obscured the skull within, but it was still visible through the inky translucence.

The audience roared in approval; there was no question as to whom they were rooting for. The deafening shouts and huzzahs of at least fifty thousand voices cheered the God-King on. Kirk's only rooting section consisted of a few hundred captured rebels who were there to witness his inevitable defeat. A shimmering gravity field confined the shackled prisoners to one small sliver of the stadium, under the scornful gaze of several Crusaders. Unlike their jubilant kin, the downcast prisoners viewed the contest as they would their own executions, which probably weren't far off. Kirk spotted Lasem among them. Apparently, the rebel leader had survived the battle in the tunnels, only to end up in the hands of the Crusade.

At least it's not his skull in the ball, Kirk thought.

That grisly possibility had crossed his mind.

He watched anxiously as the blackened ball zoomed toward the hoop. Jaenab's aim was true, but his timing off; the ball reached the hoop just as it contracted, rendering the goal too small to pass through. The ball rebounded off the twirling ring instead, much to the disappointment of the spectators, who let out a collective groan.

Kirk did not share the crowd's dismay. The winner of the bout was the first player to score four points, one for each finger on an Ialatl hand. Jaenab was already one up on Kirk, having scored an early goal while Kirk was still getting his feet wet. The God-King needed only three more points to win the trial—and condemn Kirk to death.

That was a close one, Kirk thought. *Too close.*

For himself, he had more than one reason for wanting to win. Beyond his own survival, which was incentive enough, he also hoped that a victory would shake Jaenab's divine confidence and perhaps make him more amenable to reason. Or, failing that, there was always the chance that a public defeat might weaken the God-King's standing with his own worshippers, to the detriment of the Crusade.

Kirk could see it happening. He knew from tragic experience just how quickly a populace could turn against a god who proved all too mortal. "Kirok" had learned that the hard way on a planet many light-years from here, and so had poor Miramanee. . . .

He shoved the painful memories away to keep his head in the game. The inky ball was up for grabs, rebounding wildly around the arena. Kirk tried to anticipate where it would bounce next. Spock, no doubt, would have found this a fascinating exercise in spatial geometry and kinetics; Kirk just had to rely on his own eye and instincts. He wished that he had spent more time playing billiards in zero g.

The trick was to think in three dimensions. . . .

He pushed off from the bars, flying through the hot, muggy air on an intercept course with the ball, while keeping one eye on the revolving hoop. If he timed this right, he might be able to propel it through the hoop with a well-aimed kick. All he needed was speed, coordination, and a hefty portion of luck.

Let's even out the score, he thought.

But, before he could shoot for the goal, Jaenab came zooming for the ball as well. His hip deflected the ball, even as his elbow jabbed Kirk sharply in the side. The collision sent them bouncing away from each other. Kirk grunted in pain.

"My apologies, God-Slayer," Jaenab called out insincerely. He smirked at Kirk as they drifted off in different directions. "I fear you got between the ball and me."

"Right," Kirk muttered. His side, which was already

black-and-blue from his rough treatment at the hands of the Crusaders, throbbed unpleasantly. He didn't buy the phony apology for a nanosecond. That wasn't the first time that Jaenab had "accidentally" clipped him in midair. Actual combat was against the rules, but there seemed to be plenty of latitude regarding physical contact, especially where Jaenab was concerned. Kirk seriously doubted whether anyone was likely to call foul on the God-King himself.

Fine, he thought. *If that's how the game is played . . .*

But while he was still recovering from the collision, Jaenab expertly twisted in the air and headed the black ball through the hoop. The audience rejoiced, shouting their lungs out in praise of their God-King. They jumped to their feet and threw their hands in the air. Trumpets blared. Banners bearing a silver *scrilatyl* against a black background waved back and forth. Jaenab threw out his arms in benediction, taking a moment to acknowledge the adoration of his subjects. His golden mane spread out in zero g, the weightless tentacles framing his regal face like an organic halo. Even without his crown, he looked very much the God-King.

A black kite was launched from a watchtower. It rose above the arena to join an equally ebon kite that was already twisting in the breeze. The satiny black kites, which were as large as or larger than an adult Ialatl, served to mark the score. At the moment, there were no silver kites to be seen.

Two to zero, Kirk thought. He saw the game slipping away from him. Jaenab only needed two more goals to win—and claim Kirk's head.

Not good, Kirk thought.

Sensing victory, Jaenab chased after the ball. Deftly using the bars to control his momentum and direction, he met up with the ball and kicked it toward the goal. The audience whooped excitedly, anticipating another score, while, on the opposite side of the hoop, Kirk watched with alarm. The speeding ball was right on track to pass through the goal at exactly the right angle and instant. Defeat was only seconds away. There was no way he could get around the hoop in time to block the shot.

So he dived *through* the hoop instead. Launching himself like a photon torpedo, he flew through the goal with his arms stretched out in front of him. His balled fists slammed into the ball, turning it silver, before it could it pass through the hoop, which contracted behind Kirk, nearly snaring his ankles. The ball zoomed back at Jaenab, who had to duck to avoid getting hit in the face. The ball hit the cage behind him before flying back into the arena.

The audience gasped in surprise. Kirk gathered that diving through the hoop was not a conventional move. *No surprise there,* he thought, considering the risk of being caught in a contraction. *You wouldn't want the hoop to close up on you.*

"You cannot do that!" Jaenab protested. "The ball goes through the hoop, not the players!"

"Is it against the rules?" Kirk asked.

He had realized early on that creative cheating, of the *Kobiyashi Maru* variety, was not really an option here. The Ialatl took their ancient rules and traditions far too seriously for that; any flagrant violations would surely forfeit the game and his head. But that didn't mean he couldn't look for a loophole or two. . . .

"No," Jaenab admitted. "Not technically. But—"

"But nothing." Kirk's momentum carried him across the arena. Open palms met the bars of the cage, absorbing the impact. "Your move."

He took some satisfaction from having dumbfounded Jaenab, but he knew that this trick alone was not enough to win him the match. He was still two points down, and Jaenab was already closing in on victory.

I can't just play defense, Kirk thought. *I need to get some points on the board.*

Now silver in hue, the ball was still ricocheting around the arena. Kirk waited impatiently for an opportunity to send it off in the right direction. Carrying the ball was illegal, so he couldn't just grab it and dive through the goal again. Kirk braced his heels against the bars, calculated the ball's trajectory, and pushed off into empty space.

The more shots I take, he reasoned, *the better my odds of getting one through the goal.*

The ball whooshed toward him. Kirk glanced

about, on guard against another sneak attack from Jaenab, but spotted his opponent floating in midair on the other side of the spinning hoop. Kirk seized the moment and swung at the ball with both fists.

Flesh and bone smacked soundly against the silver ball, which angled off toward the hoop. Tumbling backward, Kirk held his breath as the ball neared the goal. The hoop revolved toward the ball at just the right moment. The copper ring expanded outward and . . .

Goal!

The ball zipped through the hoop right before it started to contract again. The crowd booed furiously and stamped their feet. Thousands of angry spines stiffened throughout the stadium. Irate aliens screeched like *scrilatyl.* A silver kite was grudgingly launched into the sky, joining a pair of black kites.

The score was now two to one.

Still in the God-King's favor, Kirk thought, *but looking better.*

Maybe he was starting to get the hang of this game.

His celebration was short-lived, however. Waiting on the other side of the hoop, Jaenab effortlessly knocked the ball back in the opposite direction. Now as black as a Crusader's tunic, the ball spun through the ring. The thunderous roar of the spectators was like the shock wave from a warp core explosion.

Another kite was released to mark the score. Three to one.

This isn't going my way, Kirk realized. Only one more point stood between him and a final, fatal defeat. He kicked out desperately at the inky ball, but his shot went astray, passing below the twirling hoop. The audience laughed uproariously, letting Kirk know just what they thought of his chances. He saw their point. How could he expect to beat the God-King at this trial? He was just a novice, while Jaenab had probably been training for such contests since he was a youth. *I can't possibly learn the ropes fast enough to eke out a victory. . . .*

"It seems the ancestors do not favor you, God-Slayer!" Jaenab gloated. He took a victory lap around the cage, basking in the exultant cheers of his people. He gleefully taunted Kirk. "Did I neglect to mention that I have never been defeated in the arena?"

Kirk refused to be intimidated.

"Or maybe your adoring subjects just *let* you win," he replied, hurling back some good old-fashioned trash talk. "That ever occur to you?"

Jaenab bristled at the accusation. "My victories have always been my own!"

"Of course they were." Kirk scoffed at the notion. "As if any Ialatl would dare to defeat the God-King!"

Jaenab's tentacles flared. They flushed darkly. Kirk had no idea if there was any merit to his accusations, but he appeared to have struck a nerve. A sly smile lifted Kirk's lips as a slender hope presented itself. Maybe his best strategy was to mess with the God-King's head—and get him angry enough to make a mistake.

Kirk figured he knew just what button to push. . . .

TWENTY

Unlike the floating pyramid, the royal temple was firmly rooted in the ageless bedrock of Ialat. Vlisora led Spock through a murky network of ancient caves, cisterns, and catacombs, using her palm-light to illuminate the way. Stalactites hung from the ceilings of the larger grottos. Hieroglyphics, which bore a familial resemblance to those samples of Ialatl script Spock had glimpsed earlier, were carved into the subterranean stone walls. Empty burial niches might have once held the bones of long-departed ancestors, before the Ialatl turned their sights to the sky instead. As with the abandoned underground rail system, the venerable caverns showed clear signs of neglect. Vermin slithered and scuttled in the shadows. Cobwebs hung like tattered curtains.

A rough-hewn tunnel climbed sharply upward. Spock managed to keep up with Vlisora, despite his recent "death," but found himself fighting gravity once more. He paused to catch his breath, leaning against a natural limestone column. The air was stale and stagnant. No breeze navigated the winding passages. The temperature was chilly even by human standards, which made it uncomfortably cold by his. He shivered and strove to keep his teeth from chattering. He hugged himself to conserve his body warmth.

"Are you quite all right?" Vlisora asked. She turned back toward Spock.

"There is no cause for concern," he assured her. "I require only a moment."

Remorse played across her face. "My apologies once again for subjecting you to such duress. I gambled that your Vulcan physiology could survive the thin air of the upper atmosphere long enough for me to recover you."

"A successful wager," Spock conceded. The stolen flyer had indeed arrived in time to succor him, although his lungs still burned to an uncomfortable degree. A few moments later and he might well have expired. The chill of the upper atmosphere clung to his bones. Frostbite nipped at the tapered points of his ears. Medical treatment was advisable, provided he survived the next few hours. "Although I regret that Captain Kirk remains in jeopardy."

"It was necessary to fake your death in order to escape the Crusade's vigilance," she insisted. "And I do not deny that I contrived to bring about a direct confrontation between your captain and the God-King. I can only pray that Kirk keeps my husband occupied long enough for us to bring sanity back to Ialat."

Spock hoped the same. They resumed their

upward trek through the forgotten catacombs. The scum-coated waters of a forgotten cistern rippled beneath the glow of Vlisora's light. Mold covered the walls, and the stagnant air reeked of mildew. Spock felt the temperature slowly climb as they made their way up from the lower depths. He hoped that meant they were nearing their destination.

"It is fortuitous," he observed, "that these subterranean passages provide covert access to the palace."

"It's an ancient temple," she said wryly. "Of course there are catacombs. And the original caverns are said to predate the earliest structures on this site. Legend has it, after all, that the first God-King was adopted by a mother *scrilatyl* in these very caves, although there is some dispute as to the precise location."

Spock sniffed the air. A rank odor indicated that the catacombs remained populated by the native fauna. He raised Kirk's phaser, which Vlisora had bestowed upon him as a gesture of good faith.

"And are we likely to encounter any *scrilatyl* in the present era?"

"It appears not," Vlisora said. She swept the ceiling with the beam of her palm-light. "Typically, there would be entire flocks of *scrilatyl* roosting in the larger chambers and grottos, but I have yet to spy one." She chuckled bleakly. "I suspect they are all out hunting for me."

"Ironic," Spock noted.

"The ancestors are not without a sense of humor, unlike many of their present worshippers."

A narrow staircase, seemingly hewn from the bedrock, led them to a sealed basalt door that gave abundant evidence of antiquity. Slivers of light, less than the width of a hair, leaked around the edges of the door, suggesting habitation beyond. Vlisora lowered her voice and gestured that Spock should do the same.

"In days of old," she explained, "such hidden passages allowed the God-Kings and their immediate kin to come and go from the temple undetected, so that they might walk among the common folk in disguise, experiencing firsthand their lives and concerns." She smiled slyly. "I suspect they were also used to facilitate clandestine visits to mistresses, courtesans, and secret lovers."

Spock arched an eyebrow. "A rather cynical attitude for a High Priestess."

"I believe in the Truth, Mister Spock, but I am not blind to reality. And I was not always a priestess."

Spock recalled her earlier claim to have once been a pilot, as well as the skill with which she had disabled the flyer's tracking mechanism and landed the royal flyer in the tunnels earlier. He had no trouble accepting that there was far more to Vlisora than merely her religious station.

"My father's first consort was a priestess," he divulged, "and an accomplished biochemist as well." He refrained from mentioning the disgraced half brother that had resulted from that long-ago union; that unfortunate matter was not relevant, nor was it something he was inclined to discuss. "On Vulcan, science and spirituality are not regarded as incompatible, provided they are both governed by logic."

"Your people sound very civilized," Vlisora said wistfully. "Much as mine once were. I wish there was time to discuss your planet further, but, alas, time is not our ally. We must make haste while all eyes are on your captain's contest against my husband."

She had previously alerted Spock to Kirk's "trial by ordeal," which she had learned of via a telepathic broadcast from the God-King's crown. Spock was concerned as to Kirk's chances in the match.

"What is the probability that the captain will prevail against Jaenab?"

"Minimal," she admitted. "But, if the ancestors smile on us, he may buy us time to do what must be done."

Spock was less quick to dismiss the possibility that Kirk might defeat Jaenab. "You may underestimate the captain's chances. In the past, he has demonstrated a singular talent for succeeding against the odds."

She gave him a pensive look. "You have great faith in your captain, don't you?"

"It is not a matter of faith, merely empirical observation. Captain Kirk's resourcefulness in such situations is well documented."

A smile lifted her lips. "Well, let us hope that both faith and empirical observations can be relied upon."

A simple mechanical latch provided another indication of the door's age. Vlisora undid the latch and shoved gently on the door, which proved to be of the revolving variety. It opened easily, without sticking or squeaking, which suggested to Spock that the ancient doorway had been recently lubricated. He suspected that Vlisora had been using the hidden passageway to conduct her subversive activities.

A well-lit corridor could be glimpsed beyond the doorway. She peeked out of the secret passage before signaling Spock that it was safe to proceed. They slipped into a narrow hallway whose palatial décor contrasted sharply with the dismal catacombs they had just traversed. Elaborate plaster bas-reliefs, depicting what Spock assumed were celebrated scenes in Ialatl myth and history, adorned the wall, as well as the opposite side of the door. She rotated it back into its original position and locked it by twisting an inconspicuous piece of sculpture. Once back in place, there was little indication that the door existed at all. Its edges were effectively camouflaged by the hall's elaborate décor.

"An impressive feat of craftsmanship and concealment," he observed. "Your ancestors are to be commended for their ingenuity."

She shrugged. "It has its uses. Even today."

"So it would seem."

She doused her light and glanced about furtively. "Follow me," she whispered. "There are back passages frequented only by the royal family and a few select retainers. If all goes well, we will encounter little traffic."

Trusting her intimate familiarity with the palace and its ways, he trailed behind her. They made brisk progress down the corridor until the sound of racing footsteps, coming from around a corner ahead, forced them to flatten themselves against the wall in hopes of avoiding detection. Spock held his breath to keep from betraying their presence. He felt Vlisora tremble beside him. The spines atop her scalp twitched. Nervous fingers toyed with the pendant around her neck. His own finger lingered on the trigger of his phaser.

"Hurry! Lift your feet, you sluggard!" A pair of Ialatl in civilian attire sprinted through an intersection at the end of the hall, looking straight ahead. "We're going to miss the fall of the God-Slayer!"

The hurried stragglers passed by without spotting them. Their pounding steps receded. Clutching her chest, Vlisora sighed in relief. Spock's acute hearing picked up the rapid beating of her heart.

"Praise the ancestors! I feared they would sound an alarm."

He acknowledged that it had been a close call. "I suggest we move on rather than tempt fate by remaining."

She nodded. Her heartbeat stabilized. "This way."

They encountered no further diversions on their way up a back stairway that led to a curtained archway. Pulling back the curtain, if only by a few centimeters, revealed an elevated gallery that looked out upon a truly grandiose throne room. Spock took due note of the chamber's manifest size and splendor. There were majestic temples and monuments on Vulcan that suffered by comparison to the God-King's lair.

Vlisora quietly nudged Spock and pointed out a jade circlet resting upon a large obsidian throne. He understood that this was the God-King's celebrated crown. He spared a moment to speculate on the unknown technology that allowed the crown to radiate Jaenab's thoughts to his subjects.

Possibly a psionic resonator, such as the fabled Stone of Gol?

The Crown was guarded by precisely nine Crusaders armed with gravity-lances. Although standing dutifully at their posts, the men were all captivated by the holographic images playing out within a floating orb, where Captain Kirk could be seen competing against the God-King inside a glowing geodesic sphere. Floating in zero g, Kirk chased after a caroming silver ball in order to survive his trial by ordeal, only to be blindsided by Jaenab, who savagely rammed his elbow into Kirk's side. The guards in the throne room cheered the brutal attack on the infidel, even though Spock found it both distasteful and unsporting. He couldn't help noticing that Kirk already appeared bruised and beaten-up. The Crusade had clearly not been gentle with him.

Despite the urgency of his own situation, he was drawn to the contest on the screen as well. According to Vlisora, Kirk's life might well depend on the outcome of this match. He found it difficult to look away.

Jim. . . .

"We can aid him best by fulfilling our own role in this drama," Vlisora whispered. "Perhaps there is still time to make a difference."

Her logic could not be faulted. He forced himself to look away from the orb and focused on the task at hand.

Intent on the televised contest between Kirk and their God-King, the guards failed to note Spock and Vlisora spying on them from the gallery, yet the Crusaders' presence undeniably complicated their mission. Spock inspected his phaser. A blinking indicator revealed that the weapon's power supply was nearly exhausted, thanks to its extensive use by both Kirk and Vlisora. Spock calculated that its charge would not survive an extended battle.

He would have to make every shot count.

Vlisora stared avidly at the crown on the throne, then lifted her gaze to the vaulted ceiling high above them. She nudged him again, backing away from the gallery.

"Come," she said. "I have an idea."

They crept up another stairwell to the floor directly above the throne room, which was smaller and less opulent by several orders of magnitude. Spock could not decipher the labels and markings on the walls, but he quickly deduced that this level of the temple was devoted to more utilitarian purposes, such as maintenance and technical support. Automated machinery hummed behind closed doors. Spock was impressed that the High Priestess was even familiar with this part of the palace.

Moving stealthily, Vlisora approached a closed door at the end of the hall. She signaled Spock to position himself to one side of the door. Her fingers made a pinching motion.

Spock grasped her intent.

"Help!" she cried out, pounding on the door. "The traitor priestess is here! Seize her!"

The door slid open. An Ialatl technician, wearing a copper tunic, rushed out of the chamber, intent on capturing Vlisora. His black eyes widened in surprise at the sight of the fugitive herself standing right in front of him. His jaw dropped, followed by his entire body as Spock came up behind him and applied a nerve pinch to his shoulder. The man collapsed at their feet.

"An efficient use of your own notoriety," Spock complimented Vlisora. He was glad not to have required his phaser to subdue the unlucky technician. He needed to conserve its charge.

"One makes do with what one has," she said, shrugging. She bent to take hold of the unconscious Ialatl's arms. "Now help me drag him out of sight."

Taking the man's legs, he assisted Vlisora in pulling their victim into the chamber ahead, which proved to be a control room of some variety. A large steel-and-glass projector, whose exotic design displayed the same unfamiliar technology previously employed by the Crusade, hung from the ceiling, its bottom lens aimed at a sealed circular hatchway directly beneath it. A solitary workstation was wedged in a corner. A viewscreen on the console was presently tuned to the grueling trial under way in the arena. The resident technician had evidently been monitoring the bout as well.

Spock glanced around, curious as to the purpose of the chamber.

"This control room is used to stage the God-King's entrances when he holds court in the throne room below." Vlisora explained how Jaenab typically descended to his throne, which rose to meet him. She pointed out the sophisticated apparatus mounted on the ceiling of the control room. "We may be able to employ that gravity projector to our own advantage."

She closed and barred the door before sitting down at the console. So far, their altercation had not attracted any attention, probably because the automated systems on this level had been largely left to tend to themselves while their operators joined the rest of Ialat in witnessing the historic contest in the arena, but Spock knew they could not count on being left to their own devices indefinitely. He stepped away from the hatchway in the floor as it quietly slid open, offering a view of the obsidian throne several meters below. The God-King's crown remained undisturbed on its cushioned seat.

She glanced at him.

"I believe your people have a saying about the mountain coming to Muhammad. . . ."

She activated the gravity projector. An incandescent emerald spotlight streamed down through the open hatch to envelop the throne, which began to ascend toward them.

"That is a *human* saying," Spock corrected her, "but I see its relevance."

Distracted by the contest in the orb, it took the guards in the throne room a moment to notice that the throne—and the crown—were leaving them behind. But the glow from the beam, reflected on the polished floors and pillars, quickly caught their attention.

"The crown!" a frantic Crusader shouted. "It is being stolen!"

The guards mobilized swiftly, aiming their lances at the hatchway above. Spock peered cautiously down at them, keeping his head low and his phaser drawn. He fired first, stunning two men before they could unleash their own weapons. Concentration, and a hint of worry, was etched on his face. Although effective, the shots further depleted his phaser's waning charge.

"I suggest you deactivate their weapons as you did before," he advised Vlisora. "And with all due speed."

"I'm trying!" She spun the rings on her pendant, without noticeable results. "Kinless bastards! They've found a way to strip me of my override privileges!"

A logical precaution, Spock admitted. *Albeit inconvenient for our purposes.*

Down on the floor of the throne room, the desperate Crusaders took cover behind looming pillars while firing back at the hatch with tightly focused gravity beams. Spock ducked his head back to avoid being tagged by one of the beams. Being yanked down to the floor far below would have a significantly negative impact on their cause, not to mention his personal well-being. Even at normal gravity, a fall from such a height might prove terminal.

He did not wish to calculate the additional impact of supergravity.

On the positive side of the equation, the guards were hampered by their understandable reluctance to risk damaging the crown, which continued to ascend toward the waiting hatch. Spock assumed that it was concern for the relic's safety that prevented the guards from pulling the entire ceiling out from under Vlisora and him; no doubt the men feared sending both throne and crown crashing to floor—and burying the crown beneath a sizable quantity of superheavy debris.

Spock doubted the God-King would look kindly on such an accident. He took full advantage of the Crusaders' handicap by keeping the rising throne between himself and his attackers.

Nevertheless, a few brave Crusaders attempted to halt the throne's ascent by snagging it with their own personal gravity beams. Lambent rays of green, firing up from multiple directions, converged on the throne like cables clinging to an antiquated hot-air balloon out of Earth's early attempts to achieve flight. But the guards' beams fought a losing battle against the more powerful pull of the hijacked gravity projector. The throne kept rising, slowly but steadily.

"Faster!" Vlisora urged their prize. She dialed up the projector's power to combat the pull of the Crusaders' beams. Its verdant light increased in intensity. "Come! Rise!"

The guards fanned out across the floor, risking Spock's phaser blasts, to try to get a clear shot at Spock. His own weapon's power was all but gone. An indicator light flashed ominously. A sapphire beam sputtered and died.

"My phaser has exhausted its charge," Spock informed Vlisora. "Any assistance you could provide would prove most useful at this juncture."

"Do not fear!" she called back. "This time I shall not abandon you!"

Setting the projector controls on automatic, she hurried to join Spock at the edge of the circular hatch.

She threw out her gloved hand, splaying all four fingers outward. The delicate black mesh of her glove glowed green as an emerald beam spread out from her fingers in a wide-dispersal pattern. An irritating whine accompanied the beam.

Her radiant broadside met the oncoming beams from the Crusaders' lances, blocking them. Gravitational fluxes crackled and flared where the rays collided; Vlisora had to shield her eyes from the blinding flashes. Spock's inner eyelids protected his own vision. Feedback caused the rebel priestess's glove to overheat. Its greenish aura shifted toward red. She winced and bit down on her lip. The keening of the glove grew sharp enough to shatter crystal.

"Your hand . . ." Spock said.

She held up her other hand to forestall his protests. "I can endure this. I have no choice."

The throne bearing the crown was now less than a meter from the hatch, bringing the relic nearly within reach. Smoke rose from the sizzling glove. Tears leaked from her eyes, but she did not stop repelling the Crusaders' hostile gravity beams. The guards raged in frustration, hurling obscene insults at the former priestess. Spock wondered what hurt her more, the searing glove or the hatred of her kind.

"Only a few more moments," she whispered through the pain. "Almost there . . ."

The throne bumped into the ceiling, its solid mass shielding the hatchway from a barrage of enemy beams. Vlisora cut off her own beam and staggered backward, lowering her arm. Gasping, she peeled the searing mesh from her hand. Its red-hot touch had burned a charred black pattern into her silver skin. Her usual smoky odor took on a harsher edge.

At least the mesh was not fused to her hand, Spock thought. *That might have been far worse.*

But the crown was now within reach.

"Take it!" she said urgently. "Now is our chance!"

She had suffered much to reach this moment. Spock did not intend to let her agony go to waste. He reached down and snatched the crown from the throne. Vlisora smiled tightly.

"We did it."

Crown in hand, Spock scrutinized her injured hand with concern. He found himself actually regretting the absence of Dr. McCoy.

"You require medical attention."

"Later, perhaps," she said. "Do not concern yourself with me. You know what you have to do."

Spock nodded.

The crown was the key. According to Vlisora, it was a conduit into the mind of the God-King and all his worshippers. Spock needed to meld with it, in the hopes that Vulcan logic and rationality could provide an antidote to the unreasoning fanaticism of the Crusade.

It was a drastic, even desperate, tactic, but not without a certain logic of its own. Spock was resolved to attempt the meld for the sake of his captain—and perhaps his universe. The Prime Directive did not require that the Federation succumb to the Crusade.

"Open up!" A fist pounded on the door to the control room. Spock heard more Crusaders approaching. "Open in the name of the Truth!"

"Now!" Vlisora pleaded. "Before it is too late!"

Spock lifted the crown.

TWENTY-ONE

The ball sped past Kirk.

He ignored it.

Trying to beat Jaenab at his own game, Kirk realized, was like trying to beat Spock at three-dimensional chess. Your only chance of winning was to do something completely unexpected.

Like this, he thought.

He dived straight at the hoop again, but this time, instead of flying through it, he grabbed onto the copper ring with both hands. Clinging weightless to the hoop, he waited until it expanded to its maximum circumference, then swung inside the ring itself and braced his feet firmly against the bottom of the hoop while simultaneously pushing back against its upper half. The hoop tried to contract, but, positioned squarely inside it, Kirk held it open with his straining arms and legs. The steady rotation of the hoop was dizzying, but he had a strong stomach; he fought back against any creeping disorientation or nausea. With his arms and legs extended, his battered body filled the interior of the ring.

No way was the ball getting past him now.

The teeming audience booed and jeered at him.

So did Jaenab.

"Heathen! Is there no end to your perversions of our sacred traditions?" His spines quivered furiously. "If you think such a low, delaying ploy will deliver you, then you are even more deluded than I previously believed!"

He fired an inky black ball at the goal. The ball struck Kirk in the chest, turning silver as it bounced back toward Jaenab. The impact knocked the breath out of Kirk but failed to dislodge him from the hoop. He tightened his grip on the ring and cautiously shifted his feet to ensure their purchase.

"Is that the best you can do?" Kirk mocked Jaenab. "I would have thought the God-King would hit with a little more *oomph*!"

Spectators gasped at his blasphemy. Scandalized Crusaders and Ialatl called for his head. The skull inside the translucent silver ball grinned insolently. Kirk liked to think it was on his side.

"Do not tempt me, God-Slayer!" Jaenab fulminated. "Remove yourself from the goal or feel the full force of my wrath!"

Kirk stayed where he was. "Bring it on."

"So be it!"

Jaenab took Kirk at his word. Ricocheting around the glowing green cage, he fired the solid rubber ball at Kirk from every direction. It buffeted him again and again, slamming against his face, back, and gut, but Kirk took the punishment. Blood leaked from his nose, drifting away weightlessly. Fresh bruises mottled his abused face and chest. His limbs ached from the strain of holding the hoop open. Sweat poured from his skin, misting around him.

"Abandon this craven stalling!" Jaenab demanded. "In the name of the ancestors!"

"How about we let the ancestors make up their own minds?" Kirk said. "I don't know about you, but I'm just getting started."

Visibly frustrated, the God-King tried to spike the ball between Kirk's legs, but, in brushing against Kirk, the ball turned silver, scoring the point for Kirk instead. A second silver kite rose above the arena.

Three to two, Kirk thought. *Better.*

Fuming, Jaenab batted the ball straight into Kirk's face, knocking his head back. Kirk felt his grip start to loosen, but he shook off the blow and steadied himself inside the ring. He glared defiantly back at Jaenab, bracing himself for the ball's inevitable return. This really was a trial by ordeal now, and the only question was what would last longer: his body or Jaenab's self-control.

"Thanks for the point." Kirk brazenly provoked the God-King. "I couldn't have done it without you."

Scowling, Jaenab paused to catch his breath. His silver scales glistened wetly; Kirk had gotten him to work up a sweat.

"Your endurance does you credit, God-Slayer, but

you cannot prevail. Your foolish intransigence merely prolongs your punishment . . . and delays the inevitable."

I don't have to keep this up forever, Kirk thought. *I just have to get you mad enough to make a careless mistake.*

"What's your hurry? I've got all day."

His sarcastic tone got under Jaenab's skin, as intended.

"Cease this travesty at once! Play like an Ialatl!"

Kirk judged that it was time to hit below the belt.

"Says the God-King who couldn't even hold on to his own wife and High Priestess! What happened? Did she finally see past your supposed 'divinity' to the weak and fallible mortal you really are? The one who can't even admit that his people always let him win?"

Jaenab's golden spines tarnished with rage. He shook his fist at Kirk.

"Silence! Do not even speak of her!"

He bounced the ball off Kirk's face once more. Kirk's nose crunched noisily. His teeth were loose. He spat out a mouthful of blood that swirled in zero g like a crimson nebula.

"You didn't even have a clue, did you? That your own wife didn't believe in you anymore? That she chose *me* to overthrow you!"

Jaenab was trembling in rage now. His spines writhed angrily.

"Still your blasphemous tongue!"

Kirk guessed that nobody had ever spoken to the God-King this way before. Maybe it was time someone finally did.

"Make me!"

Jaenab screeched like an enraged *scrilatyl*. He flew at Kirk with his hands stretched out to throttle the maddening heretic. Kirk's eyes narrowed as he watched the God-King rocket toward him. His body tensed, poised for action. He needed to time this right, and he had only one chance to pull it off.

Here he comes. Ready, set . . . go!

At the last minute, he sprang out of the way. No longer held open by Kirk's straining muscles, the hoop contracted abruptly, catching Jaenab as he soared through the ring after Kirk. It closed about his torso, squeezing him like a copper-hued python. Scaly silver skin was no match for the pressure. Ribs cracked audibly. The God-King howled in agony.

All around the stadium, the stunned audience fell silent. A shocked hush descended.

How about that? Kirk thought. *It worked!*

The hoop expanded outward, momentarily relieving the pressure on Jaenab, who writhed in place at the empty center of the revolving ring. He reached weakly for something to push against, in order to propel himself away from the hoop before it contracted again, but found himself floating helplessly in zero g, too badly hurt to save himself.

"Help," he whispered.

Kirk responded without hesitation. Caroming off the bars of the cage, he grabbed Jaenab as he flew through the open hoop one more time, only a heartbeat before it contracted again. Kirk's momentum carried both men to safety. He held on to the God-King's sash, so that they wouldn't end up on opposite sides of the arena again.

They needed to talk.

"Listen to me," Kirk said urgently. "You can end this—"

Jaenab was obviously too hurt to keep on playing. He was curled in a fetal position, clutching his ribs. He coughed painfully, a silvery liquid spraying from his lips. It floated like mercury across the open space. His spines were pale and flaccid. He moaned in disbelief.

"No, this cannot be. . . ."

By now, the Crusaders were reacting to this shocking turn of events. "The God-King is injured!" a guard cried out in alarm. "Open the arena! The trial must be called off!"

"*No!*" Jaenab mustered the strength to countermand the guard's orders. Despite his grievous injuries, he hung on to his resolve. "I am the God-King! I shall not forfeit the match!"

Frantic Crusaders, who were rushing to his aid, held back uncertainly, torn between rescuing their God-King and obeying his command. Legions of spectators looked on speechlessly. Cheers erupted from the shackled prisoners, who were brutally driven to the ground by gravity beams in response. Nobody knew what to do next.

Except for Kirk.

Lowering his voice, he offered Jaenab a chance to save face in front of his people.

"Let me score one more point and we'll call it a draw. You can tell your people that the ancestors chose peace and compromise over a decisive victory or defeat."

Kirk prayed Jaenab was listening. In the past, he had often found that offering mercy to vanquished foes was the key to preventing future conflicts. He could only hope that would be the case this time as well. Maybe there was still a chance to demonstrate to Jaenab and the Crusade that the Federation did not pose a threat to their way of life. Sometimes actions spoke louder than words.

"Never!" Jaenab spat. Angry and in pain, he seemed in no mood to listen to reason. "The Truth cannot be compromised! The ancestors will not allow it!"

"Are you absolutely sure of that?" Kirk asked. "We both know that you're in no shape to stop me from scoring two more points anytime I want. So if I win this trial by ordeal, what does that say about the will of the ancestors . . . and your unerring grasp of the Truth?"

"I . . . I . ." Jaenab was at a loss for words, unable to refute Kirk's arguments. For the first time, Kirk saw a flicker of doubt in the God-King's eyes.

But only a flicker.

Jaenab's face and voice hardened. "You try to trick me, but I will not succumb to your lies. I will die for the Truth . . . and so will you!"

Kirk's heart sank. Glancing around, he saw dozens of Crusaders poised tensely outside the arena, their weapons aimed at Kirk. He suspected that he would not long survive Jaenab's willing martyrdom. Mercy, it appeared, was not enough to sway the God-King.

He wondered if anything could.

TWENTY-TWO

Spock contemplated the God-King's crown.

To his slight surprise, it felt like ordinary jade. He detected no unusual psychic energies from the artifact. A troubling possibility occurred to him: What if the relic was merely what humans termed a red herring? What if Jaenab's telepathic capacity was instead a genetic quirk inherent in his lineage?

In that case, he thought, *our efforts to secure the crown will have been pointless.*

"Hurry!" Vlisora urged him. She stood nearby, cradling her injured hand. Temple guards pounded on the locked door of the control room, which was unlikely to withstand a sustained assault. She barricaded the door with her own body. "Use the crown!"

That haste was imperative could not be denied. If he was going to carry out their plan, and attempt to mind-meld with Jaenab by means of the crown, he needed to do so promptly. They were unlikely to get a second chance.

Nevertheless, he experienced a moment of trepidation. Even an ordinary meld, if there could be said to be such a thing, was not something to embark upon lightly. To fully merge one's mind and thoughts with another's, even on the most superficial level, was a profoundly intimate act that demanded a dangerous lowering of personal barriers. The risk of losing one's own identity and emotional control was always present, and how much more so, perhaps, when attempting the meld via an unknown piece of alien technology?

"Step away from the door!" an authoritative voice shouted through the door. "We're coming through!"

An invasive green light, coming from the hall outside, penetrated the edges of the door. Vlisora backed away from the light as the metal began to buckle, crumpling under its own weight. On the floor nearby, the unconscious technician stirred uneasily. Vlisora kept one eye on him as she also stared at the door in alarm. Her rampant spines were on full alert.

"Stay back!" she yelled. "Or we'll destroy the crown!"

Spock was uncertain if she was bluffing, but the threat appeared to give their assailants pause. The green light vanished, followed by loud, muffled discussions in the hallway. If nothing else, the guards seemed to be in no hurry to risk the loss of the relic. Spock wondered how much time the threat had bought them.

Enough?

"Now," Vlisora whispered. Gold-rimmed eyes entreated him. "While they debate their next move."

Spock knew he could delay no longer. He had come too far to falter now. Overcoming his doubts and apprehension, he placed the crown on his brow. All at once, something sparked within the relic. Spock *felt* something: a connection forming between his mind and the crown.

Not a red herring after all, then.

He closed his eyes and placed the fingers of both hands gently against the sides of the crown. A tingling sensation, not unlike static electricity, greeted his touch. An intangible current flowed from the crown into his nervous system and vice versa. He cautiously opened his own mind and reached out as he would to another living being. . . .

"My mind to your mind. My thoughts to your thoughts."

The ancient mantra focused and settled him, easing what was to come. His consciousness spread from his brain to his fingertips to the crown to . . .

Ialatl.

A vast ocean of alien minds stretched before him, both breathtaking and terrifying in its churning immensity. He was poised at the shore of the ocean, the essences of billions of sentient beings lapping against him, creating a psychic undertow that was almost impossible to resist. His uprooted mind quailed at drawing any nearer the ocean, for fear of being swallowed up by its unfathomable depths forever. What training and/or natural gifts must the God-Kings of Ialat possess to be able to set their thoughts a-sail upon that turbulent ocean without going under?

He dared not emulate their feat. He could not risk spreading his consciousness that thin. Safer instead to concentrate on one specific mind with a particular affinity to the crown.

Focus.

Wading cautiously into the cerebral ocean, he sifted through its myriad currents in search of the right Ialatl. It seemed an almost hopeless task until he detected a distinct psychic imprint of the crown's illustrious owner. He seized that connection and did not let go.

"My mind to your mind. . . ."

The ocean swirled around him, rendering him briefly dizzy and disoriented, and he suddenly found himself seeing through a stranger's eyes. His ribs throbbed in agony as he floated helplessly inside the arena. Kirk was there as well, hovering nearby. He knew the cunning human was responsible for his woe.

He felt an overpowering urge to strike down the infidel and defend the timeless sanctity of the Truth. He was the God-King. It was his sacred duty and destiny to deliver both universes from lies and confusion, bringing all into harmony so that they might be reborn in the new Creation to come. To do otherwise was illogical.

A flood of utter certainty washed over Spock. There was no doubt, no unsettling dilemmas. For perhaps the first time in life, he felt no division within him, no perpetual conflict between his Vulcan and human heritages. His course was certain, his place in the universe preordained. The Truth brought clarity and peace of mind, as well as a better understanding of the need for the Crusade. Questions, diversity, alternatives, and error could not be tolerated. There could be only one Truth, eternal, immutable. . . .

No, Spock thought. *That is not the Vulcan way. That is not the Federation. That is not Starfleet.*

Caught in the meld, it was difficult to distinguish between his thoughts and Jaenab's. He fought back against the seductive appeal of the Truth's soothing certainty, calling upon not just cold, impersonal logic but also his individual life and experiences, both aboard the *Enterprise* and across the galaxy. Clinging to his own identity and purpose, he reached back to the memories and discoveries that shaped him:

Vulcan, many years ago. Only six solar cycles old, Spock observes his mother and father as they share a breakfast on a patio outside their home on the family estate. It is early in the morning, the scorching yellow sun not yet high in the sky. He struggles to find the logic behind his parents' union, and, by extension, his own existence.

They are so very different. His mother: warm and tender and human. His father: reserved and stoic and Vulcan. They appear to have nothing in common.

Even as he watches, his mother laughs and teases her husband, who sighs and shakes his head at her baffling emotionality. Even their blood was intrinsically at odds. Green and copper-based for him; disturbingly red and iron-based for her. Spock's own conception defies probability.

They are clearly opposites. Vulcan and human. Logic and emotion. Even male and female. By all logic, they should not be able to coexist, let alone thrive together side-by-side. They should be like matter and antimatter, unable to come together without explosively destructive results. Any other conclusion was illogical.

And yet . . . their verifiable differences only seemed to strengthen the bond between them, which suggested that the intersection of opposites, neither yielding to the other, could sometimes result in unexpected combinations and possibilities, as demonstrated by the indisputable fact of a boy named Spock. . . .

No, the Truth argued. That was not possible. Difference led only to dissent and turmoil and extinction. When disparate views clashed, only one could prevail or else there was chaos. One could believe in only one Truth—or nothing at all.

Not so, Spock countered. One must simply be content with the knowledge that one could not know everything—and be open to the possibility that creation itself was far too large to be encompassed by a single "Truth."

Granted, this could be both challenging and arduous, as he knew better than most. He had spent his entire life grappling with the conflicts posed by his mixed heritage. In truth, he sometimes contemplated resolving the conflict by surrendering to the ancient discipline of *Kolinahr*. Fully embracing the Vulcan way, to the exclusion of all others, might well be the only way that he would ever find peace.

But, he considered, another fundamental Vulcan principle, which had guided him all his days, encouraged him to keep exploring other possibilities. It was the same principle that helped hold the Federation together and sent starships into space to seek out new life and new civilizations, not to conquer or convert, but to learn and share. It was a conviction—a belief—that the new and different was not to be feared, but seen as opportunities for growth and progress, as well as evidence of creation's endless wonder and complexity:

Infinite diversity in infinite combinations.

Spock felt the Truth retreat. . . .

In the arena, Jaenab's eyes opened in revelation. A look of wonder came over his face, replacing the stony conviction that had hardened it before. Tendrils drifted benignly around his silver visage.

"By the ancestors," he whispered. "Could it be that I was mistaken? Did I misread the Truth?"

He looked over at Kirk, who was puzzled by the God-King's sudden change of heart. He sensed somehow that this was not his doing, or at least not entirely. Something else had broken down Jaenab's divine self-assurance.

But what?

Jaenab peered at Kirk, as though seeing him for the first time. "You are not a God-Slayer. You are . . . Jim."

A familiar cadence sparked a flash of recognition. Hope flared inside Kirk. Could it be . . . ?

"Spock?"

Jaenab nodded. "He is with me. In my soul. In my crown. His mind to my mind. His thoughts to my thoughts—"

A *mind-meld,* Kirk realized. An overwhelming wave of relief washed over him. He didn't know how, but Spock was obviously still alive. *We didn't lose him after all.*

"He is slipping away from me now," Jaenab murmured. He placed a hand to his head. "Our hearts and minds are parting, and yet . . ." He looked about him in bewilderment. "Perhaps the Crusade is not . . . logical?"

"That's what we've been trying to tell you," Kirk said. "You just needed to listen."

The Crusaders surrounding the cage had heard enough. "The God-King is delirious! We must see to him at once . . . and destroy the infidel!"

"No!" Jaenab commanded. "No harm shall come to him!"

"But, Divinity, you are not well! You know not what you are saying!"

Wincing, Jaenab uncurled himself from his fetal position. His voice rang out with surprising strength.

"I am still the God-King and my word is Truth! I declare this trial over and our visitor innocent of all charges." He grasped Kirk's hand. "Now open this cage and see to our injuries!"

TWENTY-THREE

The throne room bore few scars from the heated battle for the crown only a few hours earlier. Spock had obviously been careful with his phaser blasts, targeting only Crusaders and not the chamber's majestic décor. The towering pillars and colossal bas-reliefs appeared undamaged, looking much as they had when Kirk had last visited the premises.

But the circumstances are hugely improved, he noted.

The God-King sat once more upon his throne, which rested securely on its dais. His crown abided on his brow, which was furrowed in concentration. His face bore a pensive, less imperious expression. His beard of spiny tentacles was at rest. Cloak and scepter attested to his authority. His black eyes held a distant gaze.

Kirk, Spock, and Vlisora looked on as Jaenab shared his thoughts with all Ialatl. Prompt medical attention had alleviated their various injuries, as well as the God-King's cracked ribs. The palace guard stood at attention, taking no action against the former fugitives. It was a welcome change.

"It is done," Jaenab declared. His gaze returned to the throne room, finding Kirk and the others. He lifted the crown from his head. "The Crusade has been recalled. All rebel prisoners are to be pardoned. The High Priestess has been restored to her former glory and privileges." He looked thoughtfully at Vlisora, perhaps wondering if their more intimate relationship could be restored as well. "Furthermore, I have informed the people that I will be withdrawing from public life to seek a period of contemplation for a time, the better to ponder certain matters." He turned his gaze toward Kirk and Spock. "I have been given much to think about."

"The opportunity to think deeply without distractions is a gift to be envied," Spock said. "May your meditations be fruitful."

"If the ancestors grant me wisdom and an open mind," Jaenab said. "In the interim, I have decreed that the High Priestess is to rule in my name."

"Divinity?" Vlisora was taken aback. "You cannot be serious. Only hours ago I was denounced as a traitor to the realm. Surely there must be another better suited to the task."

"I can think of no one better," Jaenab replied. "You have proven to be the conscience of the throne, and to be willing to cast aside everything, even your own safety and reputation, for the sake of Ialat."

He stepped down from his throne, wincing slightly, and crossed the floor to them. Bandages were wrapped tightly around his injured torso. He placed his cloak upon her shoulders and handed her the scepter. She accepted them with obvious trepidation.

"But how can you truly know that I am up to the challenge? The responsibility is great. . . ."

"You'll do fine," Kirk predicted. "Like the man said, you've already proved that you'll go to any lengths for your people."

She regarded him with surprise. "You can say that, even after I used and betrayed you?"

"All's well that ends well," he said with a shrug, inclined to let bygones be bygones. "Sometimes a leader needs to make hard choices. Believe me, I know."

He figured he had some explaining to do to Starfleet where the Prime Directive was concerned, but the fact that Ephrata had been liberated, and a full-scale invasion from the Crusade had been averted, would surely weigh in his favor, no pun intended. Besides, Vlisora had been the true mastermind behind recent events, which made her ascension more of an internal matter than a case of Starfleet interference. He and Spock had merely been roped into a resistance movement that had already been under way before they'd even set foot on Ialat.

At least that was his story, and he was going to stick to it.

"It will not be easy." She fumbled awkwardly with the scepter, rolling it over and over in her shaking hands. "A social convulsion such as the Crusade cannot be rolled back overnight. And the God-King was not alone in his views—or militant devotion to the Truth." She cast an apologetic look at her husband for speaking so bluntly. "Many Ialatl will not readily comprehend this change in direction. It may be hard for them to accept."

Kirk was concerned. What if the Crusaders did not accept Vlisora or the end of their holy war? "Is there any chance of a coup? Or an uprising?"

"That is unlikely to occur," Jaenab said confidently. "The people will accept my pronouncements, even if they do not fully understand at first."

"He is right," she agreed. "Our age-old reverence for the institution of the God-King works to our favor in this respect. His decrees will not be challenged, although they will surely be controversial. It will take time and patience to convince our fellow Ialatl of the wisdom of our present course . . . and steer them toward a more generous and inclusive interpretation of the Truth. One that looks to the future, as opposed to preparing for the End."

Kirk felt optimistic about their prospects. "Progress takes time, but it usually gets its way. The history of my own planet proves that."

"For now, I am simply happy to be on the same path as my husband again." She took Jaenab's hand, eliciting a surprised reaction from the humbled God-King, but he did not let go. She gave him a hopeful look. "Even roads that diverge sharply can sometimes find their way back to each other, is that not so?"

He smiled back at her. "So the ancestors said."

Kirk wished them luck. It was none of his business, but it was nice to think that the couple might be able to overcome the betrayals and divisiveness that had come between them. He was a big fan of happy endings.

Spock, naturally, had less sentimental matters on his mind.

"And what of the portal?" he asked.

A rueful look came over her face. "I fear I must close the portal for now. My people need time to adjust to the reality of another, very different universe . . . and to recover from the excesses of the Crusade."

"And how long do you think that might take?" Kirk asked.

"Who can say?" she replied. "Years. Decades. Maybe even centuries. Enlightenment cannot be achieved in the wink of an eye, especially after all that has come before. But someday, perhaps, when we are ready, Ialat can make contact with your universe again—and we can truly share our truths with each other." She allowed herself a wistful smile. "Before the end of creation, I hope."

Kirk nodded. "I understand."

To be honest, he could live with the portal being shut down for the immediate future, despite the tempting prospect of exploring a whole new universe. The safety of the quadrant took priority.

"I can assure you that the Federation will always be ready to establish peaceful diplomatic relations with Ialat," he said, "no matter how far in the future that might be."

"On behalf of my people, I look forward to that day," the God-King replied. "When the time is right for both our realms."

"In the meantime," Kirk pointed out, "there is one small matter to attend to. Can I ask that, before you shut down the portal, you send us home first?"

Vlisora laughed. The royal cloak fit her well.

"I think that can be arranged."

TWENTY-FOUR

"Your chair, Captain."

Uhura surrendered the captain's seat to Kirk as he strode back onto the bridge, accompanied by Spock, who assumed his customary place at the science station. All seemed well at first glance. The *Enterprise* remained in orbit around Ephrata IV, which spun serenely on the viewscreen.

"Thank you, Lieutenant. I appreciate your holding down the fort for me."

He'd already been briefed, at least in broad strokes, on what had transpired during his involuntary sojourn on Ialat. From the sound of things, Uhura had done an exceptional job under extremely challenging conditions. Kirk resolved to put in for a commendation for her, as well as for Spock, Sulu, and Yaseen. And that was just to begin with; he suspected that he would find other crew members worthy of special recognition after he thoroughly reviewed the logs.

"Any time, sir." Uhura resumed her post at communications, relieving Lieutenant Palmer. "And how is Mister Scott, Captain? How is he faring in sickbay?"

"About as unhappily as you'd expect," Kirk said.

Doctor McCoy had insisted on checking out both the captain and Spock after their return from the other universe. Kirk had taken advantage of the detour to look in on the injured chief engineer, who struck him as well on the way to recovery. "He's chomping at the bit to get back to his engines, much to the doctor's annoyance."

"At least he'll have a chance to catch up on his technical manuals," Chekov said.

"If McCoy doesn't knock him out with a tranquilizer first," Kirk quipped. "Just to keep him quiet."

"The good doctor's bedside manner is often lacking in patience," Spock commented. "A regrettable failing in a physician."

"I'll be sure to let him know you said that," Kirk said.

"Thank you, Captain. That would be most obliging of you."

Kirk settled into his chair. It felt good to be back where he belonged. He noted that Sulu was back at the helm as well, looking quite at home. "What about you, Mister Sulu? Have you had enough of Ephrata IV?"

"Actually, Captain, I was hoping there might be time for a little shore leave before we leave orbit." He winked at Ensign Yaseen, who was standing nearby for no particular reason. "I hear there are some beautiful picnic spots down on the planet."

Kirk picked up on a definite vibe between the

helmsman and the security officer. When did that happen?

Good for Sulu, he thought. *And Yaseen, too.*

"I imagine the Institute is going to require some assistance rebuilding," Kirk said. "There should be time to squeeze in some shore leave, too. From what I hear, you deserve it. Both of you."

"Thank you, sir." Sulu grinned at Yaseen, who responded with a positively devilish smile that seemed to promise a shore leave to remember. Sulu beamed as though he had just won the Neptunian Lottery. "Very much, sir."

"Speaking of Ephrata, sir," Uhura said. "Doctor Collins is hailing you from the planet."

"Pipe her through, Lieutenant."

"Aye, sir."

Elena Collins appeared on the viewer. Without an inhuman silver mask, she looked once more like the shrewd and feisty older woman Kirk remembered. He heard the sound of heavy construction banging in the background.

"Madam President," he greeted her warmly. "How are things down on the planet?"

"Much better, thanks to you and the crew. I just wanted to let you know that the last of the Crusaders, including Maxah and High Brother Sokis, have been sent back through the rift, and we've begun the process of demolishing the portal . . . over the protests of some of our more fanatical physicists and researchers."

They must have short memories, Kirk thought. Or maybe their intellectual curiosity simply outweighed the abuse and enslavement they had suffered at the hands of the Crusade. *You have to admire that degree of dedication to science and the truth . . . with a lower-case T.*

"Sounds like things, and your faculty, are getting back to normal."

"Absolutely," Collins said. *"I can't thank you enough, Jim. You gave us back our most precious gift: our ability to think freely."*

"Glad to be of service," he answered. "The Institute is one of the intellectual jewels of the Federation. It didn't belong under occupation."

A voice called to Collins from off-screen. She nodded in response.

"Looks like I have to go," she said apologetically. *"As you can imagine, I have about a million items on my plate right now, up to and including finding funds in the budget for a new subspace telescope."*

Sulu and Yaseen shared a guilty look.

"I understand," Kirk said. "Don't be a stranger."

"I won't," she promised. *"And give my love to those rambunctious nephews of yours the next time you talk to them."* She moved out from behind her desk. *"Ephrata out."*

The transmission ended. The peaceful planet returned to the screen. No distress calls intruded on the moment.

"You know, Captain," Uhura reminded him, "you never really answered my question from before. Can we expect you at the holiday party?"

Kirk had been leery of the party, but not anymore. After all they had just been through, he couldn't think of a better way to celebrate their victory—and the infinite diversity of their own universe.

"Count me in," he said. "I wouldn't dream of missing it."

Acknowledgments

Strange to realize that I've been writing *Star Trek* fiction for seventeen years now. As someone who fondly remembers watching the original classic TV series back during its original run in the 1960s, and standing in line to see pretty much every *Star Trek* movie on opening night, I feel privileged to have been able to play in this wonderfully optimistic and imaginative universe so many times now—and to be able to voyage aboard the *Starship Enterprise* once again.

This time around, I want to thank my esteemed editors, Margaret Clark and Ed Schlesinger, for inviting me aboard again, and John Van Citters at CBS for offering his own input on this latest voyage. Thanks also to my agent, Russ Galen, for handling this and many other deals.

Finally, and as always, I couldn't have done this without my girlfriend, Karen Palinko, who helped out on the home front despite her own pressing deadlines and commitments. Among other things, she let me take over our (air-conditioned) kitchen during an extended heat wave, which meant putting up with stacks of *Star Trek* reference books and magazines all over the kitchen for weeks at a time. And, of course, I have to mention our four-legged family members: Henry, Sophie, and Lyla. Just because.

About the Author

Greg Cox is the *New York Times* bestselling author of numerous novels and short stories. He has written the official novelizations of such films as *The Dark Knight Rises, Daredevil, Ghost Rider,* and the first three *Underworld* movies, as well as novelizations of four popular DC Comics miniseries: *Infinite Crisis, 52, Countdown,* and *Final Crisis.*

In addition, he has written books and stories based on such popular series as *Alias, Buffy the Vampire Slayer, CSI: Crime Scene Investigation, Farscape, The 4400, The Green Hornet, Leverage, Riese: Kingdom Falling, Roswell, Star Trek, Terminator, Warehouse 13, Xena: Warrior Princess,* and *Zorro.* He has received two Scribe Awards from the International Association of Media Tie-In Writers. He lives in Oxford, Pennsylvania.

His official website is www.gregcox-author.com.

Made in United States
North Haven, CT
31 October 2022

26159233R00211